SWITCHBACK

A HENRY HOLT MYSTERY

BY THE SAME AUTHOR

A HENRY HOLT MYSTERY

SWITCHBACK

COLLIN WILCOX

HENRY HOLT AND COMPANY
NEW YORK

Henry Holt and Company, Inc.
Publishers since 1866
115 West 18th Street
New York, New York 10011

Henry Holt® is a registered
trademark of Henry Holt and Company, Inc.

Library of Congress Cataloging-in-Publication Data
Wilcox, Collin.
Switchback / by Collin Wilcox. — 1st ed.
    p.   cm.
"A Lt. Frank Hastings novel."
1. Hastings, Frank (Fictitious character)—Fiction.   2. Police—
California—San Francisco—Fiction.   I. Title.
PS3573.I395S94   1993   93-18197
813'.54—dc20   CIP

ISBN 0–8050–2104–3 (alk. paper)

Henry Holt books are available
for special promotions and premiums.
For details contact: Director, Special Markets.

First Edition—1993

DESIGNED BY LUCY ALBANESE

Printed in the United States of America
All first editions are printed on acid-free paper. ∞

10 9 8 7 6 5 4 3 2 1

*This Book Is Dedicated
to Chris's Monica . . .
and to Monica's Chris.*

SWITCHBACK

A HENRY HOLT MYSTERY

1

This, then, was the lost talisman, this single cylinder of blued steel centered on her torso. Everything else, even creation, was excluded: the beginning and the ending, everything and nothing.

But she couldn't confess it. Neither could she beg and therefore save herself. Even here, even now, she couldn't capitulate. Instead she must mock him:

"You won't do it, you bastard. You can't do it. And then you're mine. You'll never—"

Flame was erupting; the car rocked with the explosion. The orange flash centered on the revolver's maw was consuming everything. The beginning and the end, gone.

2 The speed was critical, not too fast, not too slow. The speedometer, then, focused everything: numbers on the dashboard, not a dial with a needle. The digital age had caught up with him: 27, the speedometer registered, two miles over the limit.

The limit—and beyond. He'd crossed the line, entered that far country waiting in perpetual darkness. Lift the revolver, press the trigger, see the blood blossom, vivid red on light beige wool, one of her favorite sweaters. Leave forever all that he'd ever known: the parents who never smiled, the children who turned away, snickering.

28, the numbers showed. Ease off on the accelerator. In the country beyond, his country now, danger was everywhere, waiting. One cop-stop for a traffic infraction meant death.

30, now.

The car was going faster, not slower. Was it the first sign, the first warning? He'd meant to ease off on the accelerator, but instead he was traveling faster. Downhill, could that be it? Suddenly it was essential that he know. Because mind must control the car, it was his only hope. If he'd willed his foot to lighten its pressure on the accelerator, but instead the pressure had increased, how then could he manage the rest of it? How could he escape them?

The plan. In the plan, where was he? Had he lost his place? How many times, these last days, had he gone over the plan?

First, pick up the car, stolen especially for the night, an essential component, no questions asked. Two fifties, and the Buick was his. A stolen car. Then, second, a stolen pistol. He'd intuitively known how the revolver worked, apparently the American male's birthright, something elemental, instinctive. And an effort of the will, an actor immersing himself in a new role, he'd decided to take the persona of the street hoodlum, scoring for the next fix: wait for her to park the car, wait for her to walk along the sidewalk, unsuspecting. Then, God, pull the trigger. Then run. Take the gun, take her purse, and—

—her purse.

Had he said it aloud? Was it his voice he heard, himself talking to himself?

He realized that the car had stopped. On Lake Street, in the middle, brakes locked, car bouncing, he'd come to a stop. He was bending low, searching. The revolver, yes, was on the floor in front, just as he'd planned.

Only the revolver, not the purse.

He'd followed her when she'd decided not to park on Page Street, decided instead to drive to the beach, which she often did. The parking lot had been deserted when she arrived. He'd let her park, let her get out of the Nissan, let her walk out on the beach. When she'd gotten to the surf line, he'd driven slowly, without lights, into the parking lot. As if their meeting had been arranged, he'd parked the stolen Buick close beside the Nissan, still the only two cars in the parking area. He'd—

Headlights flashed in the mirror; a horn blared. Close behind him, then beside him, then ahead: still angrily bleating. Reacting, he was reflexively stabbing at the accelerator. The Buick shot forward, struck the curb, bounced. Now his foot found the brake; the Buick was stopped, engine still running, gear selector still in Drive. He touched the lever, moved it to Neutral.

Take the purse, take the money, he'd rehearsed. It was, he knew, what a petty thief would do: take the purse, pocket the money. Then toss the purse.

And then, as a murderer would do, throw the gun through a sewer grate, gone forever.

And then, mind over matter, the actor, he would walk

3

home, the solid citizen, returning. Because the trash container and the sewer were on the same corner, two blocks from home.

But now he was miles from home. And she was miles from Page Street. She was lying among the low bushes bordering the beach.

And in her car, abandoned at the beach, someone would discover her blood-spattered purse.

Blood . . .

He'd been so careful about the blood.

He'd gotten out of the Nissan on the passenger's side and gone around. He'd opened her driver's door and let her tumble out onto the gravel of the parking lot. And then he'd—

On the sidewalk, two figures were materializing out of the darkness, coming toward him. They would see him: one man in a Buick, just before midnight. They would see him, and they would remember.

But, desperate revelation, he was suddenly immobilized, somehow held prisoner, unable to move until the other images had registered, a succession of freeze-frames: Lisa, sprawled on the gravel as inert and shapeless as a bundle of old clothing . . .

Lisa's ankles in his hands as, careful of the blood, he dragged her body faceup, arms spread wide, away from the car and into the nearby underbrush . . .

Lisa's eyes, open so incredibly wide in the moonlight, as if, surely, she could see deep into his secret self and would surely remember.

3 Jessica Farr checked her watch: time, seven twenty-five, exactly nineteen minutes and ten seconds on the lap counter. Fifty seconds, then, remained yet to jog, rounding out the mandatory twenty minutes, three times a week. An hour and a half, actually a few minutes more, would then remain in which to get in her car, drive home, shower, dress, feed Max his early morning snack, briefly skim the *New York Times* and the *Sentinel* before, at nine o'clock, booting up the computer and modem, ready to deal with her people in Los Angeles.

Forty seconds. Conscious of plenty in reserve, celebrating this bright and shimmering day, she picked up the pace for a strong finish. Beside her, tongue lolling, Max was barely keeping up. Once the dog had actually walked the last several yards, completely pooped. At age six, the standard poodle was—

Suddenly Max was veering off, making for the low-growing scrub that separated the jogging path from the beach and the parking lot just ahead. Seven seconds remained. Sprinting, kicking at full stride, she swept into the parking lot. God, she could feel the rush, those last triumphant yards, all out. At the car now she pulled up, began slowly jogging in place, coming down.

"Max—here, Max."

She waited for the dog to show himself, then repeated the command. Nothing.

"Max! Come!"

And then she saw the tip of his tail, just visible above the scrub. He'd found something concealed in the tangled vegetation. A hundred dollars spent on obedience training, and still the damn dog obeyed commands only when it suited him. Angry, she strode the fifty feet to the edge of the graveled parking lot, then continued walking in the beach sand to the dog. Consequence: it would be necessary to empty sand from her jogging shoes, an aberration that would erode a time frame that, thanks to the poodle, was already skewed.

"Max! Dammit!"

But, with his head and shoulders buried in the vegetation, the dog was oblivious. Behind him now, she grasped his collar and yanked.

Revealing, in the brambles, a human hand and wrist and part of a forearm.

Muttering an obscenity, she released the dog. She stepped back, considered for a moment, then decided to sit in the sand, obliquely facing the exposed hand. Unpredictably, instead of returning to sniff the body, Max was sitting beside her, as if to reassure her that, somehow, it would be all right.

4

Hastings smiled, nodded to the uniformed patrolman stationed at the entrance to the Hall's underground parking garage. As the barrier came up the patrolman casually half saluted, returning Hastings's smile. Hastings parked his Honda in his reserved stall, locked the car, began walking to the elevator. Ten minutes into the nine o'clock morning shift, this level of the garage was almost full.

As he walked between the rows of cars, he realized that, God, he was looking for a particular white Toyota: Janet Collier's car. He might have been a schoolboy again: a lovesick adolescent hoping to catch a glimpse of that one special girl.

Five weeks ago, a small, sad man named Anton Rivak had

invited Hastings into his apartment—and bolted the door behind them. Rivak had been a marginal suspect in the meticulously planned murders of five men. They'd talked for perhaps fifteen minutes before Hastings asked Rivak to account for his whereabouts during the preceding two hours, during the time the last of the murders had been committed. They'd been talking about Rivak's beetle collection; with great pride, Rivak had shown Hastings one of the framed, cotton-covered display boards on which the beetles were impaled. When Hastings asked Rivak where he'd been earlier in the evening, the little man hadn't answered. Instead, he'd taken a long-barreled .22 caliber Colt Woodsman from its hiding place behind the display board. For another fifteen minutes, with the pistol trained on Hastings, speaking very softly, Rivak had confessed to the murders. In the hallway outside Rivak's door, two detectives were on backup: Janet Collier, on loan from Bunco, and Jim Pomeroy, Safes and Lofts. At the first hint of trouble, the detectives would come crashing through the door, guns drawn.

But the first sign of trouble had been a shot: a single shot from the Woodsman that penetrated Rivak's right temple. The little man had sighed once, slumped back in his chair, and silently died. In death, his eyes had remained fixed on his beetles.

First Hastings had shouted that he was all right. Then he'd kicked the gun away from Rivak's still-twitching hand. Then he'd gone to the door, unbolted it, let Janet Collier and Jim Pomeroy inside the apartment.

The phone had been in the bedroom. Sitting on the bed, Hastings had made the calls to the coroner and the police lab. As he spoke into the phone, Janet had come to stand in the bedroom doorway. Turning toward her, Hastings could see it in her face: in the line of duty, this was her first dead body, with all the blood, and the empty eyes staring at nothing, and, worst of all, the odor of urine and excrement.

There were no chairs in the tiny bedroom, only a double bed. Talking to Communications, Hastings patted the bed beside him; she should sit down before she fell down. Nodding, tremulously smiling, she accepted the offer. Finished with Communications, Hastings had remained seated, letting his gaze wander over the walls of Rivak's bedroom. Three of the four walls were covered with framed displays of beetles, each board the same size and design as the one that had concealed the Woodsman. For a few awkward, stilted moments they'd talked about the beetles. Then, inevitably, they'd talked about Rivak, the meek little waiter who'd murdered five men because they'd had him fired from his job at Rabelais, the exclusive men's club. Born in Hungary, his body misshapen at birth, Rivak had always been a victim. Except for his job and his beetle collection, he'd had nothing, meant nothing.

Janet had never seen a body, Hastings had never witnessed a suicide: both of them had been shaken and were trying to conceal it.

And then, still sitting beside him on the bed, she'd touched his hand. And she'd—

"Frank," a voice called out. "Hold the elevator, okay?"

Turning, Hastings saw Jerry Kennealy, just locking the door of his vintage '66 Mustang, lovingly restored.

Conscious that he felt something like relief, Hastings waved in return. Yes, he'd hold the elevator.

5   At the Inspectors' Bureau reception desk, Hastings scanned his phone messages and slipped them into a thick file folder filled with interrogation reports, FBI workups, and documents from the crime lab and the coroner's office.

"Anything else?"

Seated behind the desk, Millie Ralston said, "Lieutenant Friedman is having a root canal, I think. Anyhow, he's at the oral surgeon. And Inspector Canelli was looking for you."

Hastings thanked her, went down the glass-walled hallway of the Bureau to his office. Seated at his desk, Canelli waved for attention. Hastings nodded, pointed down the hallway to his office. He unlocked the door, left it open for Canelli, dropped the file folder on his desk.

In the doorway, Canelli said, "Lieutenant Friedman's having a root canal. He says he's planning to come in later this afternoon, unless he's hurting too bad. He's got to see the DA at three o'clock. Then he'll come by here. He said to tell you." Canelli was a big, swarthy, earnest man. Because he didn't look like a cop or think like a cop or act like a cop, Canelli was Homicide's premier stakeout specialist. In a pontificating mood, Friedman had once labeled Canelli an innocent abroad, the only Homicide detective in recent memory who periodically got his feelings hurt. Like Friedman, Canelli weighed about two hundred forty, not all of it muscle.

"Okay—" Hastings nodded. "Anything else?"

"Yessir. That's what I really wanted to tell you. There's a dead one out at Baker Beach, in the Presidio. I got it about ten minutes to nine, but I thought I'd wait for you."

Hastings glanced out into the inspectors' squadroom. Of the thirteen men who worked Homicide, only three were at their desks. Three, plus Canelli.

"Is the scene covered?"

"No problem. There's about four units there. Rafferty, from the Park Station, is in charge. They've got the tapes up, and everything, and there aren't many rubberneckers around, especially at this time of day—a few dog walkers and some joggers, that's about it. So everything's cool. Some jogger, she found the body—or her dog, I guess. Rafferty's holding them at the scene. The jogger's pretty pissed about it. She's very up-

9

scale, Rafferty says. Drives a BMW, and everything. She's got a poodle, too. In fact, according to Rafferty, the poodle sniffed out the body."

"Why don't you go out, get things started? I'll call the lab and the ME. I've got maybe five other calls I've got to make. Then I'll be out."

6

Hastings pulled the unmarked car to the curb, opened the glove compartment. Except for a plastic-coated registration certificate, the compartment was empty. Someone had taken the city map, probably the same slob who'd left the floor littered with take-out food wrappers.

Baker Beach . . .

Drive to the foot of Thirty-fifth Avenue, he'd thought, enter the Presidio, turn left, and the beach was right there.

Thirty-fifth Avenue?

Or Twenty-fifth?

Yes, dammit, Twenty-fifth. If it wasn't Thirty-fifth, it must be Twenty-fifth. He signaled for the turn, found himself on Clement Street, driving east toward the green hills of the Presidio, a verdant contrast to the surrounding urban sprawl. Built in the nineteenth century, the Presidio originally had served to guard the entrance to San Francisco Bay. Now the Presidio was the garden-spot headquarters of the Sixth Army, plush duty for officers and enlisted men with retirement on their minds. One of San Francisco's pleasant little surprises, Baker Beach offered a picture-postcard view of the Golden Gate Bridge, curving over the narrows and into the Marin

County headlands to the north. Because Baker Beach was open to the public, it was policed by both the Sixth Army and the San Francisco police.

Twenty-sixth was next, then Twenty-fifth. He signaled, made the turn. Yes, the waters of the bay were just down the hill, sparkling blue beneath a cloudless sky. Just out to sea, a container ship was maneuvering to pass beneath the Golden Gate Bridge.

At the bottom of the hill he turned into the Presidio, then turned down to the beach and the shoreline. In a graveled parking lot he saw the familiar array of official vehicles: the coroner's van, the forensics van, two black-and-white sector cars, two MP cars, and Canelli's unmarked cruiser. Yellow crime scene tape outlined a white Japanese sports coupe and bracketed the low shrubbery on the east border of the parking lot. On the beach, a few random figures strolled along the shoreline, a few dogs frisked at the water's edge. Facing the taped-off section of low brush, Canelli stood with a lab technician. As Canelli pointed, the technician was nodding. Yes, he understood Canelli's instructions. Out of long habit, Hastings took his plastic ID plaque from his jacket pocket, clipped it to his lapel. Sensing a superior officer's presence at the scene, Canelli turned as Hastings approached. The two homicide detectives stepped carefully over the yellow tape, solemnly walked side by side to the white sports coupe, a Nissan 240 SX. According to protocol, the technicians drew back out of earshot, busying themselves at their work.

"The first thing I should tell you, I guess," Canelli said, "is that the lady who found the body—she's the one in that dark gray BMW, with her dog—she's pissed. She discovered the body about seven forty-five, when she was jogging. She's got a car phone, naturally, and she called it in about eight o'clock, give or take, I haven't checked that out yet with Communications. But, anyhow, she's some kind of a real high-powered business consultant, the way I get it. And she's got to get to her computer, she says, start making deals. The sector guys didn't want to cut her loose until I got here, and I didn't want to cut her loose till *you* got here. So, like I said, she's steamed. She's been on her car phone the whole time."

Hastings glanced at the BMW, parked a hundred feet away. Sitting on the far side of the car, the woman was indistinct. The poodle, sitting behind the steering wheel, stared steadily at Hastings. The woman was talking into her car phone. After a moment, Hastings turned his attention to the Nissan.

"Don't worry about her. Tell me how it goes, here."

"Right." Canelli stepped closer, pointed to the car's interior. The seat on the driver's side was blood soaked, the window and door on the driver's side were blood spattered. Blood ran in three rivulets down the inside of the windshield above the steering wheel.

"The way I get it," Canelli said, "this beach is the only part of the Presidio that's in our jurisdiction. The duty commander went off duty at eight o'clock, so I don't have anything solid. But Callahan—" He pointed to a patrolman, arms folded, leaning against the side of his unit. "Callahan says we make it maybe twice an hour. The MPs, I guess they do better than that, but they aren't saying much, at least not to me." Canelli shot an aggrieved look at the two MP units. In each unit, two white-helmeted MPs sat stiffly, both men staring straight ahead. "The way I get it, they don't talk until there's an officer with them. Anyhow, they aren't talking to me."

"Don't worry about them. Go ahead."

"The way I figure it," Canelli said, "she parked here sometime between eleven o'clock and midnight. Like I say, we should be able to pin it down once we get the sector reports for last night. But, anyhow, it's a pretty good guess that she was sitting behind the wheel when she was shot. Maybe the assailant was sitting beside her, or maybe he was outside, shooting through the open door, or maybe the window. The lab'll tell us if there're powder burns, I guess. But then the assailant probably walked around the car and opened the driver's door and pulled her out. There's blood beneath the door outside on the driver's side. So then—" He pointed to the taped-off section of low-growing scrub that began about twenty feet from where they stood. "Then he dragged her in there, and that's where Jessica Farr found her. That's the jogger with the poodle. Jessica Farr. And the victim's name was Lisa Franklin, by the way."

"How do you know that?"

Canelli pointed to the car. "Her purse is on the floor, which is hard to figure. I mean, jeez, the car was apparently here all night, all bloody, with the doors unlocked and a purse with money in it on the floor in front, just sitting there, and nothing was touched. And what's more, our guys didn't even bother to check it out, shine a flashlight inside, nothing." Canelli shook his head dolefully. "It makes you wonder."

"How much money did she have?"

"About sixty dollars. No credit cards, though, so I'll check on that. And there's a can of Mace."

"So she wasn't expecting foul play."

"Or else didn't have time to react."

Hastings nodded agreement, circled the car to examine the bloodstains beneath the driver's door, then pointed to the shrubbery that was bracketed by the tapes. "Is she still in there?"

"Yessir. I figured I'd wait for you, to move her."

Hastings pointed to the taped-off section of the graveled parking lot that led into the underbrush. The trail was clear: a continuous shallow depression where the victim had been dragged. "Has all this been processed?"

Plainly registering pride in his job performance, Canelli's soft-eyed face broke into a shy smile as he said, "Three sets of pictures, everything labeled. Plus dirt samples. Blood, too."

"So it's okay to walk between the tapes."

"Yessir. And the body, everything's done there, too. She's all set to go."

"You go ahead."

Canelli began advancing. Neither man stepped between the parallel furrows. As they came close to the underbrush, Hastings saw dried blood on branches and leaves. Gingerly Canelli grasped a branch, pulling it back to reveal most of the body. Still holding the branch back, Canelli moved aside, making room for Hastings.

The murderer had left her lying faceup, with her arms extended over her head, feet together. She was probably in her middle twenties, dark haired, slim, full breasted, dressed with a free-spirited flair. From her throat to her waist, her vividly styled clothing was blood soaked. Her eyes were open wide, staring up at the bright blue October sky. Her features were regular; if her facial muscles hadn't been contorted by death's final agony, she might have been beautiful. Because she'd been lying for so long in the open air, and because a stiff breeze was blowing in from the ocean, there was no odor.

Stepping back, over the tape, Hastings signaled for Canelli to let the branch spring back into place.

"What's the ME say?"

"Pretty much what you'd think," Canelli said. "Dead for eight to twelve hours, probably. They'll know better when they move the body, get her clothes off, take her temperature. He says it looks like two gunshots, one through the thorax, one maybe through the heart. He'll know more when he gets her downtown." Canelli paused, then added softly: "He says she had a real nice body, as much as he could see."

"It doesn't look like sex."

"And if it wasn't robbery, then someone just wanted to kill her, it seems like."

"Do you have an address for her?"

"Yessir, I do." Canelli began exploring the pockets of a

14

badly fitting corduroy sports jacket, finally found his notebook. He flipped through the pages, frowning. Finally, a pleasant surprise, he nodded. "Yeah, here it is. Eighteen thirty-two Page Street. It's in the Haight, I looked it up."

"Is the car registered to her?"

"Yessir. Same address. Nice car. Twenty, twenty-five thousand, out the door."

"You finish up here. I'll start at her place and see how it goes. I'll meet you at the Hall, let's say about four o'clock."

"What about Jessica Farr?"

"You deal with her."

"What about the MPs? There's supposed to be a couple of officers on the way. They'll want to talk to someone with a little rank."

"That's easy. Tell them to get in touch with Lieutenant Friedman, at the Hall."

Doubtfully, Canelli frowned. "Lieutenant Friedman's having a root canal this morning."

"All the better. See you about four."

"Hmmm."

7 Many of the buildings in the eighteen-hundred block of Page Street had narrowly escaped the earthquake and fire of 1906. They'd originally been tall, narrow, dignified post-Victorian houses, all of them at least two stories, some of them built as single-family dwellings, some two-family flats. Located in the heart of the Haight Ashbury district, Page Street had aged gracefully until the sixties when the flower children had come,

the vanguard of the drug culture, and the area had declined. A decade later, after sodium streetlights had been installed on Haight Street and the shop fronts had been barred and the city had allocated more money for garbage collection and the aging hippies had either burned out or moved on or else begun wearing three-piece suits, the Haight Ashbury began its slow climb back.

The house at 1830–32 Page Street reflected both the scars of neglect and the hope for something better. Four names were posted on the mailboxes, and two names above the buzzers for each street number: C. J. Kirk and J. Thomas for 1830, Lisa Franklin and Barbara Estes for 1832. Hastings pressed the buzzer for 1832, waited, pushed it again—and again. Nothing. Like most Victorian residences, the building was attached on either side, and was built close to the sidewalk, with space for a tiny front garden. But there was no front garden here, only a slab of concrete. Hastings walked across the concrete to the side of the building and the service door. Predictably, the door was locked, probably bolted from the inside. Hastings returned to the small front stoop, climbed the three stairs, and pressed the buzzer for 1830, the lower flat. Just as he was pressing the button a second time, the door swung open. Dressed in washed-out jeans and a badly wrinkled black T-shirt, barefooted, a man in his haggard, hollow-eyed late twenties stood in the open doorway. His face was pale; his dark blond hair, earlobe long, was disheveled. Of medium height, he was as slim as a teenager. His face was deeply etched with unmistakable lines of anguish. His sunken eyes were smudged by something that could be despair. When he saw the gold detective's shield that Hastings held in his open palm, the man in the doorway winced, drew back an involuntary half step.

"Mr. Thomas?"

Quickly, the other man shook his head. "N-no. That's Jamie. James Thomas. I'm C. J.—C. J. Kirk."

"I'm Lieutenant Frank Hastings, Mr. Kirk. I'm co-commander of the Homicide Detail."

The elusive eyes shifted sharply from the badge to Hastings's face, then back to the badge. Then Kirk suddenly looked back over his shoulder, as if to seek retreat, a way out. It was, Hastings knew, a textbook example of guilt response upon being unexpectedly confronted by authority. Watching Kirk carefully, Hastings stepped back to the edge of the stoop, giving himself room. Pocketing the badge with his left hand, moving slowly and deliberately, he used his right hand to surreptitiously unbutton his jacket. He let his hand linger at his belt line, close to the service revolver holstered at his belt on the left side.

"I'm making inquiries about Lisa Franklin. Your upstairs neighbor."

Kirk frowned, as if he were puzzled. "Lisa? You want Lisa?"

"You know her, then. She lives here. Upstairs."

The puzzled frown deepened. "Well, sure, I know her." As if grateful for the chance to affirm something, Kirk nodded anxiously, repeating, "Sure."

"Can we—" Hastings gestured to the open door. "Can we go inside? There're a few questions. It won't take long."

As if the query confused him, Kirk blinked. Then, with obvious effort, he focused his dulled stare on Hastings. Every uncertain gesture, every retreat from direct eye contact, every oddly disconnected body movement suggested that Kirk represented no direct threat. Kirk was a victim, a burned-out case.

"Questions?"

"Mr. Kirk—" Purposefully, Hastings stepped one pace forward. "Please. Let's talk inside."

"Ah—" As if he'd just heard the request, Kirk nodded, stepped back from the door, made room for Hastings to enter the ground-floor flat.

"After you." Hastings gestured politely. It was a situation

17

taken directly from the police training manuals: working alone, in unfamiliar territory, an officer never turns his back on a stranger.

In his bare feet, shuffling along, Kirk walked into the long, narrow corridor of the lower flat. The first door opened on a front living room.

"Here?" Kirk asked.

"Fine." As if he were the host, Hastings gestured for Kirk to sit on a lumpy sofa that faced three tall, narrow bay windows fronting on Page Street. One glance confirmed the predictable: the room was a mess, a haphazard collection of mismatched salvage shop furniture, with newspapers, magazines, paper-back books, and tape cassettes scattered everywhere. There was no ventilation; the room reeked of dust and decaying food—and, most certainly, marijuana smoke. To himself, Hastings nodded. If he should need leverage, the marijuana would help. He unburdened a rickety ladder-back chair of a stack of yellowing newspapers, dropped the papers on the floor, and sat facing C. J. Kirk, who was staring down at the threadbare carpet. His hands were slack, dangling dispiritedly between the blue denim of his skinny thighs.

"I'm afraid," Hastings began, "that I've got some bad news, Mr. Kirk." He waited for Kirk to raise his eyes, the unfailing response to this prelude of the blow that was about to fall: death descending.

But Kirk gave no sign that he'd heard. Freeing Hastings, therefore, to get on with this grim game that he'd so often played out, everyone a loser:

"Lisa Franklin was found dead this morning, in the Presidio. We think she died late last night." He let a moment pass, then said softly: "She was murdered."

When Kirk finally raised his head, he was once more frowning, unable to comprehend.

"Murdered?" As he said it, he failed again to directly meet

Hastings's gaze. "Did you say murdered? In the Presidio?" Perplexed, he shook his head. Repeating: "Murdered?"

"Yessir."

"Do they—did you—" He broke off, sighed once, began again: "Did you—do you know who did it?"

"We're still checking it all out, trying to establish what happened last night—what happened, and when. That's why I'm here."

"But I—I don't understand. I—"

Hastings raised a hand to cut him off. He put an edge of authority on his voice as he said, "Let's make this simple, Mr. Kirk. What I'd like from you, first, is for you to tell me about Lisa Franklin. How long have you known her? How well did you know her? Start with that."

"Well, I—" Kirk licked at his lips, a pink tongue-tip circling a pale, tight mouth. "It's been—I guess it's been about three years that I've known her. We moved in here about the same time. We—" Abruptly, he broke off. Then: "I—would you like some water? I—I need some water."

Hastings decided to nod. "Fine. Thanks." He watched the other man get to his feet, watched his shambling progress out into the hallway. What could account for C. J. Kirk's obvious distress? It wasn't just the news of Lisa Franklin's death. From the first, Kirk had been anxious, frightened. Was it drugs on the premises, and the fear of discovery? The craving for water suggested drug dependency. And the muddy eyes and the uncoordinated arm and leg movements. And the—

In the open doorway Kirk reappeared, holding two glasses of water, neither glass quite clean. Concentrating, Kirk managed to give one to Hastings, took one for himself, returned to the sofa. Greedily he drained his glass, wiped his mouth, put the glass on the floor beside the sofa. Then, once more staring down at the floor, he began shaking his head, mumbling, "Dead. My God, murdered."

"What I want," Hastings said, "is for you to tell me about her. What'd she do? What kind of work? Was she married? Divorced? What about her friends? What about enemies?"

"She didn't have a job, not that I know about, anyhow."

"Then how'd she live?"

"I—I think her parents gave her money. And there were—" He broke off, frowned. "There were friends."

"Friends?"

"Oh, Jesus—" Suddenly he shook his head, a blind, desperate denial. As if he'd been touched by a hot wire, his scrawny body jerked spasmodically. "Jesus, it's just hitting me, that she's dead."

In silence Hastings watched the younger man struggling to tame his demons. It was a losing struggle, a struggle that had long ago been lost. Why? When, and why?

"What d'you do, Mr. Kirk? What kind of work?"

As if the question puzzled him, Kirk managed to raise his head, make cautious eye contact. His expression was anxious. "I—I'm not working right now. I used to work at Carter Labs."

"Carter Labs?"

"They do photo finishing. They're not like Fotomat, though. They do work for professionals."

"So you're a photo finisher."

Kirk nodded.

"But you're not working now."

Once more the pink tongue-tip circled the pale lips. "It's been six months since—" He let the rest of it die, let his eyes fall. Now Kirk's body had gone slack again, listless.

"Did Lisa Franklin have a roommate?"

"Barbara—Barbara Estes. Barbara had the place first, and then Lisa moved in. That's about the time I moved in here."

"You have a roommate, then. Both of you had roommates." As he spoke, Hastings took out his notebook and began writing.

"Yes."

"Who's your roommate?"

"It's James Thomas."

"Is he at work, now?"

"I—I'm not sure."

"What about Barbara Estes? I rang her bell, but there wasn't any answer. Do you think she's at work?"

Kirk nodded. "I think so. She works nine to five, anyhow. So if she isn't upstairs, then she's probably at work."

"In an hour or so there'll be a lab crew upstairs—photographers, lab technicians. Before they come, I'd like to look around, up there." He gestured to the rear of the building. "Is there a back stairway to Lisa Franklin's flat?"

Kirk nodded. "It might be locked, though."

"I'd like to take a look." He gestured again. "I'll go through your place. You'll be here when I get back, won't you?" It was a command, not a question.

8 The outside rear stairs leading up to the second-floor landing were badly weathered; the landing was small, its floorboards warped, its railing in need of repair. A few red clay flowerpots contained only dry, cracked dirt. Small panes of wood-framed glass surrounded the solid wood door. Through one of the windows Hastings saw a cluttered back porch. The door was fastened securely, but one of the panes was cracked. Hastings stepped close, drew his revolver, used the butt to break out the cracked pane. He looked at the neighboring buildings on either side, then reached through the window and retracted the bolt that secured the door. He was in what had originally been a small sun porch, enclosed now to house laundry tubs, a washer and

dryer, and miscellaneous storage. An inside door led into the kitchen and was unlocked.

When he'd walked through the downstairs flat he'd taken his policeman's automatic inventory: the bedrooms with beds unmade and discarded clothing everywhere, the dining room that was apparently used for haphazard storage, the kitchen with its greasy walls, tattered curtains across the single window, and dirty dishes stacked on every surface. The evaluation: two men who didn't give a damn about their surroundings and probably didn't give a damn about their lives.

The upstairs flat was better furnished, better organized—and better dusted. Except for a few dirty dishes stacked neatly in the sink, the kitchen was clean and orderly. From his hip pocket Hastings took a pair of surgical gloves, an essential tool of the detective's trade. He slipped on the gloves, began going through cupboards and drawers. The labels on the food and wine suggested a trendy, upscale bias. The pots and pans hung on the wall beside the stove looked expensive. There was a cork bulletin board beside the refrigerator, with a notepad attached and a ballpoint pen hung on a string: *Call Cecil, 824-4076,* and *Call Victor. Lily is ready, 2 P.M.* and a dozen other slips of notepaper. The messages had been written in two distinctive scripts, one strong and large and bold, one neat and cramped. Which handwriting, Hastings wondered, would match which woman?

Like most turn-of-the-century flats, this one was long and narrow, with kitchen and dining room across the rear, followed by bedrooms opening off the single hallway. Most of the hallway wall space was covered with travel posters and poster reprints of modern art, some of them paintings, some of them photographs of statuary and ancient buildings. The living room and entryway took up the front of the flat.

The two bedrooms were small, each with its door standing open, each with a single window opening on an airshaft. The bathroom was next. Like the kitchen, the bathroom was clean and marginally neat. The medicine cabinet yielded no apparent surprises. Hastings went back into the long, narrow hallway and retraced his steps to the first bedroom. It was small; with a double bed there was room only for a small dresser, a chair, and one floor-to-ceiling bookcase. The bed was made, covered with an expensive-looking spread. Over the dresser, a large cork bulletin board shared wall space with a gilt-framed mirror. The bulletin board was covered with snapshots, advertisements, a magazine picture of a bright red Ferrari, a centerfold of a beautifully bronzed, dramatically muscled man (totally naked), two black-and-white Ansel Adams photographs of Yosemite, several clips of newspaper headlines, and a variety of picture postcards, most of them obviously sent from foreign countries. On top of the dresser Hastings saw a collection of small perfume bottles, a matching tortoiseshell comb and brush set, and two photographs facing each other in a hinged silver frame. One photograph was a full-face snapshot of a middle-aged woman with hard-edged features; the other photo was of a young girl cuddling a black-and-white puppy.

Quickly Hastings went through the bureau's drawers. In the top drawer he found a checkbook, a bill from Macy's, and a bill from Chevron. The Macy's balance was seventy-eight dollars. The Chevron bill, overdue, was for eighty-three dollars. The checkbook showed a balance of less than three hundred dollars. The checks were imprinted to Barbara Estes, 1832 Page Street.

Hastings closed the drawers and glanced at his watch. At the office, with Friedman still at the dentist and both Canelli and Lou Marsten out in the field, he'd left Bill Sigler in charge. In his fifties, with retirement on his mind, Sigler had no interest in making decisions or enforcing orders.

Hastings checked to make sure the beeper clipped to his belt was switched on, then walked down the hallway to Lisa Franklin's room. He would give it a quick toss, then phone for the technicians.

Her bedroom was a mess. The double bed was a tangle of blankets and sheets that clearly outlined the nest where the victim had once slept. Magazines and newspapers were precariously stacked on the floor. But, a contradiction, three walls were hung with large oil paintings, each one obviously an original, each one signed and dated. Before the Lisa Franklin file got much thicker, Hastings would recruit an art expert to evaluate the paintings. And, before that, he would get a woman's appraisal of the victim's clothing and effects.

A woman detective . . .

Janet Collier.

Who could fault him for calling her in, getting a second opinion? In Homicide, it was standard practice.

Still staring at one of the paintings, a large, complex abstract, his eyes went out of focus.

Janet . . .

He could call her, all business, order her to meet him here. As they'd been only a few weeks ago, together in a murder victim's bedroom, so they would be together again, here. But this time there would be no corpse in the next room, still bleeding from a self-inflicted head wound. Instead, there would be this intriguing room, so intensely female, with its unmade bed and the dramatic paintings and its air of mystery. If he chose, he could easily arrange for them to be alone together, without the lab crew.

At the thought, he could feel himself sexually quickening.

When would he admit it?

When would he face the truth? When would he admit that, yes, he wanted Janet. Badly.

With an effort he blinked, brought the room back into focus. Resolutely he turned to the closet. The bifold doors were standing open. Garment by garment, Hastings went through her clothing. The conclusion: Lisa Franklin had dressed for the action, whether it was the ski slopes or dancing at the clubs or dining at whichever restaurant was trendy.

Glossy illustrations torn from magazines and thumbtacked to the inside of the closet confirmed the conclusion: hot-eyed, go-for-broke models wearing thousand-dollar clothing with a million-dollar flair. The floor of the closet was a jumble of shoes, boots, tote bags, small luggage, and a cane picnic hamper.

Hastings stepped away from the closet, turned, let his gaze traverse the rest of it: a small desk and a bureau jammed together on one wall together with a small chair. There was a telephone, a digital clock radio, and a tiny TV on the desk. The bookshelves over the desk contained telephone directories and an untidy stack of catalogs and periodicals on its bottom shelf. A large spiral-bound Sierra Club appointment calendar had been placed on the telephone directories, which were laid flat on the shelf. The calendar was a standard format: a large page for each month, a two-inch square for each day, with room for notations. For October, this month, most of the squares contained at least one notation, many of them two or three, usually a single word followed by a single number, probably representing the time of an appointment. Sometimes there was an address, or a phone number.

For yesterday, October fourteenth, Lisa's last day of life, there was only one notation:

Reggie's 7

Hastings put the calendar aside, opened the center drawer of the desk. There, the answer to a homicide detective's fondest wish, he saw them: a checkbook, an address book, a scattering of bills, and a sheaf of bank statements secured by a thick rubber band. Lisa's room might be disorganized, but she'd apparently kept records.

The address book was medium size, made of red Moroccan leather. On the cover, at the lower right, L.M.F. was stamped in gold. Like the calendar notations, the entries in the address book were cryptic, often only a single name followed by a phone number. The handwriting was bold and sketchy. In the

25

whole address book there were probably less than fifty names. Hastings flipped to the "F" section—F for "Franklin." The first entry was simply "Dad" followed by a phone number but no area code. The second entry was "Mom," followed by a 212 area code, followed by a number. Conclusion: Lisa Franklin had been unmarried, or at least probably used her maiden name, married or not. Secondary conclusion: her parents probably lived apart, the mother in New York City. Without an area code, it was impossible to determine her father's place of residence.

Sitting down at the desk, more methodically now, Hastings began at the As and went through the book page by page. A few pages were empty; others had only one or two entries, usually with the predictable single cryptic name followed by a phone number, usually no address. Most of the entries confirmed Hastings's first impression: in her with-it twenties, Lisa Franklin kept in touch by phone. Letter writing took time. Lisa had moved fast and hadn't looked back.

The checkbook was next. Again, only names and numbers, with almost no explanatory notations on the check stubs. At a glance, during the thirty days between September tenth and October twelfth, the date of the last check, Lisa Franklin wrote twenty-odd checks, most of them for amounts of less than a hundred dollars. There was one deposit, on September twenty-first, for five thousand dollars. The last balance, taken on September fifteenth, showed almost nine thousand dollars.

Hastings glanced at his watch. Already the time was past noon. With a gloved hand he picked up the telephone from its cradle on the desk and called Communications. He identified himself and ordered a two-man lab team and a photographer to the scene. He cradled the phone, considered, then turned to the three bookshelves that went the full width of one wall, extending over the desk and the bureau. About half the books were hardbacks, half paperbacks. Unlike the rest of the room, the bookshelves were carefully arranged. Most of the books on

26

the top shelf were novels. Serious novels, by their titles. The lower shelf was glass and displayed a collection of primitive clay statuary and clay artifacts that looked as if it could be a museum display. Hastings guessed the statues were Mayan or pre-Columbian. Were they copies or originals? Were they valuable?

The middle shelf, which also contained some primitive sculpture, held a considerable collection of outsize books, most of them art books, as well as many books that were obviously antique, some of them leather bound. They were the classics: Dickens, Tolstoy, and Dostoyevsky, not complete matched sets but random titles and sizes. Two or three feet of shelf space was devoted to poetry: original works, plus criticism, all of them hardback, all of them obviously well read. Directly above the desk, Hastings saw three large leather volumes that were plain, with no printing on the spine. They were notebook size, a matched set. Slipping one of the unmarked books free, Hastings saw the small brass lock and leather strap that secured it. The volumes, then, were diaries. He took out his Swiss army knife, selected the screwdriver blade. Three tries, and the lock sprung open.

The bound pages were unlined and were covered with handwriting. Unlike most diary entries, the entires were undated. Standing at the desk, skimming the pages, Hastings realized that the entries were not the ordinary accounts of day-to-day life. Instead, they were impressions, deeply emotional fragments, many of them poetic. He turned to the first page:

Petals underfoot in a dusty lane, as fragile as memories of childhood, and just as lost. Only the images of smiles remain— twisted smiles, grotesque smiles, predatory smiles. If only the petals had remained, then the smiles might fade. Forever.

Hastings blinked, reread the passage, then turned at random to a back page, reading:

Their hands: fingers like slugs, probing, finally penetrating. Talons, tearing the flesh, paralyzing her, crushing her beneath the monster's weight. But she must not cry out. Instead, she must remember their faces, remember their rutting grunts. And, most of all, she must remember their eyes, made transparent by the lust, revealing the beast within.

Was it poetry? Was it fact? Fiction? Who was the "her"— Lisa Franklin? Someone else? Frustrated, he shook his head. The homicide detective's first task was to discover everything possible about the victim. For this case, to do the job right, it might take an art consultant, a poetry consultant, and a fashion consultant. He decided to take the calendar, the checkbook, the address book, the bank statements, and the three journals with him. Using the calendar as a folder, he secured the documents, then took a last long, reflective moment to look around the room, his last moments alone with the victim and her worldly possessions. Then, with a half nod of farewell, he went out into the hallway, finally into the living room. Predictably, the feeling of the living room was a meld of the two bedrooms: more orderly than Lisa Franklin's room, less orderly than Barbara Estes's room. The furnishings, too, were uncoordinated: not quite matched, not quite mismatched. There was a sizable collection of tapes and discs; the sound system and the TV were both top of the line.

Carrying the journals and the documents, Hastings was walking back to the kitchen when he heard the faint sound of voices from the downstairs flat. He stopped long enough in the kitchen to find a plastic shopping bag to carry the documents, then went out the back door and down the rickety outside stairs to the ground-floor flat. C. J. Kirk and another man were standing in the kitchen, in urgent conversation. Seeing Hastings, Kirk flinched, drew back toward the hallway. But the newcomer turned, smiled, offered his hand. It was a cheerful, open, comradely gesture. In his forties, thin and slightly stooped, nondescriptly dressed, the newcomer showed a face deeply etched in a pattern of chronic defeat. His hair was thin and unkempt, his graying beard sparse and badly trimmed. His eyes, though, were alive with a spontaneous pleasure that matched the generously outstretched hand.

"You're Lieutenant Hastings. Frank Hastings."

Hastings nodded, tried to visualize the names on the mailboxes as he shook the man's hand. "Are you Mr. Thomas? James Thomas?"

"That's right, Frank." Thomas's thin lips twisted in a mischievous smile. Then, teasing: "You don't remember me, do you?"

"Afraid not."

"How about Jamie? You remember Jamie Thomas? From about—what—almost thirty years ago, give or take."

It was a guessing game that, during the past several years, Hastings had often had to endure. In addition to his aversion for exercise, departmental brass, and politicians as a class, Friedman also systematically dodged media exposure in all its forms. Leaving Hastings, Homicide's co-commander, to deal with the press and the TV crews. It was an arrangement that Hastings secretly savored—especially since, lo, he could often see himself on the six o'clock news. The downside was the occasional hanger-on, a face from the past, sometimes the long-distant past, when Hastings had been growing up in San Francisco.

A face like James Thomas. AKA, apparently, Jamie.

Almost thirty years. Making them teenagers, then, he and Jamie Thomas.

"Was that Hamilton?" Hastings asked, naming the high school he'd attended for four years.

Owlishly, Thomas nodded. "Right. Hamilton. I was a year behind you. But I accept it, that you don't recognize me now. I've changed, a lot more than you have. You're still the same guy you were then, Frank—the same all-American boy.

29

God—" Marveling, Thomas shook his head. "God, I can still see you, walking down the hallway in your letter sweater, with those love-struck girls following you. I used to wonder whether you even knew they were there, trotting along, hoping for just one little smile. Now, of course, I realize that, sure, you knew. But back then, how could I know? I was so insecure, so fucked up by all those hormones. To me, you were a—an icon. It's incredible, you know, what a difference a year makes, in high school. Like, when I was a freshman and you were a sophomore, you were already playing varsity football. You—" Thomas shook his head in ancient wonderment. "You had it all together. I thought you were the essence of cool, man—even before you were all-state quarterback, or whatever it was."

"It was fullback."

"Whatever." Thomas shrugged his bony shoulders, ran not-quite-clean fingers through his not-quite-clean hair. Still gazing quizzically at Hastings, Thomas shook his head, an expression of wry resignation. "I suppose this happens to you all the time, doesn't it? How's it feel, to see yourself on TV?"

Hastings considered, then decided to say, "It feels a lot like making all-state fullback, if you really want to know. It feels great—but not as great as you thought it would. It never does."

"Oh, yeah—" As if he were resigned to whatever memories Hastings's answer had evoked, Thomas shrugged again, nodding deeply, regretfully. Repeating: "Oh, yeah."

As they'd been talking, C. J. Kirk had surreptitiously moved down the hallway, disappearing into a bedroom, closing the door. Hastings gestured to the door that led out to the rear porch. "Let's go out here. I've got some questions for you."

Instantly Thomas's manner changed. No longer reminiscing, he now projected an overwrought despair. His body language, his deep, bitter sigh, everything expressed an exaggerated, theatrical sadness. Jamie Thomas, Hastings was deciding, was an unstable personality, an older version of C. J. Kirk, both of them lost.

When they were standing to face each other on the small back porch, door closed, Hastings said, "C. J. told you about Lisa."

"God, yes. How—how did it happen?" Thomas's pale, washed-out eyes searched Hastings's face.

"We don't know, Jamie. That's why I'm here. I want to find out how it happened, and why."

"Was it a thief? Was that it? A mugging?"

Pointedly not replying, Hastings said, "You've lived here for—what—three years, something like that?"

Thomas nodded. "C. J., me, and Lisa, we all came about the same time. Barbara'd been here for a while."

"Were the four of you friendly?"

Thomas's eyes narrowed; the muscles of his face tightened. Was it caution? Fear? Or was it a mood swing? Was it possible that Thomas was on drugs? Yes, Hastings decided, it was possible. Very possible. And C. J. Kirk, too. Definitely possible. What was the new age phrase—symbiotic relationship? Did that describe the connection between Kirk and Thomas?

Covertly watching Thomas's face, Hastings waited for the other man finally to speak.

"Sure, we were friendly."

"How friendly?"

"I—I don't know what you mean."

"I think you do, Jamie."

"You mean sex, like that?"

"I mean everything." Hastings gave it a hard-eyed pause, then put an edge on it: "Like that."

"Yeah—well—" Inside the tattered beard, Thomas's mouth twisted into a sardonic, crooked-tooth smile. "Well, whatever the game was, I was a spectator, if that's what you mean."

This time the edge was sharper, bit deeper: "Listen, Jamie, quit dancing around this. You know what I want. Give it to me. We're wasting the taxpayers' money."

"Yeah, well, like I said, I was outside the loop. That hap-

31

pens, you know. They're all in their twenties, these kids. Us, you and me, we're in our forties."

Hastings made no reply. He was waiting, impatiently now.

"Well," Thomas said, "the way it goes—or, anyhow, the way it went—Lisa seems to've swung both ways."

"She liked men and women both. Is that it?"

"That's it," Thomas said heavily, adding, "What a waste, someone who looked like that."

"So it was she and Barbara Estes—and then she and C. J. Is that what you're saying?"

Suddenly Thomas guffawed. "Jesus, no. I mean, not Lisa and C. J., except once in a while when she was high, and looking for someone to drive crazy, amuse herself for an hour or two, like that. Otherwise, she just ignored C. J.—the way everyone else does."

"Lisa and Barbara Estes, then."

"Oh, yeah—" Thomas nodded emphatically. His skin, Hastings noticed, was like yellowed parchment, an unhealthy sign.

"Did they always get along, Lisa and Barbara?"

Thomas's lips twisted again, this time wryly. "They got along the way everyone got along with Lisa—Lisa's way, take it or leave it."

"Like that, eh?"

"Definitely, like that."

"Did Lisa work?"

"God, no. Lisa was above work. That was for ordinary mortals. Lisa just—just *was*."

"Come on, Jamie. Lisa had rent to pay and car payments and I. Magnin bills. Where'd the money come from?"

"Men," Thomas answered promptly.

"Men?"

"Men," came the firm response. "She used to say she was a courtesan—and that's what she was, no question. She could pull it off. She was one of those women who drove men mad. She was beautiful, you know. Really beautiful."

"No," Hastings said, "I didn't know. When I saw her, she wasn't very beautiful."

Thomas blinked, swallowed, then spoke in a voice that was meant to be defiant: "Well, she *was* beautiful. She had an unbelievable body, and the face of a goddam angel—all that, plus a brilliant mind. Add it all up, and then factor in that driving men mad was probably the only turn-on that ever really interested her, and you've got Lisa. She let men buy her things—all kinds of things. For which, if she didn't feel like it, she delivered nothing in return. Which, as I say, was probably the real turn-on for her."

"Did a man buy her car—the Nissan?"

"Sure—" Thomas gestured negligently. "Sure, the Nissan. She's had at least three different cars, since I've known her. But cars never really interested her."

"What *did* interest her?"

"Art," Thomas answered. "Art, and poetry."

Deciding not to reveal what he'd already discovered in the victim's room, Hastings pretended to be intrigued as he asked, "Poetry? You mean she wrote poetry?"

"If she did," Thomas said, "I never knew about it. She read it, though."

"Did she draw? Paint?"

"I don't think so."

"Could you identify a specimen of her handwriting?"

Thomas frowned, thought about it, finally shook his head. "No, I don't think so. Why?"

Ignoring the question, Hastings said, "You say she was a courtesan. What's that mean? Was she a call girl? Is that it?"

"Not if you mean she went with a lot of guys, turned tricks for a hundred bucks, no, that wasn't Lisa."

"So what'd she have, three or four guys on the string?"

"Exactly."

"These men—can you identify them?"

"You mean by name, like that?"

33

"By name, or visually."

"By name, no. Visually—" He shrugged. "I doubt it. Lisa usually went to them, they never came here. I guess, over the years, I saw a lot of them. But it was mostly—you know—they'd come by, ring her bell, pick her up, take her somewhere in their Mercedes or Jaguar. I never talked to them."

"You never knew these guys, and yet you know how she treated them. How's that?" Asking the question, Hastings let doubt surface, a reproachful doubt, as if Thomas, his old high school chum, had disappointed him.

"Hell, Lisa'd have a few drinks, or maybe sniff something, and she'd boast about how she diddles these guys. She had nothing but contempt for them. Which, probably, was why they kept coming back for more."

"But she didn't mention any names."

"Well, yes and no. I mean, she'd talk about—you know—Charlie or Bill, or whoever she'd just done a number on. But it was all for laughs. Lisa was a terrific storyteller. She'd mimic these guys, and it was a hoot. It really was."

"What would you say if I told you that Lisa kept a diary with some pretty heavy-duty prose in it?"

Thomas shrugged. "I'd believe anything about Lisa. *Anything.*"

"Last night she was meeting someone named Reggie. Does that ring a bell?"

Thomas shook his head. "Sorry."

"She was going to meet him at seven, apparently. Did you see her leave the house anytime between six and seven?"

"No."

"What kind of background did Lisa Franklin come from?"

"A pretty ritzy background. She said one time that her father had a seat on the New York Stock Exchange."

"Do you think she was telling the truth?"

"I don't think Lisa ever lied. She just wasn't *involved* enough to lie, if you know what I mean. Whatever she had on her mind, she came right out with it. Lisa just plain didn't give a shit. That was her charm. You always knew exactly where she stood—and where you stood, as far as Lisa was concerned."

"So where'd you stand with her, Jamie?"

Thomas thought about it. Then, reflectively, wistfully, he said, "I suppose I stood with Lisa the way I would've stood with you in high school—if you'd bothered to notice me. She tolerated me, let me hang around. It's the story of my life."

9

Here, with the door closed, he was safe.

Not locked. Closed, but not locked.

Because a locked door would itself be an admission of fear, therefore of guilt.

With disproportionate effort, he lifted his left wrist, consulted his watch. The time was two-fifteen in the afternoon. The date, October fifteenth.

Midnight to noon had been twelve hours. Plus two hours and fifteen minutes. Total elapsed time, fourteen hours, fifteen minutes. Plus another ten minutes, the time between her death and midnight.

How long had it been, how many minutes, since he'd last checked his watch? Why was it so terribly important that he know precisely the time that had elapsed since she'd died?

Was there a clue in the Bible: the elapsed time since Christ's birth, A.D., Anno Domini?

The birth of Christ.

The death of Lisa Franklin.

From Christ's birth, everything, for everyone, began.

Just as for him, from Lisa's death everything had begun—and ended.

He'd first suspected it as he was driving down Lake Street, with the revolver on the floor of the car, on the passenger's side. He'd intended to drive at twenty-five, the limit. Because if he were pulled over by a patrolman, and the policeman saw the gun, it was finished. Everything, finished. But the car, an inanimate object, had betrayed him, had gone thirty, not twenty-five. And in those moments before the car had finally responded, he'd felt the first terrible pang of vulnerability, felt the numbing realization that he was alone, that when he'd stepped over the line and then looked back everyone was arrayed against him: the police with their heavily belted burden of pistols and handcuffs and radios and batons, the lawyers with their briefcases, the black-robed judges, and—finally—the jailers, with their keys.

And then came the executioner, his hand on the lever that would drop the cyanide pellets into the vat of acid beneath the chair.

Once more, he was checking the time. It was another involuntary gesture, independent of his own volition. Just as he'd caused the car to break the speed limit last night, thus placing himself in mortal danger, so now was he lifting his wrist, gazing at the dial of his watch. Last night, he'd paid no penalty for his inability to control the car—just as, now, he paid no penalty for the compulsion that caused him constantly to consult his watch. Here, safe in his sanctuary, with the door closed but not locked, he paid no penalty.

But soon, very soon, he must venture outside, take up his role of the innocent abroad. And for that role, take off one mask and put on another mask, he must be ready.

Therefore, with great effort, he must lower his arm until, yes, it lay in his lap. Then he must rotate the arm until the palm was up, rendering the watch invisible, turned facedown.

And then, having established control, he must pronounce the word. First it would be hardly more than a breath, not even a whisper. But then, with determination, mind over matter, it would be a whisper. Until, finally free, he could say the word aloud:

Murderer.

10   The three-story brick building was a turn-of-the-century warehouse that had been reinforced against earthquakes, then rehabilitated and finally upgraded to become a part of the trendy south-of-Market real estate boomlet. The directory for the upper two floors listed a number of businesses, many of them architects, industrial designers, and commercial artists. The entire street level was occupied solely by the Jamison Coffee Company, specializing in quality coffee from all over the world. Like the exterior, the interior walls of the ground floor had been sand-blasted to expose the natural brick. Overhead, above the partitions that had been newly constructed, ancient rafters and trusses had been taken down to the natural wood, then varnished. The floor, too, was seasoned planks, also varnished. The aroma of roasting coffee filled the building.

The reception space for Jamison Coffee was small and functional: two contemporary visitors' chairs, a contemporary desk, and a contemporary young woman seated behind the desk. The partition that separated the reception room from the working area was hung with three very large, very grainy framed photographs of horse-drawn drays. The unsmiling drivers and helpers wore derbies, leather aprons, and mustaches. The background building in each photograph was the warehouse.

"I'd like to speak to Barbara Estes, please. My name is Hastings. Lieutenant Hastings."

The young woman behind the desk studied Hastings's face for a long, bold moment, then deliberately dropped her eyes to the gold shield held in Hastings's left hand. Now she raised her eyes to Hastings's face—and smiled.

"A lieutenant," she said. "Impressive." Her voice, too, was bold. Her eyes had turned speculative. Violet eyes. Provocative violet eyes.

"Is she here?"

The receptionist nodded. "She's in the office, at the rear of the building." She pointed to a door. "If you'd like to go back, I'll tell her you're coming."

"Fine. Thanks." A buzzer sounded; Hastings pushed open the partition door and walked through the long, narrow shop floor where a dozen men and women worked at roasters and packaging counters. Here the odor of the roasting coffee was oppressive, no longer a pleasure. Some of the workers glanced at Hastings, some didn't. At the rear of the building a small, glass-walled office had been partitioned off. As Hastings approached the office, he saw a woman rise from behind one of the two desks. She was tall and slim, with an athlete's trim, spare, wiry body. She was dressed in tight designer jeans, running shoes, and a loose sweater that suggested small breasts. Her sand-colored hair was cropped close. In her eyes, even at a distance, Hastings could clearly read tension. The line of her body was drawn taut. Then, as Hastings opened the door and entered the office, he saw tears in her eyes. She knew then.

"You've heard." He spoke quietly.

"Jamie just called. Five minutes ago." She dropped her eyes to the telephone on her desk. There was a computer, too, displaying color graphics. She stared at the display for a moment before she touched a series of keys and the graphics faded away.

"I'd like to check some things out with you," Hastings said. "Have you got a few minutes?"

She shrugged but said nothing, made no gesture of assent. She put one hand on her desk and lowered herself back into her chair as some of the tension went out of her body. Her eyes, in soft focus now, were going blank as she stared at the telephone. Hastings took a chair from behind the office's other desk, rolled it clear, and sat facing Barbara Estes. How should he begin? Should he pretend not to know that she and the dead woman were lovers? *Were* they lovers? How reliable was Jamie Thomas's information? How reliable was Thomas?

"Did you see Lisa Franklin last night?" Hastings asked.

For a long moment she made no reply, her blank eyes still resting on the telephone. Her face was oval, with regular features. She wore no makeup; her forehead and cheeks were slightly freckled. Her mouth was small, her lips compressed. Whatever Barbara Estes felt, she would not reveal—not, at least, to a stranger.

Hastings decided to wait for her reply. Finally, shrugging, she nodded. "I got home a little before six. She went out about quarter to seven. Most of that time, though, she was in the shower. We just had a quick glass of wine and then she left."

"Did she say where she was going?"

"Out to dinner, she said."

"Who with?"

"I don't know."

"Did she know a man named Reggie?"

"I couldn't say." It was a brittle response. When the questions touched Lisa Franklin's relationship with men, Barbara Estes froze up. It was, Hastings realized, the predictable response of a lover.

"On her calendar for last night she'd written the numeral seven, then 'Reggie's.' Does that mean anything to you?"

"No. Nothing."

He decided on another turn of the screw: "Jamie said Lisa had something going with three or four men. He said they gave her money. Is that true?"

"Oh, yeah . . ." The two words were sharply edged with contempt. But contempt for whom? Lisa—or the men? "Oh, yeah," she repeated. "That's true."

"Could Reggie have been one of those men?"

Suddenly her eyes glazed, her voice grated fiercely: "God-dammit, I *told* you, I don't know any Reggie. And I don't know any of the others. *None* of them."

"Jamie says you knew Lisa better than anyone else." He spoke without inflection while he watched her face for a re-action. He saw both anger and desolation, both defiance and the numbing pain of sudden loss. But all of it was kept rigidly in check, internalized. Whatever he got from Barbara Estes he would work for.

Finally she said, "I don't know how to answer that, Lieu-tenant. Lisa was the most complex person I've ever known. She was different with everyone she was with."

"Did she have any enemies?"

"Not that I know of."

"Was she involved with drugs?"

For the first time her lips upcurved in a smile. But it was a smile without humor. "Lisa did everything at least once."

"But she didn't have a habit."

"No. Never."

"And you don't have any idea what she did last night."

"I already told you. No."

"Did you expect her home at any particular time?"

"My God—" The bitter smile returned. "My God, no. You think I kept track of her—had strings on her? Is that what you think?"

"I'm collecting information, Miss Estes. Data. I'm a long way from trying to put it all together."

"Well, the answer is that I expected Lisa when I saw her—just like everyone else she knew."

"She had three leather-bound journals. You knew about them."

"Yes . . ." It was a guarded response.

"I skimmed the entries. They're very—" He searched for the word. "Very poetic."

Her eyes hardened. "Those books were locked."

"Miss Estes—I'm trying to find out who killed her."

She made no response, but her eyes were hostile.

"You say the two of you had a glass of wine last night. Did she seem different when you saw her? Worried about anything? Afraid?"

Barbara let a moment pass before she said, "For the last week or two, Lisa seemed—" She frowned, searching for the word. Then: "She seemed preoccupied, like she had something on her mind. It wasn't anything specific, it was just a feeling. Usually Lisa let everything hang out. You always knew exactly what she was feeling. But lately . . ." She let it go unfinished.

"So something *was* bothering her."

"Something was on her mind."

"What kind of a relationship did she have with her parents?"

She grimaced, shook her head. "Not much of a relationship, that's the quick answer. They're divorced. Lisa grew up in New Canaan, in Connecticut. Her father's a financier, very wealthy, very high powered, a real asshole it sounds like. Her mother lives in Manhattan. She's a socialite, goes to parties, gets her name in the columns. She and Lisa never got along."

Hastings thought of Lisa Franklin's address book, locked in the trunk of his cruiser. There'd been both an address and a phone number for "Mom," but only a phone number for

"Dad." Conclusion: she'd memorized her father's address, but not her mother's.

"How long did you know Lisa Franklin?"

"A little less than three years."

"How old was she when she died?"

"Twenty-seven. She was a year younger than I am."

"Where'd she live before you met her?"

"She lived in New York—around New York. She went to two or three girls' schools, two or three colleges. And she spent some time in Europe—a year, give or take."

"She was restless—looking for something. Is that it?"

She nodded, a weary inclination of her close-cropped head. "Always. That's what Lisa was all about. She never quit looking."

"Money was never a problem."

"No—" It was a soft-spoken reply. "No—not unless too much money is a problem."

"Did she ever marry?"

"No. Never."

He hesitated momentarily. Then, deliberately formal, as if they were being recorded, he said: "What was the nature of your relationship with Lisa Franklin, Miss Estes?"

Her response was a small, bitter smile. "I knew you'd ask that. From the time you walked in, I knew you'd ask."

"That's what my business is all about, Miss Estes. It's about asking questions—and getting answers."

"Yeah—well—I've got an answer for you, then."

"Good." He challenged her with a smile. "Let's have it."

"The answer is, Lisa shared the best part of herself with me." She spoke quietly, defiantly.

Hastings considered and finally decided to concede: "That's not a bad answer. Not bad at all."

11

With Lisa Franklin's address book, bank records, appointment calendar, and the three journals open on his desk, Hastings turned to the address book's "A" section and began methodically turning the pages. If "Reggie" was a man's first name, then the last name could be anything—anywhere in the book.

But a page-by-page scan yielded nothing.

He put the address book aside, went to the calendar. He folded it back month by month to July, then began recasting the day-by-day entries for the last three and a half months. There was no other entry for "Reggie." At least once during each month, usually more often, "Barbara" was entered, followed by a number. As he closed the calendar and was reaching for one of the journals, the phone warbled.

"It's Canelli, Lieutenant."

"Where are you?"

"I'm out at Baker Beach still. See, I figured if the word got out that she was killed, maybe somebody'd come by out of curiosity and have some information, like that. You know how they do, sometimes. Rubberneckers, they're a pain, we all know that. But still I figured that, what the hell, I'd—"

Gently Hastings interrupted yet another of Canelli's long-winded reports from the field. "So what's the status out there, Canelli?"

"Well, that's why I'm calling. I mean, it's pretty well wrapped up here. Everyone's gone but me and a sector guy, I forget his name. He's only been out of the Academy for a year, something like that. Anyhow, I told the lab guys to take their time, get everything covered. I mean, a good-looking, well-dressed victim driving a fancy car, I figured there's going to be questions, maybe reporters. You know. But the truth is, Lieutenant, there's nothing you didn't see when you were here. By the way, how'd Lieutenant Friedman do with his root canal?"

"I don't know. He'll be here in a half hour, just for a few minutes. He's got to see the DA on the Fowler case. Why?"

"No reason. I was just, you know, wondering. I had a root canal a couple of years ago, and it's the shits."

"So what d'you think, Canelli? You want to take down the tapes out there and come in?"

"Yeah, Lieutenant, that's what I'm thinking."

"Okay, come on in."

"Yessir. Right."

Hastings broke the connection—only to have the phone warble again.

"It's Jim Burke, Lieutenant."

Sergeant James Burke, sector supervisor for the eleventh precinct—the Baker Beach sector. Burke had been on duty last night from eleven to seven. Meaning that he was off duty now, probably calling from home.

"Have you got something?" Hastings asked.

"Not a hell of a lot that you don't know, Lieutenant. But Canelli left a message on my machine. So when I got up and had some coffee, I called Scottie Frazer. He covered Baker Beach last night."

"Has he got anything for me?"

"Well, we make the Baker Beach loop about twice an hour, give or take, and Scottie thinks he made that parking lot about eleven-thirty. He's got to check his log to be sure, but that's what he thinks. Anyhow, he remembers seeing the Nissan. There were maybe three cars in the parking lot at the time. Neckers, mostly. We give them until midnight, and then we shine them, clean them out. The Nissan, Scottie remembers, was way off to the east end of the parking lot. Is that right?"

"That's right," Hastings echoed.

"Yeah. Well, Scottie says there was another car parked right alongside the Nissan. It was like the two drivers had arranged to meet there, and then they'd gotten into one car and

44

started making out. That happens a lot, you know, at those neckers' places."

"But Frazer didn't check them out?"

"No, sir, he didn't. Not that round. Like I said, we wait until after midnight, unless there's something that looks fishy. Which, at eleven-thirty, or whenever it was, there wasn't. And then, the next time Frazer made Baker Beach, there was just the Nissan. That was a little after midnight. So he pulled up beside the Nissan and shined it, just with the spotlight. It was empty."

"It sounds like she was killed and dragged into the bushes by whoever met her between eleven-thirty and midnight."

"I guesso, yeah."

"What kind of a car was parked beside her?"

"Frazer said it was a GM product. A Buick, maybe. Like I said, he didn't check it out on the eleven-thirty round. And the next round, it was gone."

"When he shined the Nissan on his midnight round, didn't he see the blood inside the car?"

"No, sir, he didn't. I don't know why."

"Most of the blood was on the driver's door and the seat. So if he was on the driver's side, outside looking in, he could've missed it."

Burke made no reply.

"So what happened next?"

"On his next round, he figured the car was probably stolen and abandoned. So he reported it."

"What time was that?"

"It's only a guess, Lieutenant, without the logs. But I'd say about twelve-thirty, something like that."

"When we got to the scene both doors were closed but unlocked. Is that the way Frazer found them?"

"Gee, Lieutenant, I just don't know. Without the logs—"

"I know. Listen, thanks for calling, Jim. I appreciate it."

"No problem, Lieutenant. Any leads yet?"

"Not yet. We're still trying to put it together, see what we've got."

"Okay, I'll let you get back to it."

"Thanks again, Jim." He broke the connection, checked the time, looked out through the glass walls to the squadroom. In the Homicide section only Marsten and Sigler were at their desks. Hastings consulted his list of extensions, buzzed Sigler.

"Have you got a few minutes?"

"Sure, Lieutenant. Be right there." Sigler dropped a file folder into his Out basket, rose, stretched, made his way between the desks to the hallway, then into Hastings's office. In his late forties, Sigler was tall, gaunt, and stoop shouldered: a lean, spare man. For Sigler life had been a disappointment, and it showed in his face. His voice was pitched low and diffident: "I'm waiting to hear back from Connecticut on her father. I just heard from New York, Manhattan North. They sent a guy named Gonzales, a detective second grade, right out to the mother's place. It's at Sutton Place South, which is very posh, I understand. Gonzales finally got it from the management at Sutton Place that Leslie Franklin—that's the mother's name—left for Europe about a week ago. They're holding her mail, but they don't have a forwarding address yet. Apparently she had reservations in Italy, but something went wrong, and she never showed up where she was supposed to be. Anyhow, Gonzales is still trying. He seems real conscientious. Which is more than I can say about the guys in Connecticut. I told them it was our policy to notify the relatives of homicide victims in person, never by phone. But the guy I talked to, his name is Hanson, he said they gave it one try in person, but then they left a note at the door saying call the detective bureau. They also left a message on the father's answering machine. But that's it. The father'll get the note or the message on his machine and he'll call in, and they'll tell him that his daughter was killed last night."

"Connecticut is having money problems," Hastings said. "Big money problems."

"Yeah, well, I told them to call me back, collect, keep me advised. But they didn't even do that."

"Well, you did all you could. Tomorrow, try Hanson again. Tell him I want some action. Meanwhile—" Hastings began collecting the victim's effects. "Meanwhile, make ten copies of all this stuff, then put the originals in the property room before you go home."

"Yessir—" The bleak acknowledgment was followed by a resigned nod. There were two copying machines for the Detective Bureau, but it was rare that both were operating properly.

"Here—" Hastings handed over the standard receipt form for the transmittal of evidence. As Sigler signed, Hastings said, "Leave me two sets with Millie—no, three sets—before you go home. Then, tomorrow morning, I want you to identify the people in her address book. Right now we've got entries like 'Dad,' followed by phone numbers, so you'll be putting in a lot of time on the phone. Then, see if you can tie in the people in the address book with names on the calendar. You'll see what I mean when you get into it—everything's cryptic as hell. See if the check stubs tie into anything, too. And see what her bank says about her. You know, the usual."

"What're these?" Sigler pointed to the three leather-bound volumes.

"Journals. Very heavy going."

Without comment, nodding dispiritedly, Sigler collected everything, then looked pointedly at his watch. His shift, Hastings knew, ended in a half hour.

"Come in late tomorrow," Hastings said.

"Whatever." Sigler sighed, left the office. Moments later, Lieutenant Peter Friedman appeared in the hallway that connected the commanders' offices to the squadroom. Friedman's resemblance to Canelli was remarkable: both men were swarthy, overweight, and amiable. Each man was indifferent to his appearance, each man was both conscientious and diligent. But their personality differences were dramatic. Canelli rambled, Friedman was laconic. Canelli was naïve, Friedman was the perpetual cynic. Canelli's emotions were constantly on display, an irresistible target. Friedman's defenses were always manned. When Captain Krieger, commander of Homicide, had died of a heart attack while urinating in the department's fourth-floor men's room, Friedman had been a lieutenant and Hastings had been the ranking sergeant. Friedman had been offered a promotion to captain, and the commander's job. Friedman, who despised departmental politics, and whose wife had just come into a sizable inheritance, had declined. Instead, he'd recommended that Hastings be promoted to lieutenant. The two of them, Friedman said, would then share command. The arrangement, he'd continued, was a natural. Hastings preferred to work in the field, he preferred to work inside. Hastings liked action, Friedman liked to theorize. And, finally, for the media, Hastings looked the part.

"So how's the tooth?" Hastings asked, gesturing Friedman to a chair.

"The root canal itself actually didn't hurt," Friedman said, lowering his two hundred and forty pounds into Hastings's visitors' chair. "When the Novocain wears off—" He shrugged. "We'll see. That'll start happening in about a half hour."

"So the dentist knew his business."

"I guess I'll know in a half hour." Reflectively, Friedman smiled: his characteristic small Buddha smile. "This guy is an oral surgeon, I'd never seen him before today. When his nurse was getting me ready—prepping me, as they say—she told me to take off my jacket. So, of course, there was the gun and the cuffs, all hanging out. And it turns out that the oral surgeon is a cop freak, one of those. So, Jesus, there he was with his fifty-dollar hair styling, and his tools in my mouth, asking me how many people I killed, all that shit." He shook his head. "I couldn't believe it."

"So how many'd you tell him?"

"I changed the subject to dentistry." He consulted his watch, then said, "This Lisa Franklin thing, how's it looking?"

"Have you got time for the rundown?"

"As long as my jaw is numb, sure."

Without interruption, Hastings talked steadily for twenty minutes. As he talked, he saw anticipation warming Friedman's dark brown eyes, tugging gently at the corners of his mouth. Finally, approvingly, Friedman nodded. "This case might have promise," he pronounced. "You know, 'Beautiful Young Heiress Slain in Lovers' Tryst,' like that." He nodded again. "Yeah, it's definitely all there. Including the lesbian lover. Very nice. Very with it, no question, obviously not one of our usual garden-variety muggings that went wrong. Just two neat bullet wounds, nothing stolen, nobody raped."

"You're feeling pretty chipper, considering."

"I told you, I'm still numb. Although—" Gingerly, he touched his jaw. "Now I'm starting to get twinges. A two-Martini twinge, minimum."

"Martinis and painkillers? Be careful."

"I'm kidding—at least about the painkillers."

"Do you know anything about poetry?"

"In a word, no. I read a few pages of Walt Whitman once. And the truth is, in limited doses, I like Shakespeare. But overall the answer is no."

"The three notebooks filled with stuff she's written—we've got to get a handle on them. I've skimmed through them, and they seem like fragments, reflections. No dates, usually no titles. Just impressions. We need someone to go through them, study them."

Friedman's small smile turned subtly elfin. "Even if we've got some guys who've read poetry, I doubt they'd admit it."

"Guys, probably. I was wondering about a woman. In

fact—" He cleared his throat. "In fact, I was thinking we need a woman's slant on this." But, as he said it, he could hear the cadence of his own speech, evaluate the rhythms of his own body language. It was a performance that lacked conviction, therefore lacked credibility. Any rookie conning a street-corner hood could have done better. And yes, there it was: the good-humored derision registering on Friedman's face. Derision and, yes, friendly disapproval.

"You're referring to Janet Collier, I suspect."

Looking away, Hastings made no reply. God, what was happening to him? Earlier in the day, in the parking garage, he'd acted the part of the mooning schoolboy, hoping for just a glimpse of her. And now, acting the fool, he couldn't make full eye contact with Friedman.

As if to accommodate his friend, Friedman let his gaze wander noncommitally away, let his voice drop to an easy, casual cadence as he said, "You've always exercised good judgment, Frank. On those few occasions when we were careless enough to get out there in the line of fire, I've always found you to be calm and collected. And, luckily, you guessed right, at least most of the time. And off duty you're not in the habit of making a fool of yourself. However—" Friedman winced, touched his jaw. "However, you're in your forties, and that's the dangerous time. Most guys allow their eye to wander, especially if they're married or otherwise committed. My theory is that—"

"Listen, Pete, this isn't exactly the time to—"

"My theory is that, in our forties, we get our first glimpse of our own mortality. Whereupon instinct, down at the bottom of our brains, sends the message to the top of our brain saying that we'd better take another shot at repopulating the planet. Whereupon the upper brain sends a message to the hormones telling them to go to work again. But it's a coded message. So—"

"Jesus, he's a neurologist. Plus, of course, a half-ass psychiatrist."

Unperturbed, Friedman said, "In my opinion, Janet Collier is the most beautiful, most desirable lady detective we've ever had here. She's also intelligent and she tells the truth, and she doesn't take any shit from anyone, I've noticed. And, most of all, she's been smart enough not to play any sex games with any of the guys here. At least—" A carefully calculated pause. "At least, not until now."

"Listen—" Hastings gestured to his overflowing In basket, picked up a pencil. "Listen, I've got an hour, at least, before I can—"

"She's also," Friedman said, front-loading the two words with significance, "she's also ambitious. Very ambitious."

"What's *that* supposed to mean?"

Friedman spread his beefy hands. "It means," he said, "that she'll undoubtedly rise in the department." Another pointed pause. Then: "One way or the other."

"For Christ's sake, a few weeks ago the dispatcher screwed up, and I drew Janet for backup when I went in after Anton Rivak, who turned out to be a mass murderer if you recall. Rivak got the drop on me before he blew part of his head away. Janet'd never seen a dead man, except at the undertaker. I held her hand, helped her handle it. So what I wish, what I *really* wish, is that you'd just goddam try to—"

Friedman raised a placating palm as he said, "We are detectives. We're surrounded by detectives. And detectives make their living by seeing things that ordinary mortals aren't trained to see. And the squadroom rumor is that you and Janet Collier have the hots for each other. The basis for that conclusion is what's called reduced cues. Which means that—"

"I know what reduced cues are," Hastings interrupted angrily. "And I'd like to—"

Still with his palm upraised, a sign of peace, Friedman said,

"What I'm doing, basically, is trying to forewarn you. I'm trying to—"

"You're trying to run my goddam life for me."

Friedman smiled amiably. "That, too." Then, abruptly: "I'm going to take my empty socket home. More follows."

"I'll bet."

12

At the elevators, Hastings hesitated. It was almost five-thirty. If Janet had been working at her desk, she would probably have already left. If she was in the field, she would doubtless go directly home after she'd finished her mission. Meaning that, if he continued down the hallway of the Inspectors' Bureau to Bunco, there was little chance he'd see her. She would—

The elevator arrived; the doors slid open. The sole occupant was Jeffrey Christopher, the deputy chief for external affairs. In his left hand Christopher held an attaché case.

The decision, then, had been preempted; chance had called the turn.

"Frank—" Christopher nodded. It was a remote, unsmiling acknowledgment. Over the elevator, the red Down light bar glowed. Without doubt, Christopher was bound for the basement parking garage.

"Chief . . ." Waywardly aware of the relief he felt, the decision having been made by external forces, Hastings stepped into the elevator.

"Garage?"

"Yessir."

Christopher nodded; the correct button had already been pushed.

"I understand," Christopher said, "that there was a homicide at Baker Beach."

"That's right."

"Is it one of those lesbian things, is that what I hear?"

Hastings shrugged. "Right now it could be anything. We're still trying to put the pieces together."

The elevator doors slid open. Hastings stepped aside for Christopher to precede him.

"Well," Christopher said, now affecting a small, frosty smile. "Good luck. You and Friedman, you do good work. Good night."

"Good night. And thanks."

Christopher nodded, strode briskly away toward his waiting Saab parked in its private space. Hastings turned in the opposite direction—

—and saw Janet Collier.

She was standing at the rear of her white Toyota Tercel. She was looking directly at him. She wore jeans, a suede leather jacket, and scuffed running shoes. Her dark shoulder-length hair was caught in a ponytail. She was smiling: a small, grave smile of welcome. As he came closer, she half turned to face him squarely. She carried a large saddle-leather bag slung over her shoulder. The bag would contain her revolver, handcuffs, and her detective's shield, pinned to the bag's inside flap.

A gun and a badge . . . the tools of their trade, symbols that bound them together, a small band of men who could kill to defend the law, and who therefore must stand apart from other men.

Men, and—now—women.

It all began at the Academy, with its diabolical tortures designed to test them. And then, with their guns and their badges, rookies, they'd ridden the sector cars, hours of boredom, minutes of danger, seconds of terror, momentary decisions that meant life or death, kill or be killed. And then, afterward, the shakes, the vomiting, the nightmares.

These things they shared.

These things, and the touch of her hand on his, sitting side by side on Anton Rivak's bed, each avoiding the other's eyes.

All of it, inarticulately verbalized now in a one-word banality:

"Hi."

"Hello." Her smile stayed steady. The eyes were steady, too—dark brown eyes. She stood easily, both hands gripping the strap of her shoulder bag. She wore only one ring, a slim band of gold on her little finger. Beneath the lightweight suede jacket, he was aware of the swell of her breasts. Up close now, he saw that the leather jacket was fringed at the bottom and beneath the sleeves. He saw, too, that the jacket wasn't quite clean.

"You've been out in the field."

The smile widened. "I'm glad you noticed. I wouldn't want you to think I didn't clean my clothes."

"That's not what I was thinking."

"Good." She nodded.

A moment of silence passed—and another moment, lengthening. Was it a companionable silence? Or had they already run out of words?

"Do you—" He frowned, began again: "Is it a problem for you, if you're out in the field? With your son, I mean, leaving him alone, especially at night."

"It *was* a problem when he was younger. But he's fifteen. I can leave him now. Besides, we have a dog."

"What kind of a dog?"

"A yellow Lab. Lu Lu." Her smile widened. Plainly, the thought of the dog pleased her.

"Ah . . ." He nodded. He realized that they were closer

now. If he reached out, he could put both hands on her waist, draw her to him, her body touching his. At the thought, he felt his genitals stir, begin to tighten. Did she sense the quickening, an elemental male-female awareness?

"And in Bunco," she was saying, "there's not much night work. That's one reason I applied for it."

"It makes sense."

"Yes . . ."

"Where were you before Bunco? In the cars?"

"Yes . . . the cars." Another moment of silence. Then: "Do you have children?"

He nodded. "They're older, though. Seventeen and twenty. They live in Michigan with their mother."

She made no reply. He realized that they were no longer standing so closely together. Whatever the magic, it was fading. As if to confirm it, she moved a step to her right, closer to the door of her car.

"Listen—" He moved with her. Artlessly repeating: "Listen, have you got time to have a drink? Coffee—whatever. There's—there's something I want to ask you, about a case."

Unsmiling now, calmly, she studied his face. Never— ever—had Janet Collier been seen after hours with another policeman.

She looked at her watch. Then, speaking deliberately, she said, "Coffee would be fine. Not at Smitty's, though."

Smitty's, the high-volume cops' bar, one block from the Hall. It had been more than a year since Hastings had been inside the place. Drinking ginger ale in a cops' bar somehow felt ostentatious, a presumption of virtue he'd never felt.

To disguise the sudden, irrational rush of elation he felt, Hastings drew a deep breath before he said, "How about that Chinese restaurant on Harrison—the Jade Temple."

"Perfect." She turned, began walking toward the garage's exit. Even though she was a small, compact woman, she walked with long, purposeful strides, swinging her arms. For

Hastings, the movement of her buttocks and thighs expressed the essence of the woman: concise, controlled, even aloof, therefore doubly desirable, a prize to be offered, never taken.

"What I should do," Janet said, "is get a set of Xeroxes from Sigler and take them home with me. I can't imagine reading poetry in the squadroom tomorrow."

"I'm not sure 'poetry' is what I mean. The entries in her journal are—well—they're complex. 'Almost poetry,' maybe."

"Still . . ."

"Will you have time tonight?" Hastings asked. "At home?"

"I'll make time," she answered.

They shared a small round table, a pot of tea, and an order of Chinese pot stickers. At five forty-five, the Jade Temple was still almost deserted, preparing for the inevitable dinnertime rush. To give herself time to decide what to say next, she sipped her tea, watched him over the rim of her cup. Finally: "I'm like every inspector in the Bureau—I'd do anything to get a shot at Homicide."

He smiled meaningfully. "Anything?"

Looking for a clue to the question's real meaning, she studied his face. Was he, after all, like the rest of them: a big, muscular, macho male cop looking to get his rocks off, easy come easy go? Was it, after all, no more than a con, telling her he needed a woman on the Franklin case? For four years, ever since she'd made inspector, she'd been aware of Frank Hastings. He was part of the departmental mythology: Hastings and Friedman, that legendary duo, Hastings the calm, brave, photogenic field commander, Friedman the inside man, the shrewd tactician. Hastings the introvert, always so serious. And Friedman the extrovert, always ready with a flip theory or a wry quip. She'd always—

"Sorry," he was saying. "I didn't mean—" He broke off, frowning slightly, obviously irked with himself. His discomfort pleased her, a sudden surge of warmth, an irrational pleasure. Because this was her image of Hastings: so serious and conscientious—and, God, so attractive.

So attractive and—once more—so close, just the two of them, separated only by this small round table. Did men like Hastings realize the effect they had on women? Did Hastings cultivate his strong, silent image? Or was he, at bottom, really an egotist, no more than a skillful actor?

No, not an actor. In the moments after Anton Rivak had turned his gun away from Hastings and on himself, Hastings hadn't been acting. He'd been shaken, yes. Devastated, momentarily. But he'd been calm and steady: always the officer in charge.

"Do you think Sigler's still at the Hall?" she asked. "If he is, I could go back, pick up the Xeroxes."

"He'll leave three sets on Millie's desk for me. You can take one set."

"Fine."

"Do you have to cook dinner when you go home?"

"It depends. Sometimes Charlie cooks. Chef Boyardee, mostly."

"Charlie—your son?"

Was it a casual question, idle curiosity? How much did he know about her? If she lived with a man, would Hastings know—as she knew that he lived with a woman and her two sons, a long-standing relationship?

She nodded. "Right. My son."

"You're—what—divorced?"

"Yes. You, too?"

He nodded. "For a long time, now. Years." He spoke heavily, an admission of defeat.

"Me, too. It's been—God—twelve years. I was only twenty-three when I was divorced." In her own voice she could hear the same heaviness, the same flat, toneless admission of failure so plain in his voice, his manner. This, too, they shared.

"So—" He smiled. "So twenty-three plus twelve—thirty-five?"

Something in the way he said it, a suggestion of intimacy in his voice, his smile, the subtle, knowing slant of his eyes as he watched for her response—all of it confirmed that, between them, this was their first face-to-face, man-to-woman exchange. How often, in the past twelve years, had she come to this moment with other men? How often had she backed away?

As now she leaned slightly back in her chair, away from him as she said, "Can I ask you something, Lieutenant?"

"If you'll call me Frank you can ask." Followed by, yes, the same meaningful smile. Did men know how predictable they were? Even Hastings—a serious, straightforward man—even Hastings was playing the game: Call me Frank now. Call me darling later, in bed.

Unsmiling now, still holding her body rigid in the chair, she said, "Is it all business, the reason you want me to help with Lisa Franklin? Is that the whole story?"

For a long, solemn moment, neither of them moving, they looked at each other, one long, speculative exchange. Then he said, "The truth?"

She nodded. "Please."

"Okay—the truth is, I—I'd like to see more of you." He spoke as he always spoke: evenly, directly, but now almost shyly, trusting her with a confession, his gift of conscience. *Was* this man different from the others?

Drawing a deep breath, she decided to trust him, too: "Maybe I should tell you my life story." She smiled as she said it, lightening the mood.

"Please." He returned the smile.

"It's really pretty simple. My dad had a fairly successful auto body shop in the Mission. When I was ten, he died. It was lung cancer, probably from paint solvents, the doctors said. My mother got cheated when she tried to sell the business, and there wasn't much money, except for a little insurance. They never really got along, my mother and dad. She thought she was better than he was, because her father sold real estate and drove big—"

Suddenly Hastings laughed, a spontaneous eruption. Surprised, she broke off. He raised his hand, shook his head.

"Please—go on. I'm sorry."

"Why'd you laugh?" It was a quiet, firm question, a demand.

"*My* father sold real estate and always drove big cars," he answered. "Except that the cars were never paid for."

"God—really? That's my grandfather. Big smile, nothing behind it."

"Go on."

"Well," she said, picking up the thread, "the point is, my mother married again, a little more than a year after my dad died. I hated him. My stepfather, I mean. He—I hate to say it—" She looked at him apologetically. "But he was a salesman, too, all flash. Anyhow, I got married when I was eighteen, mostly to get out of the goddam house. I'd been riding streetcars out to State College for a couple of years, taking journalism and working my way through, when I met a guy—Collier—and I married him. Two years later, when I was twenty, I had Charlie. And three years after that, when I found out that Collier was screwing every woman in sight, I got a divorce. My mother was divorced, too, by that time. So we moved in together. Between us, we managed to raise Charlie. That's when I was driving a cab while I waited for my name to come up for the police exam."

"You drove a *cab?*"

"Sure. I liked it. Flexible hours, fresh air. It's a great second job. I drove twenty hours a week even when I was going to the Academy." She hesitated, then said, "The reason I'm telling you all this is that I'm supporting a child, and I'm partly supporting my mother. I need money—more money than I'm making now. I took the sergeant's exam two years ago—and I

59

flunked. I flunked because the only cop I ever fooled around with all the time I've been on the force saw to it that I flunked. We went to bed once. When I said no more, he never forgot it, the bastard. He swore he'd get back at me."

She saw him frown, saw his eyes lose focus as he calculated. Then he said, "I could probably figure out which guy you're talking about."

She nodded grimly. "You probably could."

"But I won't."

"Good."

"Go on."

She smiled, cheerfully spread her hands. "There isn't much more left to tell. You've got my whole life story."

"So what you're saying is, no office romances."

She drank the last of her tea, took up the pot, poured tea into his cup, then into her own. As she set aside the pot she said, "What's your life story? It's your turn."

"It's a little like your story. You grew up in the Mission, I grew up in the Sunset. You already know about my dad, what he did for a living. Except that when I was fourteen, he disappeared with his girl Friday in his big shiny car—that the finance company was trying to foreclose on. He turned up in Texas, eventually. That's where he died—he and his girl Friday, in the big shiny car, on a two-lane road in west Texas. They'd been drinking. A lot."

"Ah—I'm sorry."

He nodded acknowledgment, a wry, resigned inclination of his head.

"You were a football hero," she said, gently prompting him.

"Hero?" He spoke ironically. "In high school, maybe. But then it gets tougher—a lot tougher. Still, I can't complain. I got into Stanford on an athletic scholarship. And then I played a couple of seasons for the Detroit Lions before I got my knee screwed up."

"So then what?"

"Before I hurt my knee, I got married. She was a socialite—and it was a mistake. A very big, very painful mistake. When I was cut from the Lions, I went to work for her father, who manufactured auto radiators. It was a PR job, so-called. Which meant that I got a good salary for doing nothing but meeting VIPs at the airport—and then entertaining them. Drinking with them, mostly."

In protest, she shook her head. "I can't see you as a glad hander."

"I was for a while. It was all there was to me, for two or three years. But then—" As if the memory caused him physical pain, he winced. "Then, surprise, I discovered that I couldn't stop drinking. I also discovered that my wife was fooling around with one of her doubles partners. That's when I decided to leave town. My father-in-law offered me a check, to leave.

"No," he said, answering the unspoken question in her eyes. "I didn't take it. A year or two later, I wished I had. But—no—I didn't take it."

"So you're divorced. Your wife lives back east with your kids. She married her doubles partner."

Surprise showed in his face—and pleasure, too. Did he know how handsome he was, with his dark, serious eyes and his generously proportioned mouth? Did he realize how urgently his trim, muscular body invited her touch?

"How'd you know?" he asked.

"I guessed." She smiled. "Honest." She caught herself almost touching his hand.

"Well," he said, "good detectives make good guesses. It's an established fact, as Friedman would say."

"Listen, I've got to—" She raised her wrist, checked the time. Then, amazed: "God, it's almost seven. I've got to pick up those Xeroxes, then get home." She moved her chair back, began putting on her jacket.

"I'll come with you, to get the Xeroxes," he offered.

"You don't have to come with me." She spoke firmly. "You'll probably be late getting home as it is."

"I was just getting to that part. Home, I mean. My—ah—situation."

She waited while he dropped money on the table, then she rose with him, saying, "I already know your situation."

"Do you?"

"You're a departmental celebrity, Lieutenant. And celebrities pay the price of lost privacy."

He sighed—then smiled. "Frank. Remember?"

"Frank," she agreed.

Also smiling.

13 On the TV screen, white blobs of clouds overlaid a multicolored map of the western states. The California coast was clear, the coast to the north was overcast. The words of the razor-cut TV weatherman, personality plus in his three-piece suit, were indistinct, merely sound, no sense. Yet if he chose, he could focus on the words, extract the meaning. His powers of concentration, he knew now, were prodigious. Actors learned their lines, costumed themselves, became someone else: themselves, separated from themselves.

Just as last night he'd become someone else, a stranger to himself.

Soon he would forget, he knew that now.

Soon the mind would smooth over the memory, eventually cause it to disappear, forgetfulness forever, the power of time's eternal passage, the cross-currents of hate and love and greed and envy, all of it would soon allow him to rest, himself the savior of himself.

On the TV screen, numbers had replaced pictures. A high of sixty-two degrees today, a probable low of forty-two. For October, the announcer intoned, the weather was unseasonably warm.

But the weather, normal or not, signified nothing. The weather was far across the chasm that had opened behind him last night, part of an existence divided now: himself here, the rest on the far side.

Murderers to the left, all others to the right. The princes, the paupers, and, yes, the policemen. All of them were standing on the edge of the chasm, staring across.

He raised the stem glass, drank half the wine, replaced the glass on the side table.

Soon, as it came to every actor, it would come to him: put on the costume, slip on the mummer's mask, draw a deep breath, and walk the few short steps that remained before the chasm's edge.

14

"No—" Barbara raised her hand as Thomas offered the bottle of wine. "No more."

In the downstairs flat at 1830 Page Street, they sat around a huge wooden spool that had once held electrical cable and now served as a coffee table. Eyes glazed, a wineglass precariously held in slack fingers, C. J. Kirk sat slumped in a canvas director's chair, his chin on his chest, legs spread wide, toes out. Watching him, Barbara felt the rise of contempt more bitter than bile. Whatever images were flickering in C. J.'s head, whatever his mumblings meant, C. J. was out of it.

Putting the wine bottle on the table, Jamie Thomas settled back in a frayed rattan chair and propped his feet on the table. Thomas's eyes were clear, his voice only slightly blurred by the joint they'd just shared—the first joint for Estes and Thomas, the second, at least, for Kirk.

"I had the feeling," Thomas said, "that Hastings thinks it was a random killing, some freak with a gun, driving around looking for someone to kill. Lisa just happened to be the one he picked. That's what I think."

"I don't think Hastings has a clue," Barbara answered. "I don't think you've got a clue, either."

Thomas's seamed, ravaged face twisted into a thin counterfeit of a smile. "Grief hasn't softened you, I see. Same warm, cuddly Barbara."

"Fuck you, Jamie."

He shrugged indifferently, made no reply. Barbara half turned to face C. J. She watched him for a moment. Then she put her glass on the table, suddenly clapped her hands. C. J. made no response.

"*Hello. Anyone home?*" She clapped again. Nothing. She took the glass of wine from his inert fingers, put it aside. Then she slapped Kirk, hard.

"Ah—what?" Briefly C. J. focused his attention on her, then lapsed back into his stupor.

"*Hey!*" Another slap. And another. On her feet now, she grasped his shirt front with both hands, pulled Kirk up straighter in his chair.

"Do you hear me, asshole?" She shook him so hard his head bounced. "*Do* you?"

"Sure," he mumbled. "Shit."

"Look at me, then."

Kirk blinked vaguely.

"You want more?" She braced herself, drew back her hand.

"Ah—no. Stop."

"When'd you get home last night. *Tell* me."

"Midnight, maybe. I dunno. Ask Jamie."

"I asked Jamie. All he knows is that you were bombed this morning. Completely bombed."

"Hmmm . . ." His eyes were closing. Another slap, another glimmer of attention. Across the table, an interested spectator, Thomas watched attentively. For more than an hour, Barbara had been building to this. Next, he knew, she would use her fists.

"Tell me when you came home last night." As, yes, she clenched her fist, drew it back. Soon, Jamie was sure, the blood sport would begin. He was conscious of a deep, primitive stirring of anticipation. Angry, aroused, Barbara was capable of anything. How many others realized that?

"I told you," Kirk was mumbling, "midnight, one o'clock, something like that."

"Where'd you go? Where *were* you last night?"

"Just—just hanging around. You know—" As he spoke, Kirk tried to bring her into focus.

"You saw Lisa last night. *Didn't* you?"

"Wh-why d'you—" He broke off. Then, mumbling: "No, I didn't see her."

"You know something. You know how she died. *Don't* you?"

His response was unintelligible.

She swung, hit him flush in the cheek. *"Don't* you?"

Half rising out of his chair, staggering, arms flailing wildly, he lunged for her. She stepped back, brought her knee up, and caught him full in his face. His head snapped back, then came forward. He fell on all fours, head hanging, the crouch of the defeated fighter. Eyes tightly closed, he was sobbing.

"Tell me, you son of a bitch."

"Hey—" On his feet, Thomas grasped her shoulder, pushed her back. "Hey—enough. Jesus, Barbara. There're cops outside."

"They should be arresting the bastard."

"You're hallucinating. You think he killed her? My God, look at him—" On the floor, still sobbing, eyes squeezed shut, Kirk was drawn up into the fetal position, hugging his knees with scrawny arms. "*Look* at him. Can you see him killing anyone?"

She looked down at Kirk, then turned angry eyes on Thomas. Her voice was low, choked by fury. "You're disgusting, the two of you. Do you know how disgusting you are? What d'you see when you look at him—" She stared down at Kirk. Beneath his nose, a small pool of blood was forming. "He's—Christ—he's what you were, twenty years ago. That's why he can't stand to look at you. You're degenerates, both of you. Acid heads. That's why you hated her. She—Christ—she blinded you, she was so pure. So you destroyed her. You—"

Suddenly she choked. Her hand was drawn back, fist clenched, as if to attack Thomas. Then, blindly, she flung herself away. She went through the hallway into the kitchen and on up the outside back stairs. At ten o'clock, the surrounding buildings were beginning to go dark. She was in her own kitchen now, then in the hallway. In moments, she would *know*. Past the dining room door, the bathroom door, her door. Lisa's door stood half open. The room was dark.

Why had she waited until now to do it? Was it the police, with their key to the padlock they'd put on the front door and their yellow "crime scene" tapes? Was it C. J. and Thomas, those spaced-out husks of decay and corruption?

Or was it part of the ritual: death and its message must be measured, calculated, assigned equal weight, the damned and the damning together, the quick and the dead, united at last.

She put out her hand, flipped the light switch. She'd known the police would take the address book and the calendar and, yes, the leather-bound journals. She'd known it and, yes, Lisa would have known, too.

Third shelf, she'd said. *Right over the desk.*

She began with *The Poems of Gerard Manley Hopkins,* letting the pages hang down, riffling the pages, back and forth, repeatedly. She put the book aside, took down a second book, and a third, making a stack of books on the desk.

Then, riffling through *Sylvia Plath's Imagery,* she found it: a single sheet of heavy bond paper, folded twice. Lisa never wrote on anything but bond paper.

She set the book aside, left the paper where it had fallen on the desk. She drew the desk chair closer and sat down. She was aware that, after the rush of rage only minutes before, her body was not quite coordinated. Her fingers trembled as she took the sheet of paper, opened it—

—and read the name.

Only his name, written in Lisa's unmistakable handwriting, bold and beautiful.

15

Somewhere nearby, a mile or less, a siren sounded. It was an ambulance siren, not a police siren. For each emergency service, the sirens had characteristic notes, the sounds that defined the city: lives in danger from disease, or fire, or mayhem. When he'd been riding in the cars those first two years, he'd once calculated that he'd hit the siren, code three, about once a week, fifty times a year, give or take. Now, in Homicide, the siren switches were never activated. Sirens were meant for those still clinging to life.

Beside him, Ann stirred, said something indistinguishable in her sleep, subsided with a contented sigh. Hastings turned away from her, lay on his back, adjusted the bedclothes under his chin, stared up at the ceiling. Tonight, sleep would come slowly. A half hour ago, they'd made love. As they always did when Ann's two sons were in the house, they kept their passion fiercely to themselves. Afterwards, sated, they whispered endearments. Then came that inevitable postcoital necessity: sighing, Ann kissed him lightly, slipped out of bed and into her robe, went barefooted down the hall to the bathroom while Hastings got into his pajamas. Returning to the bedroom, Ann got into her own pajamas, got back into bed, kissed him again, yawned, and promptly fell asleep.

They'd met more than two years ago. Ann Haywood's older son, only fourteen then, had been a witness to a homicide and briefly a suspect. It had been a cold, rainy winter night when Hastings had rung the Haywoods' doorbell. He'd had his coat unbuttoned, had his service revolver loose in its spring holster, had his right hand at belt height, ready. The Haywoods lived in a huge ground-floor Victorian flat in Cow Hollow, a prestigious address just down the hill from Pacific Heights. When Ann opened the door she was wearing faded blue jeans and a Norwegian ski sweater. Her dark blond hair was caught in a ponytail; she wore no makeup. When he'd shown her the shield and stated his business, her violet eyes had grown large; she'd raised one hand to the base of her throat, the classic gesture of maidenly distress.

Dan, Ann's son, was quickly cleared of suspicion, but Hastings had contrived to see Ann again—and again. Finally, feeling like a teenager asking for his first date, he'd invited her for dinner at a small Italian restaurant only a few blocks from her flat. Over dinner, companionably, they'd told each other their stories. She was a fourth-grade teacher. Yes, she liked teaching. But, no, she didn't plan to always be a teacher. And, no, she had no desire to become an administrator. She'd graduated from U.C. Berkeley, where she met Victor Haywood, a pre-med student. They'd gotten married the day after graduation. She'd worked for two years while her husband went to medical school. Dan, their first child, was unplanned. Billy's arrival, four years later, had been scripted.

Victor Haywood had taken a residency in psychiatry, and for ten years, give or take, the Haywood family had flourished. The two boys did well at private schools, where they made many friends. After five years on staff at Pacific Union, Victor had gone into private practice, specializing, Ann had said bitterly, in the emotional problems of well-tended but unhappy matrons in their thirties and forties, most of whom had been divorced at least once. When Billy was settled in school, Ann had decided to get a teaching credential. When she got the credential, two years later, Victor Haywood had told her he was taking his Porsche and leaving them. Yes, the other woman was one of his patients: very rich, very beautiful, very neurotic.

Before she and Hastings finished their first dinner together at the Italian restaurant, they'd both known that they would become lovers. It had happened a month later, when she'd come to his apartment for dinner. *Fire and ice* was the cliché, a wonderment. Outwardly a calm, quiet, reflective woman, Ann was a fiercely passionate lover—passionate and, once aroused, incredibly bold.

After that first time, she regularly came to his apartment. And, on those rare occasions when Victor Haywood took the children for the weekend, Hastings would stay with her overnight, for them a rare treat.

Yet, even after a year together, they'd never discussed the possibility of his moving in with her and the boys. Without once having talked about it, they both knew why they hesitated. For both of them, the wounds left by divorce were still unhealed.

And then, a little more than a year ago, Hastings had made the mistake of turning his back on a scrawny, spaced-out cultist who had already been searched for weapons. Instantly, the cultist had grabbed a ceremonial sword from a wall display and swung. Twelve hours later, Hastings had awakened in the hospital. The diagnosis: a severe concussion complicated by a fractured cervical vertebra. The treatment: a week in traction, then complete bed rest for three weeks.

He'd gone from the hospital to Ann's flat; there was nowhere else to go. It was a long, narrow flat, three bedrooms, a bath-and-a-half. The only place for him to sleep was in Ann's room, a fallen warrior. It was perfectly natural for Ann to sleep with him, with no objections from her sons, who seemed to consider the inert Hastings an interesting new project, not a threat. A month later, when Hastings was ambulatory, Ann had suggested to Dan that, soon, Hastings might leave them. Dan's response was simply "Why?" accompanied by a puzzled frown.

And so, a year later, here—now—he lay beside Ann while she slept.

While she slept, and his thoughts flicked to Janet Collier, and then flicked away, the mind wrestling with the mind, temptation glimpsed, then denied.

He'd always been monogamous. Even after his divorce, that season of madness, he'd almost always been with only one woman at a time. During the year he and Ann were lovers, before he moved in with her, he'd never been tempted to stray. Even during his first year on the pro football tour, playing for the Lions, he'd never collected scalps. A few scalps, yes—a few incredible hours in strange hotel rooms, hours and minutes he'd never forget, the gladiator accepting his tribute from adoring maidens.

He'd never forget those hours of utter abandon—but he'd never remember the names of the women, or their faces.

Along with every man in the Inspectors' Bureau, he'd been aware of Janet Collier. Even when she'd been riding the cars, wearing her equipment belt, her hair twisted in a short, bouncy ponytail, she'd been incredibly desirable, constantly trailed by the sidelong lust in the eyes of her fellow officers. But never—*never*—had she given any of them the slightest encouragement. A polite smile, a few pleasant words, and it was always back to work. Over their tea and pot stickers, she'd told him the reason, a one-word statement of goals: advancement. She'd already made one mistake, in bed with a superior officer. And Janet wasn't one to repeat mistakes.

Did she have a sex life? Had her fifteen-year-old son suffered through a succession of weekend "uncles"? Or did she do what Ann had done: dinner at his place, an hour of love, then get dressed, get back in the car, drive home?

His place . . .

It had been a one-bedroom apartment in the Marina. A fireplace, a small balcony with an oblique view of the Golden Gate Bridge, a bedroom barely large enough to take a double bed and a chair and bureau. He'd hung a large cork bulletin board on the wall beside the bureau and pinned photos and memorabilia to the cork: snapshots of his father and mother, newspaper clippings from high school football, the wire from the Lions instructing him to report for training camp. And, yes, a dozen pictures of his children: Claudia with her puppy, Darryl wearing a football helmet and pads, both of them in swimsuits, squinting against the sun.

When Ann had first come to his apartment after dinner, he'd taken her into the bedroom and stood behind her as he showed her the bulletin board, identifying his parents, his children, the various mementos of his life. When she'd finally turned to face him, her eyes had been misted. He'd put his arms around her. They'd kissed only once before he'd helped her undress.

16

"What happened yesterday," Sigler said, "was that both our goddam copying machines were down, and there was a goddam line for the machines in Traffic. And meanwhile, I didn't mention it last night, but my son was in town just for the night and was coming by for dinner. So when Janet Collier showed up, and said you'd assigned her to the case, and I told her what happened, she said she'd take the stuff downtown to a copy shop and do the job. Well—" Sigler gestured to the two sets of photocopies on Hastings's desk. "Well, it all worked out, obviously. I checked with Property, and the original evidence is there, everything signed off."

Eyeing the other man sternly, Hastings spoke quietly, gravely: "You took a chance, Bill. That stuff was signed out by me to you, for transmittal to Property. If anything had happened to it—" Their eyes locked. Hastings let an uncompromising beat pass, then shook his head.

"I tried your pager," Sigler said. "It was turned off."

During the time Sigler was trying to reach him, Hastings realized, he and Janet were together at the Jade Temple. Anxious that nothing interrupt them, he'd switched off the pager—and forgotten to switch it back on until at least an hour later, after he'd arrived home.

If Sigler's record hadn't been impeccable, Hastings would have taken it further. Instead, all's-well-that-ends-well, he dropped his eyes, riffled through the copies. The reproduction was perfect, sharper than the originals. "So you've got—what—seven sets?"

"Right. Janet Collier took one set home with her."

"Okay—" Seated behind his desk, Hastings raised a hand, signifying dismissal. "Okay—so how're you doing on those phone numbers?" As he spoke, he glanced at his watch: ten o'clock. Time was passing.

"There're ninety-two separate entries," Sigler said, "counting both the address book and the phone numbers on the calendar. I had to recopy a lot of it, then I faxed the numbers to the phone company an hour and a half ago. It's going to take time, that many names. By the way, Marsten's got some slack, and he said he'd follow up on Franklin's parents, try to run them down. Dealing with those guys in Connecticut and New York is turning out to be a full-time job."

Hastings shrugged. "Whatever it takes. I want to keep the heat on this, though. It's been twenty-six hours since she was found. And all we've got're zeroes."

"Twenty-six hours . . ." Sigler shook his head, raised his bony shoulders. The unspoken message: Hastings was pressing too hard, too early in the game. But, without comment, he left Hastings's office, went to his own desk, took up the telephone.

Hastings turned to his own phone, consulted a slip of paper, and punched out Janet Collier's extension in Bunco. Then, as the phone rang the first time, he realized that he hadn't decided how to identify himself. "Frank" was out of the question. "Lieutenant Hastings," then? Should he—

"Collier." Her voice was crisp, all business.

"Yeah—ah—it's Frank Hastings, Janet."

"Ah . . ." The single word was layered with a complexity of pleasures. Then, quickly recovering: "I was just going to call you, Lieutenant."

Lieutenant . . . Yes, inevitably, *Lieutenant*. Last night, though, saying good-bye, it had been *Frank*. And then she'd smiled: one quick, brilliant, off-duty smile.

"You had the stuff Xeroxed last night, Sigler said. Downtown."

"He had to be home for dinner. His son was in town just for the night. His son does lighting for Fluid Drive."

73

"Fluid Drive?"

"That's a rock group. They're very successful."

"Ah—"

Was she a rock fan? What would she think when she discovered he didn't like rock?

"Well," he said, "be sure and put in a chit for the Xeroxing. Give it to me. I'll approve it."

"Yes—fine." Then: "I've got some ideas, on Lisa Franklin."

"Good. Can you come to my office? I talked to Lieutenant Cutler this morning. He's going to loan you to us."

"I know. Thank you."

"Well, bring the stuff, come on over."

"Yessir. Is fifteen minutes okay? I'm waiting for a call from a Bunco snitch."

"Fifteen minutes is fine." As Hastings broke the connection, Canelli and Marsten materialized in the hallway. Physically and psychologically, the two men were direct opposites. With his dark hair, swarthy complexion, and roly-poly body, Canelli was the squadroom innocent, the only Homicide detective in recent memory who could consistently get his feelings hurt. His hair was carelessly cut, his tie carelessly knotted, his clothing carelessly worn.

Marsten had his shirts tailored, kept his body lean, kept his blond hair militantly cropped close—and kept his hard-focused gray eyes fixed on the prize he sought: the rank of sergeant in Homicide. It was a promotion that neither Hastings nor Friedman would ever approve.

Hastings beckoned the two inspectors to chairs while he pulled the photocopies of the Franklin documents closer to him, leaving desktop space for the manila folders each inspector carried.

As always, Marsten spoke first. He lifted his chin a parade-ground half inch, cleared his throat, spoke clearly, concisely: "Apparently the New Canaan police tracked down Lisa Franklin's father—his name is Eric Franklin—about six P.M. yesterday evening their time. They didn't bother to get back to us, though, I'm not sure why. But Eric Franklin was apparently able to get a red-eye flight out of New York about three hours later. So he's probably in San Francisco right now."

"Pretty fast," Canelli offered.

Speaking to Hastings, not Canelli, Marsten said, "He took a cab to Kennedy as soon as he heard."

"Jeez," Canelli said, "a hundred-dollar cab ride, I'll bet. Easy."

Still ignoring his fellow inspector, holding himself erect in his chair, Marsten said, "I talked to a Captain Hollowell in Manhattan. He's going to keep trying to run the mother down. But it's probably going to take time. Money, too, if they do much trans-Atlantic calling. Which, in my opinion, won't happen."

"Let's see what the father says," Hastings said, speaking to Marsten. "It's ten-thirty. If he took the red eye, we should be hearing from him soon." He considered, then added: "When he contacts us, you pick him up at his hotel, have him make the identification, then see what he has to say. While you're waiting"—Hastings gestured to the photocopies—"get a set of these from Sigler, see what you can make of them. Sigler'll fill you in, tell you what he's done. Got it?"

Plainly deciding whether the assignment was worthy of his talents, Marsten hesitated, finally nodded. "Got it."

Hastings turned to Canelli. "Sigler's got a set for you, too. See what you think. Stay close, though. There're a couple of guys living downstairs from Lisa Franklin. I want to squeeze them when I get a chance."

"Yessir."

"What about the lab and the ME? Anything?"

"They've got the two bullets," Canelli said, "and one of them has good rifling marks. The weapon was a Smith and Wesson thirty-eight revolver, so there aren't any ejected cartridges. The lab, I already told you, they've got soil samples, sweepings from the car, everything. And, of course, they're working on the fingerprints. But the thing is, Lieutenant, it all doesn't add up to anything. Zero, pretty much."

"What we need are witnesses. What about that jogger?" He glanced at his notes. "Jessica Farr. Anything there?"

"I don't think so, Lieutenant. I could be wrong, but I think she was exactly what she seemed to be—a yuppie with a poodle and a BMW and an upscale running outfit. She—" As Canelli broke off, he smiled. Following the other man's gaze, Hastings saw Janet Collier in the corridor. As their eyes met, still all business, she nodded a brisk greeting.

"Ah," Marsten breathed, "the sexy Inspector Collier. Look at those boobs. Not too big, not too small. Perfect."

Hastings beckoned her into his office, then gestured for her to leave the door open. Manila folder in hand, Marsten stepped close to Janet in the doorway, smiled meaningfully as he greeted her, then left the office. In contrast to Marsten's smooth, self-confident moves, Canelli's departure was a bumbling mix of mumbling and shoe shuffling. His soft brown eyes turned shy when Janet smiled cordially at him.

"Shall I close the door?" Janet asked. Added to the customary clutch of manila folders she also carried a set of the Lisa Franklin papers.

"Yes. Please." Hastings gestured for her to sit across the desk. She wore a simple blouse under a loose-fitting jacket. Her skirt, the jacket, and the blouse were different shades of brown and beige. As always, her brown hair was worn simply, drawn back. Today, though, the lines of her face were softer, as if she'd taken extra care with her makeup.

"So how'd you do?" Hastings gestured to the Franklin documents.

"God," she answered, her eyes coming alive, warmly animated. "God, it's fascinating. I have to tell you, I stayed up till one-thirty this morning."

"Jesus, Janet. You should've slept in."

"Tomorrow, maybe."

"Be sure and keep track of your hours."

"Sure. *Oh*." She produced a cash register receipt. "That's for the Xeroxing."

"Good." He took the receipt, glanced at it. Yes, it was signed and dated.

She set the photocopies aside, opened a second folder, withdrew a length of accordion-folded computer printouts.

"You've got a computer?"

"I've only had it for a few months," she answered. "It's for Charlie, mostly. Kids, if they don't know computers, they're off to a slow start."

Hastings smiled. "You're something else, Janet. When we were trying to get to Anton Rivak, and we had to deal with a Chinese couple, it turns out you speak Chinese. Now it turns out you're a computer whiz."

"I speak a *little* Chinese, because I was on the Chinatown beat before I went to Bunco. And Charlie, believe me, is a lot better on the computer than I am. I just—"

Hastings's phone warbled, an interoffice call.

"It's Marsten, Lieutenant." A pause. Then, insolently: "Enjoying yourself?"

Angry, Hastings made no reply.

"I just wanted to tell you that Eric Franklin called. I've got him on the other line. He's in town, staying at the Stanford Court."

"How's he sound?"

"Hard-nosed, I'd say. A prima donna. Demanding his rights. You know."

"Why don't you take him to the morgue to make the identification. That should cool him off."

"He wants to see the person in charge. Immediately."

"All the more reason to haul his ass down to the morgue. Then you can bring him by here. I'll talk to him."

"Right." The line clicked dead.

"Is the father in San Francisco?" Janet asked.

Hastings nodded. "He took a red-eye flight from New York. He's staying at the Stanford Court."

"Rich, eh?"

"Apparently." He gestured to the printout. "Go ahead."

"You've looked over the stuff," she said. "You know how it goes."

"Just a bunch of first names and numbers. 'Reggie, seven' on the calendar, and 'Dad' with a phone number in the address book."

She nodded avidly; her eyes were bright. This, plainly, was what Janet Collier had dreamed of at the Academy. "Right. So the first thing I did was do a computer list of all the names on the appointment calendar. I decided not to put in the numbers or addresses, or whatever, just the names, going back to the first of the year. I went day by day—" As she spoke she held up three sheets of perforated paper. "Almost ten full months, and it comes to three hundred eighty-three entries, a little more than one entry a day, in other words. When I was doing it, making the entries, I was aware that a lot of names were repeats. Men's names, mostly."

"What about 'Reggie'? Was he repeated?"

"Wait—" She held up a schoolmarm's hand.

Indulgently, Hastings waved in return. "Sorry."

"After I got the list done," she said, "I went back and scanned for repeats. I won't go through all the numbers, but there were three names that popped out." With obvious satisfaction, she tapped the printout. " 'Victor' was noted down exactly forty times. 'Walter' was thirty-seven, and 'Clay' was thirty-six. Those were the three. Number four, to give you a basis for comparison, was 'Barb' at seventeen."

"That's her roommate, probably. Barbara Estes."

Janet nodded, noted the name in pencil on a separate sheet of lined yellow legal paper.

"What about 'Reggie'?"

" 'Reggie' appears just once, Lieutenant. The night she died. By the way, it's 'Reggie's,' not 'Reggie.' Somebody's place, maybe. Or maybe a restaurant, that's the way I interpreted it. I checked the phone book, though. Nothing under Reggie's in the white pages."

"Maybe it's unlisted. I'll see what Sigler can find. He's running down the phone numbers. Which reminds me, were Victor and Walter and Clay in her address book?"

"Yessir. Just the names and phone numbers, as always. At least she was consistent. Incidentally, the 'Victor' entry was in the Cs. 'Clay' was in the Ws. And 'Walter' was in the Ds. So we can cross-check whatever Sigler gets."

"Good." He nodded emphatically, lifted the phone, punched Sigler's extension, saying: "How're you doing on those phone numbers, Bill?"

"Nothing yet, Lieutenant. I'm leaning on them as hard as I can. I think they're short a supervisor."

"Well, keep on them. And tell them that you especially want to know about 'Clay' and 'Victor' and 'Walter.' The rest, we can wait for. Also, check out anything they've got on Reg-gie's—" He carefully spelled out the name, then repeated it. "Collier's checked the white pages, but not the new listings, I gather." He questioned her with a glance. She responded with a shake of her head. No, she hadn't checked the new listings. "So," Hastings said into the phone, "those three names, first. Then 'Barbara.' Then 'Reggie's.' If the phone company won't cooperate, let me know."

"Yessir."

Hastings cradled the phone, nodded for Janet Collier to go on.

"There're other things on the calendar besides just names. April fifteenth is circled in red, for instance. And in February, I think it was, she wrote 'New car. Wow!' But that's the exception."

"However," Hastings said, "what you turned up confirms

what the guy downstairs said. Jamie Thomas. He said she was a courtesan—her word, incidentally. Apparently she kept three or four guys on the string. So those three names could mean a lot."

"A courtesan who writes free verse?" Plainly she was thinking it over, the woman's view of life and death.

"A courtesan who writes free verse and apparently came from an affluent background. Her father is supposed to have a seat on the New York Stock Exchange. That's the big time."

"And he's here, identifying the body of his daughter . . ." Janet spoke quietly, reflectively. Out of focus, her eyes wandered far away. It was a mannerism that Hastings could easily recognize. In Bunco, the victims were little old ladies who might have been bilked out of a thousand dollars. In Homicide, the victims were dead.

As if she could divine his thoughts, she said, "God—it's the dominion of death, isn't it. Nobody gets off."

"Nobody." Deliberately, he put an edge of cold finality on the word. He watched her face, watched her eyes. Whatever else a homicide detective did or didn't do, he must be able to handle death. He—or she.

As if, once more, she had tuned in to his thoughts, she blinked, brought her eyes sharply back into focus. She waited for him to speak.

"What about her bank records and the journals?"

"The check stubs and statements both go back about three months. The deposits were almost all in round numbers—a thousand dollars, two thousand. The last one was for five thousand."

Hastings nodded. "It looks like she took gifts from individuals, which would confirm that these guys were paying her for services rendered. If she was depositing payroll checks, or dividend checks, whatever, they'd be for odd amounts."

"I know . . ." She spoke softly, with regret: one woman's reaction to another woman's betrayal of herself. "I was thinking the same thing." Then: "There was one deposit for an odd amount." She riffled through the photocopies. "Ninety-one hundred seventy-six dollars, a month ago. Altogether, in three months, she deposited a little more than twenty thousand dollars."

"That's a pretty good cash flow."

"But there's no paper trail. Almost all the checks she wrote were for cash, also for round numbers. Big checks. Five hundred, a thousand dollars."

"I noticed that, too," Hastings said. "She apparently paid the rent and the phone company by check, but everything else was cash-and-carry. She probably didn't even have a credit card."

"No credit card, but an annual income of maybe eighty thousand," Janet mused. "This was a one-of-a-kind lady."

"And now she's dead. And her rich father is in town. And we haven't got a clue. All we've got is 'Reggie,' written on her calendar."

" 'Reggie's,' " she corrected absently.

" 'Reggie's,' then." He drew a notebook closer, found a pencil beneath a stack of interrogation reports. "What were those three names again?"

"Clay, Victor, and Walter," she answered promptly. "Four days ago—Monday—she had 'Clay, skeets,' and the number 'one' written down. And a week ago—Friday—she'd written 'Walter,' followed by 'seven-thirty.' "

" 'Skeets'? If it means they were skeet shooting, that'll be easy to check. As far as I know, there're only two skeet clubs in the area."

"I know," she answered. Then, tentatively: "I checked."

He smiled, nodded approval. Sex aside, desirable though this woman was, she was also proving herself an imaginative, intelligent investigator—an asset to him, professionally. The squad leader was only as good as his squad.

"How about the diary entries?" Hastings asked. "Anything there about Clay or Walter or Victor?"

"Ah, the diaries . . ." Her dark eyes came alive; a current of spontaneous excitement animated her face and her gestures, even the line of her body, that taut, infinitely desirable line. "That's the best part, the diaries. I couldn't put them down. I ended up taking them to bed, to read. God, what a woman she must've been."

About to tell her how Thomas had described Lisa Franklin, Hastings decided instead to say, "How do you mean?"

"First of all, I think she was brilliant. And very, very manipulative. I also think she was totally neurotic, really screwed up."

"And beautiful. And unbelievably sexy, apparently. And, if I didn't mention it when we talked yesterday, also apparently bisexual," Hastings said.

Signifying that, yes, he'd told her, she nodded, saying, "God, I'll bet she'd drive a lover crazy. The way I imagine her, she was totally self-centered. She didn't give a damn about anyone but herself, and she didn't care who knew it." She paused, to frame her next thought: "I also think, basically, she hated men. So she drove them crazy. Really crazy. She—"

The phone warbled again, another interoffice call.

"It's Sigler, Lieutenant. I just heard from Pacific Bell."

"Ah—" Hastings smiled, nodded to Janet, signifying a positive development, finally some action. He drew the notepad closer. "Let's have it."

"Well, first, the numbers for the three guys you just gave me. It turns out they're mostly businesses, not individuals. Which is kind of interesting. For instance, the number for 'Walter' actually belongs to the Pacific Trust. They're at twelve sixty-seven Sacramento Street. 'Victor' is a law firm— Cameron, Schott, Birely and Whittager. They're on Montgomery Street, three-oh-five. 'Clay' is the only one that checks out. That's Clayton Wallis. It's an unlisted number, and the address is one-oh-one California Street, right downtown. So I figure that phone's at his place of business. The last one is—"

"Wait a second," Hastings interrupted. "Let me get this down." He continued to write, checked what he'd written. Then: "Okay, that's Victor and Walter and Clay. What about Reggie's?"

"The only thing I found for Reggie's, spelled the way you spelled it, is a restaurant. It's a new listing, only four months old."

"Ah—" With his eyes on Janet's face, Hastings smiled, nodded. Her guess had been a good one. He took down the address and phone number for Reggie's, then ordered Sigler to call the other three men, get their last names, identify their business and home addresses.

"Well, Lieutenant, the thing is, I got to be in court in two hours. It's the Huff case. And I really should review my notes, if they should put me on the stand. Plus, I've got to eat lunch."

"How long do you figure, for the Huff case?"

"The DA's guys say a week."

"Crap."

Sigler made no reply.

"Have you got the other numbers matched up with names?"

"Yessir, all of them. They just came over the fax."

"Okay—thanks, Bill. I'm going to have Janet Collier get them, see what luck she has. Good luck in court." Hastings broke the connection. Across the desk, Janet was already arranging her papers and putting them in the right folders. Her hands were small, moving deftly, efficiently. The message: she was anxious to leave, anxious to get the information from Sigler, anxious to get to work. All business.

As, in the squadroom, on the far side of the glass-walled corridor, eyes were watching them. Prying eyes, speculating.

17

Hastings put the sandwich on its plastic wrapper, gulped coffee from the Styrofoam cup, picked up the telephone, switched to Intercom. Looking out across the squadroom, he saw Marsten standing at his desk, phone raised as their eyes met. A civilian stood beside Marsten, a man of medium height and build, bareheaded, dark haired. The newcomer was dressed casually but elegantly: an expensive-looking trench coat over an expensive-looking turtleneck sweater. His eyes were in constant motion, avidly sweeping the squadroom.

"Mr. Franklin is here, Lieutenant. He's identified the victim."

"Ten minutes. I'm just finishing a sandwich."

"Ten minutes. Right."

As Hastings bit again into the sandwich, a pastrami and Swiss cheese on dark rye, his phone warbled again, another interoffice call. He let the call go to three rings as he swallowed the pastrami, took another gulp of the coffee.

"It's Janet, Lieutenant."

"Yeah—" He cleared his throat, swallowed. "How's it going?"

"I think maybe I've got something." In her voice, he could clearly hear the tightness, the excitement she was feeling. He knew that feeling: an elemental quickening, the excitement of the hunter, sighting the prey.

"The victim's father is here. Why don't you come over to our squadroom? When Franklin leaves, you're next. I'm trying to finish a goddam sandwich and coffee."

"Yessir." The line clicked dead.

Another five minutes, and Marsten was escorting Eric Franklin down the hallway to Hastings's office. Just as, from the opposite direction down the hallway, Peter Friedman materialized. Friedman pointed to his own office. Translation: he would attend to his In basket after his day at the dentist, then touch base.

As he rose behind his desk to greet Eric Franklin, Hastings realized that his coffee cup had left a brown ring on an extradition document from the state of Ohio. He shook hands with Franklin, gestured him to a chair, took a tissue from the bottom drawer of his desk, and tried unsuccessfully to blot the stain. Realizing that Marsten intended to sit down, take part in the interview, Hastings caught the inspector's eye, moved his head toward the door. Gracelessly, Marsten departed.

Seen close, Eric Franklin's face conveyed an uncompromising impression of forcefulness and command—a face, certainly, that perfectly fit the stereotype of an eastern financier with a seat on the New York Stock Exchange. The lines of his face were squared off, suggesting a kind of regal arrogance: royalty, accustomed to command, at ease with the uses of power—and the misuses. What Eric Franklin wanted, he most certainly had gotten.

Until now.

Until thirty-six hours after the death of his daughter, when death had raked Eric Franklin with skeletal fingers, the wound that would never heal.

"I'm sorry about your daughter," Hastings said. "If there's anything we can do for you, we will."

"The only thing you can do for me," Franklin answered, "is find the one who killed her." His voice was roughened by exhaustion. Beneath a country club tan, his face was drawn and pale. But his gray eyes were uncompromising, fixed steadily on Hastings.

"Is there anything you can tell us, Mr. Franklin? I assume you were in touch with your daughter. Did she indicate that she thought someone wanted to kill her? Was she worried? Was she in trouble? Any kind of trouble?"

As if he were analyzing a complicated problem and would

soon render a decision, Eric Franklin sat motionless, staring at Hastings. Finally, in measured phrases, he spoke:

"Lisa came to San Francisco a little more than three years ago, when she was twenty-four. Since then, except for the occasional call at Christmas time, or on her birthday, we haven't spoken, haven't communicated."

"Were you estranged, sir? Is that what you're saying?"

" 'Estranged' isn't really the word. We just—just grew apart. Or, more accurately, we were never as close as we could've been, even when she was a child."

"That's all? I mean—" Frowning, Hastings broke off, began again: "I mean, there was no rupture—nothing specific that blew the top off?"

"Not between Lisa and me. Her mother—" His hands moved in a gesture of futility. "Her mother, that's something else."

"Her mother, I understand, is traveling in Europe."

Franklin nodded. "That's correct."

"And she can't be reached."

"Apparently her reservations were screwed up. I've got people in New York, trying to locate her."

"You're divorced?"

"Yes . . ."

"But you're on good terms, I assume."

"Let's say we're in touch."

"Was Lisa an only child?"

"Yes . . ." Reacting to a sudden spasm of ancient pain, he winced. "There was never any question of having another child."

"Were Lisa and her mother on good terms?"

"No. Not at all."

"Did either you or your wife remarry?"

Franklin's decisively sculpted mouth twisted bitterly. "We both remarried. Leslie married twice after we divorced. I tried it once. Now we're both single. I doubt that either of us will try it again. I'm wealthy, as you probably know. But I'd be a hell of a lot wealthier if I'd stayed out of divorce courts." He looked shrewdly at Hastings. "Are you divorced, Lieutenant?"

Caught off guard, Hastings laughed spontaneously, ruefully. "Yes, sir, I am. I've never gotten up the courage to do it again. And I *didn't* lose a fortune."

"The goddam lawyers. You can't even die without lining a lawyer's pocket."

Across the squadroom, Hastings saw Janet Collier sitting at an empty desk. Nodding to him. Not smiling. Yes, she was carrying her manila folders. And, yes, now Marsten was smiling meaningfully as he got up from his own desk and crossed the squadroom to half-sit on the edge of Janet's desk, one elegantly pressed leg swinging.

". . . get the body released?" Franklin was asking. As he spoke, another spasm tore at his face, this one more damaging than the first. His voice was low; his pale eyes were stricken.

"By tomorrow, probably. I'll talk to the coroner. They have to—" Displeased with himself, he broke off, frowned.

"They have to do an autopsy. Is that what you were going to say?"

"Yes," Hastings answered. "Yes, that's what I was going to say."

They sat in silence, looking gravely at each other. Finally Franklin cleared his throat, spoke in a low, carefully modulated voice. He was, Hastings knew, struggling for self-control. And succeeding.

"Inspector Marsten wouldn't commit to saying much about the, ah, nature of the crime. But I gather you're handling it as premeditated murder, not a robbery attempt that went wrong, or a random killing."

"It's still early in the investigation, Mr. Franklin. So far, we haven't even been able to account for your daughter's movements Wednesday night. But you're right: we're investigating it as a premeditated murder. Her purse wasn't taken, and neither was her money."

"She was murdered as she sat parked at a small beach near the San Francisco end of the Golden Gate Bridge, Inspector Marsten said."

"Yessir."

"About midnight."

"Yes."

Suddenly Franklin's voice rose, a shrill, anguished plea: "But *why*? My God, I've got to know *why*."

"We've got to know why, too, Mr. Franklin."

Once more fighting for self-control, Franklin nodded: one dip of his head, as if the muscles of his neck had suddenly gone slack. Then, head still lowered in defeat, he began speaking in a low, leaden monotone:

"I blame her mother. I've always blamed her. That's an easy out, I know—except that it happens to be true." Even though Franklin's face was still averted, Hastings saw the spasm of pain, now a continuing affliction.

"Lisa was a noisy, willful, demanding baby—and, so help me God, she never changed. And my wife, Leslie, didn't—or couldn't—help. She and Lisa just didn't get along. That's not supposed to happen, but it did. By the time Lisa was two years old, she'd learned how to drive Leslie absolutely wild. So Leslie hired nurses and nannies. They took care of Lisa while Leslie went back to her parties, and her charities, and her tennis. She went to her parties, and I went to the office. It—"

He drew a deep, unsteady breath, then moved his hand, as if to protest the sudden pain of memory, push the pain away. The movement of his eyes was random now, unmoored. His voice was low and clotted: "It's a cliché, isn't it—the poor little rich girl, neglected by her parents, raised by strangers. But, God, it happens. The clichés, you know—they turn out to be the truth, don't they?" Now he managed to steady his eyes on

Hastings, as if to find some solace, some hope in agreement.

"Marriages come apart, Mr. Franklin. And the children suffer." Hastings let a moment pass, then decided to say, "My marriage came apart. And I'm sure my children suffered."

As if he hadn't heard, with his eyes once more cast down, Franklin began speaking in the same cowed, clotted monotone: "Even when Lisa was very young, it was obvious she was going to be beautiful. And so, when she was a teenager, the world was hers—plenty of money, plenty of boys, plenty of everything except parental supervision. By that time, we'd moved from Manhattan to New Canaan. We thought—erroneously, as it turned out—that the suburban life might be good for Lisa."

"People are the same wherever they are," Hastings offered.

Once more speaking autonomously, taking no notice of Hastings's remark, Franklin said, "I kept an apartment in Manhattan, and that's where I spent most of my time—getting rich. Leslie, meanwhile, was amusing herself with booze and men. As for Lisa—" He shook his head. "God knows what she was doing."

"My impression," Hastings said, "is that Lisa was very intelligent."

"Intelligent—Christ—" Bitterly, Franklin shook his head. "Of course she was intelligent. That's what I'm *telling* you. She was too smart for her own good. And too beautiful. And too willful. And—" Once more he shook his head despairingly. "And too cruel, too. I always thought—believed—that she hated her mother and me, and took it out on everyone. Including us."

"Did your daughter have an independent income, Mr. Franklin?"

"God, yes—" It was another bitter rejoinder. "Her grandfather—Leslie's father—gave her a trust fund when she was eighteen."

"She couldn't touch the principal, that kind of a fund?"

"Exactly."

"What did the fund pay her a year?"

"Ten to twelve thousand, depending on the markets. It's all in bonds. T-notes, mostly."

Hastings nodded. Ten, twelve thousand a year—accounting, doubtless, for the odd amounts deposited in Lisa's bank account.

"Was Lisa ever involved with drugs, Mr. Franklin?"

"I doubt it. But I simply don't know." As he spoke, Franklin began to shift restlessly in his chair; his eyes sought the door. Hastings rose, gravely thanked the other man. As Franklin also rose, Hastings said, "Inspector Marsten will take you to your hotel—or anywhere else you want to go. I'd like the two of you to stay in touch. As much as he can, Inspector Marsten will keep you current on the investigation. Okay?" He offered his hand. Franklin's grip was hard, competitive. A glance at Franklin's face confirmed that, yes, he'd recovered his natural assertiveness, his financier's persona.

"Okay," Franklin answered. Not smiling.

18 Even as she came down the glass-walled hallway, Hastings could clearly see the excitement in Janet's face, in the swing of her stride, in the purposeful set of her shoulders. He beckoned her into the office, nodded for her to close the door, gestured her to take the chair Eric Franklin had just vacated.

"So," he said, smiling encouragement—and more. "What've you got?"

"What I've got," she said, her eyes shining with excitement, "what I *think* I've got, is a handle on Lisa's movements on the day she died. I also think I can pin down three guys she's been seeing."

"Ah . . ." Pleased—surprised—Hastings nodded, gesturing for her to go on.

"It's the phone numbers, really. Sigler and Pacific Bell. Except that it took more. And it—God—this is *fun*, Lieutenant. This is *great*."

"It's great when the pieces fit together," Hastings said. "Which, usually, they don't."

"Well—sure." She made an obvious effort to speak more laconically, more professionally. "Well, sure, I understand that. It's the same in Bunco. But—"

"Go ahead," Hastings interrupted. "What've you got?"

"Well, first, the phone numbers. One was for the Pacific Trust. That was the 'Walter' number. So I assume Lisa was seeing some guy named Walter at the Pacific Trust. But the other two were individuals. Big-shot individuals, as it turns out. Victor Cameron, for instance—his private line at his law office." As she said it, she questioned him with a look. Did he recognize the name? He nodded: Victor Cameron was a super-successful personal injury lawyer. Feeling the first glimmer of the same excitement that was animating Janet, Hastings nodded again, said, "Victor Cameron. Sure."

"And the other one—the third one—is also a personal line at a company. The name is Clayton Wallis. The company is Palmer and Wallis. They're venture capitalists. It just so happens that I've heard of them. They made it very big in Silicon Valley ten or fifteen years ago, backing a couple of startup computer companies."

"So—" He glanced at the notebook. "So Clayton Wallis, Victor Cameron, and Walter Something are the three guys that alternated on her calendar."

"Well—" Her nod was cautious. "Well, that's my assumption."

"Did you talk to any of them directly?"

She shook her head. "No. I wanted to check with you, first. For Palmer and Wallis, I got as far as their secretaries, and I backed off. Walter, though—" As she shrugged, the light material of her jacket drew taut across her breasts. "He could be a dud. But, like I say, I wanted to get a game plan from you."

"What about Reggie?"

Now humor enhanced the animation in her eyes. "That's 'Reggie's,' Lieutenant."

"Jesus—all right—Reggie's."

"Well—" Obviously, now, she was having difficulty keeping her professional cool. "Well, Reggie's is the best part."

"So you saved it for the last."

"Something like that."

"So?" He gestured broadly; the floor was hers.

"Well, the only Reggie's in the new listings is a restaurant. It opened four months ago. I have a friend who goes out a lot, very trendy. And she says Reggie's is suddenly the place to be. It's a seafood restaurant south of Market. I called them a little before noon and asked them if they took dinner reservations. They said yes, but when I asked them about specific reservations for Wednesday night, they said they were too busy with lunch today to check, could I call back? They were very nice about it, very cooperative. So I called back and got the maître d'. I asked whether Lisa Franklin was there night before last, whether she'd made a reservation. The answer was no reservation—and the maître d' didn't know her by sight. So I asked him to run down the reservations at seven o'clock. And guess what?"

This time he tried to engage her with an intimate smile as he said, "I give up. What?"

Ignoring the overture, she gave herself a last prideful moment, building the suspense. Then: "There was a reservation for two at seven o'clock—for Wallis."

Hastings glanced at his list of names and phone numbers. "Clayton Wallis."

"They didn't have a first name. But the maître d' said he remembers the couple. The guy was about fifty, very well dressed, very sure of himself, very smooth. And the woman with him—" Another suspenseful pause. "She was in her twenties—and very, very beautiful. Rather tall, dramatic looking, dark hair, a model's face and figure—with the flair to match. A really smashing couple, was the way the maître d' put it. He's British."

"British, eh?" Calculating his next moves in the investigation, Hastings spoke absently. Just as, again, his phone rang on Intercom.

"It's Canelli, Lieutenant. Hey, I got something interesting, maybe."

"What's that?"

"The lab called. They apparently lifted some pretty good prints from the car. And the thing is—good news, maybe— some of the prints are in the blood that splashed on the inside of the Nissan's driver's-side door. So if the prints aren't the victim's, then maybe they're the murderer's, from when he dragged her out of the car. I mean, whose else could they be, assuming our guys didn't screw up and touch the door?"

"Well," Hastings demanded. "*Are* they her prints?"

"I don't know, Lieutenant. I told the lab guys to hotfoot it over to the morgue and get her prints. It shouldn't take too long."

"Okay—you stay on this, Canelli. Keep me posted. Right?"

"Yessir. Right."

"And what about a picture of the victim? Do we have one?"

"Gee, Lieutenant, I don't know. I thought you'd—I mean—" Uncertain of his ground, Canelli broke off.

"No," Hastings answered. "I didn't find any pictures at her place. So you'd better tell the lab to take her picture while they're getting her prints."

"Yessir." The line clicked dead. Hastings turned to Janet Collier. Now he spoke rapidly, concisely:

"Did you get that—about the picture of the victim?"

"You're going to take a picture at the morgue."

He nodded. "As soon as that's done, get copies. Or, better yet, get a Polaroid, for yourself. Don't wait for the lab, that could take a couple of days. Then take your picture to the restaurant, see what the maître d' says."

"Yessir." She began gathering up her documents and file folders.

"Also," Hastings said, "there's her bank account." He glanced at his watch: almost three o'clock. Before she finished at Reggie's, more than two hours would have passed. "Tomorrow, first thing, I want you to contact her bank. Tell them we want the maker of every check deposited to her account, going back three months."

"Anything else?"

"Not for now."

"Do you think—I mean—I was wondering about overtime, tonight. Whether it'll be necessary."

He knew why she'd asked. She was thinking about her son, about making arrangements for him.

"How old is Charlie?" he asked. "I forget."

"He's fifteen. But that's not why—"

"Don't plan on working tonight, Janet. You read her diary all last night. Remember?"

"Still, if anything develops at Reggie's . . ." She let it go meaningfully unfinished. The message: If, in fact, she'd gotten a handle on Lisa Franklin's movements Wednesday night, a development that could break the case, she had a right to follow the trail. Janet was learning fast.

"Get the picture of the victim," he ruled, "and see what

they say at Reggie's. Then call my pager." He opened his desk drawer, found the insider's card with his page number. "Here. Hang on to that."

"Yessir. Thank you." Then she smiled directly into his eyes and said spontaneously, "I feel like I've been initiated."

"You have been, Janet. You have been."

19

"In my opinion," Hastings said, "you should go home. You look terrible."

"Actually," Friedman said, "the tooth—socket—feels a lot better than it did yesterday at this time. But I didn't sleep much last night. The doc gave me pain pills but nothing to put me to sleep." Friedman yawned, then began a familiar ritual: extracting a cigar from a vest pocket, lighting the cigar, sailing the still-smoking match into Hastings's wastepaper basket. The ritual was years old, beginning when Hastings first made lieutenant and rated a private office. At first Hastings had complained, citing the danger of fire. Then, as the years passed, he realized that, secretly, he'd begun to hope for a fire, anything to disconcert the supremely unflappable Friedman.

"The fact is," Friedman said, drawing on the cigar, "I'm on my way home. I just came by to check out this Franklin case."

"While you enjoy a cigar." His voice heavy with irony, Hastings waved a plume of smoke aside.

"Exactly."

For almost a half hour, consulting his notes, Hastings updated the case. When he'd finished, Friedman, still puffing contentedly, allowed a long moment of thoughtful silence to pass before he finally said, "This Janet Collier—in addition to being a dish, which everyone knows, she's also smart. And ambitious, it sounds like."

"You're right. She *is* ambitious."

As Hastings said it, a question surfaced: could Janet be using him to further her ambition? Was it possible?

"She also seems to have good intuitions," Friedman observed. "Which, in this business, is better than being smart, sometimes."

When Hastings pointedly made no reply, Friedman drew on the cigar, blew a lopsided smoke ring, obligingly changed the subject: "What's needed in this case is a motive. So far, all we know is that she possibly knew her assailant. We can also surmise that it was premeditated. But that's about it."

"If the assailant was parked beside her at Baker Beach, we could also surmise that he was her lover."

"Why?"

"Well—" Hastings waved. "That's where lovers go, to places like Baker Beach. And they typically park side by side. And then they get into one car and start making out."

"Muggers also go to places like Baker Beach."

"Muggers go everywhere."

"And it's a well-known fact," Friedman pronounced, "that muggers can turn into murderers, if things don't go to their liking. However, I'm with you. I think we should be squeezing her lovers. To begin with, anyhow."

"Which is why—" Hastings consulted his watch. The time was almost four o'clock. "Which is why I'm going to give Clayton Wallis a call."

"You're going to call first? Not surprise him?"

"Types like Wallis, I don't think they surprise very well. I also plan to call Walter Something and Victor Cameron."

"Victor Cameron—" Friedman nodded wryly, at the same time brushing haphazardly at the cigar ash that had fallen on his vest. "You're taking on a very big job when you try to sweat

Victor Cameron. The guy's one of the best trial lawyers in the country. By the way, the guy's a swinger, I think. A real hotshot with the women. I seem to recall that he's had multiple marriages."

"Is he married now, do you know?"

"No idea." Friedman heaved himself to his feet. "Too bad you're hard at work. I was going to offer to buy you a glass of mineral water while I enjoy a double martini."

"Some other time."

"You AA guys—" Mock dolefully, Friedman shook his head. "No fun." He flipped a hand, left the office as Hastings glanced at his notes, dialed the number that Lisa Franklin had assigned to "Clay" in her address book.

"This is eight-two-four-four-oh-seven-six." It was a cool, guarded female voice.

"Yes. I'd like to speak to Mr. Wallis, please."

"Who shall I say is calling?"

"My name is Hastings. Lieutenant Hastings. It's a police matter."

"Concerning what, shall I tell Mr. Wallis?"

"Tell him I'm the co-commander of Homicide."

"Just a moment, please." The line clicked, went dead for no more than thirty seconds. Then: "Lieutenant Hastings?"

"Yes. Mr. Wallis?"

"Just a moment, Lieutenant." Once more, the line went momentarily dead. Then: "I think I know why you're calling. It's about Lisa Franklin."

"Yes, sir, that's correct. I'd like to talk to you about it. As soon as possible."

"If I'd known who to call at police headquarters, I'd've called. But I don't have a number—a contact. You understand." It was a statement, not a question. Plainly, Clayton Wallis expected his pronouncements to be accepted at face value.

"You were with her Wednesday night."

A quick beat passed before Wallis said, "Did you want to

get together, talk about this? Is that the purpose of this call?"

"Yes, sir, it is."

"Fine. I'll be tied up until a little after six o'clock. Why don't you come here, to my office, at six-thirty?"

Six-thirty, downtown. Add an hour for the interview and a half hour to get home to Ann. Meaning that he must call Ann, tell her he'd be late for dinner—again. He would tell her to eat with her two sons, without him. Otherwise, all-important homework schedules could be compromised. Therefore, before he got home, Hastings would make the Burger King stop.

"All right," Hastings was saying. "What's your address, Mr. Wallis?"

"It's one-oh-one California. The thirty-ninth floor."

"The whole floor?"

"Yes, the whole floor," Wallis answered curtly. Then, just as curtly: "Will you be coming alone, Lieutenant?"

"Probably. Why?"

"Obviously, I want to help. But we've got to be—ah— diplomatic. You understand." It was another flat statement, this one an order.

But Wallis had miscalculated, left an opening: "Would you rather I come to your home?" Hastings asked the question blandly, innocently: the public servant, trying to help.

"No—no. What I'm saying is, let's keep this low-keyed. Which is why I'd like to know whether you're coming alone."

"I'll see you at six-thirty, Mr. Wallis." Click.

The second call, to Victor Cameron, was remarkably like the first call. It began with a short conversation with a secretary, followed by a terse, hard-edged question-and-answer session with Cameron. His office, too, was in the financial district, only fifteen minutes from the Hall of Justice. Yes, Victor Cameron readily admitted knowing Lisa Franklin. And, yes, he would gladly meet with Hastings. In precisely thirty minutes, Cameron would be available for a twenty-minute interview. Click.

Hastings quickly ordered Canelli to get their car and wait

on Bryant Street, curbside. With fifteen minutes available, Hastings punched out the phone number for "Walter" at the Pacific Trust. On the fourth ring, a woman's voice answered: "The Pacific Trust."

"Yes. This is the San Francisco Police Department calling. Lieutenant Hastings. Who am I talking to, please?"

"Pamela Jordan. Will you hold, for a moment?"

"Yes." Hastings checked the time. In exactly ten minutes he must be in the car, on his way to Victor Cameron's offices. Thirty seconds passed. A minute. Another minute. Finally: "Yes, Lieutenant. Sorry. This is one of those days. Now, what can I do for you?"

"How many do you have on staff, Miss Jordan?"

"On staff? You mean everyone?"

"Everyone."

"Well, there's—" Counting to herself, she broke off. "There's eleven, including Mr. Drake. Is this about parking— our white zone? Are you—?"

"Mr. Drake," he interrupted. "Is that Walter Drake?"

"Yes." It was an I-thought-you-knew response. Puzzled now. Cautious.

"Is Mr. Drake there now?"

"Well, I—" Unsure, plainly over her head, she fell silent.

"Let me talk to Walter Drake. Tell him it's police business. He'll thank you for putting me through, Miss Jordan. Believe it."

"Really?" There was an innocence to the question. He could visualize Miss Jordan: in her forties, probably. Pigeon breasted, never married. Round, anxious eyes. Nervous hands. At home, in a tiny apartment, there would be a cat.

Another wait, minutes ticking away. Finally: "This is Walter Drake."

"My name is Lieutenant Frank Hastings, Mr. Drake." He let one beat pass, and another. Then, delicately timed, the single word: "Homicide."

For a moment there was no response, only silence, the phone line softly sizzling. Then, speaking softly, cautiously: "I think I know why you're calling, Lieutenant. I—I've been expecting a call."

"You knew Lisa Franklin. You—"

"Please." It was an urgent plea, half stifled. "Not now. The phone—" Desperately, Drake let it go unfinished.

"When, then? Your choice. Quick, though. I'm running late." He checked the time. In two minutes, he should be under way.

"Could—could you come here? After five?"

An after-five appointment sandwiched between a six-thirty appointment with Clayton Wallis and a twenty-minute audience at three forty-five with Victor Cameron. It could work.

"Where're you located, Mr. Drake?"

"On Sacramento near Leavenworth."

Russian Hill . . . only fifteen minutes from the financial district, traffic permitting.

"All right, I'll be there between five and five-thirty."

"Not before five, though." In Drake's voice, Hastings could clearly hear the tension, the anxiety.

"When everyone's gone home. Is that it?"

Drake's silence was eloquent.

20 Victor Cameron rose from behind his desk, perfunctorily shook hands, gestured for Hastings to sit across the outsize rosewood and walnut desk. The cost of the desk, Hastings calculated, had certainly run to five figures.

In his fifties, Cameron was a short, muscular, bellicose man. Like his body, Cameron's face was thickly fashioned: a heavy jaw, heavy brow ridges, a large, truculent mouth that denied the frivolity of laughter. He was almost totally bald. The dark eyes moved quickly, constantly probing, seeking even the smallest advantage. His rolled-up white shirtsleeves revealed muscle-corded forearms, thickly matted with dark hair.

"I was expecting you to call, Lieutenant. At first I'd considered calling the DA, to touch base. Then I decided there was no need, since I've got nothing material to contribute."

"Just the fact that you knew Lisa Franklin is material, Mr. Cameron."

Impatiently, Cameron nodded. His voice, too, was impatient: "I suppose so."

"You're a lawyer—a famous lawyer. You know what I'm after." Hastings decided to smile. "Why don't you tell me what I need to know? It'll save time."

It was the right gambit. As if to acknowledge his own superiority, and accordingly accept the tribute due him, Cameron nodded. He let a moment pass, then began what might have been a summation to a jury:

"I'm fifty-four years old. I've had four wives and ten children. I'll never—ever—marry again. Luckily, I'm rich enough and successful enough and self-absorbed enough to attract a lot of very interesting women, one of whom was Lisa Franklin. Ever since I learned of her death, I've been thinking back over our relationship. That's inevitable, I suppose." He paused briefly, as if to critique what he'd just said, whether he'd revealed an unacceptable weakness. Then he continued: "I met Lisa about two years ago, give or take. It was at the Oakland airport, on the flight line. I keep an airplane there, and so does Clay Wallis." He broke off, looked quickly at Hastings. When Hastings's face revealed nothing at the mention of the name, Cameron continued smoothly: "Clay and I keep our airplanes on the same hangar line. He and Lisa were just getting ready to get in his airplane and taxi out. The three of us talked briefly, got through the introductions. But the overcast was just lifting, and Clay was anxious to beat the VFR backup to the runway. I had Lisa's name, though. And, lo, she was in the book. I called her the next day, which was a Monday. And I must tell you, Lieutenant—" As if he were taking Hastings into his confidence, man to man, Cameron momentarily focused completely on the detective. It was, Hastings realized, a disconcerting experience, as if Cameron were in direct contact with his inner self and could somehow control his thoughts. Was this how a member of the jury felt, confronted by Victor Cameron? "I must tell you," Cameron continued, "I've never—*never*—known a woman quite like Lisa Franklin. She was an incredible study in contrasts. She was unbelievably complex, and therefore often utterly unpredictable. She was sophisticated, but at the same time almost childlike, once her guard was down. Except that her guard was almost always up—at least with me."

"You saw her—what—once a week?" Asking the question, Hastings tried to visualize Lisa Franklin's appointment calendar. Yes, "Victor" appeared about once a week. And, confirming it, Cameron nodded.

"Something like that."

"Can I ask what—" Hastings broke off, began again: "What'd you do, when you got together?"

"Well, Lieutenant, I think I'll just leave that to your imagination." Cameron's smile was brittle, his expression inscrutable.

"I'm not asking about your sex life, Mr. Cameron. I'm asking what you did together—who you saw, what restaurants you went to, what you talked about. What'd she like to do? What didn't she like?"

"Ah . . ." Cameron nodded knowingly. "The list game, is that it? Well, she couldn't abide small talk—and she never laughed unless something really amused her. She didn't like music, especially—at least, not rock. I think she liked the classics, the hard-core classics. She liked books. She'd spend hours in a bookstore. She liked the movies—all kinds of movies. She'd always eat popcorn at the movies, even though we might've just eaten dinner. She didn't much care about clothes—about fashion. But the way she dressed, she had an incredible flair. She'd find something in a surplus store and combine it with something from Neiman-Marcus, and every head would turn when she made an entrance. Not that she noticed, especially. She was like royalty. She *expected* heads to turn."

"Did you go to restaurants much?"

Cameron nodded. "She liked good food. And she *knew* good food. She didn't eat much, though, just picked at her food. But she had a superb palate."

"The reason I mentioned restaurants, I was wondering about someone like Clayton Wallis—whether there'd be a problem, having someone like him see the two of you on the town together."

"It might've been a problem for Clay," came the prompt reply, "but not for me. And not for Lisa, either. And Clay's married. I couldn't imagine him doing anything stupid."

"*Did* you, in fact, ever see Wallis when you and Lisa were together?"

"No. Never."

"Flying?"

"I told you, no." Cameron spoke irritably. Plainly he wasn't accustomed to having his statements questioned. But then, a switch, he smiled. "The fact is, Lisa and I only went flying together once. It turned out that, yes, Lisa loved to fly. But she didn't like my airplane especially. I have a Beechcraft, which is a top-of-the-line four-place single. You know, glove leather interiors, soundproofing, deep carpets, two-hundred-thousand-dollar price tag. All of which didn't interest Lisa in the slightest. Clay, on the other hand, has a Citabria. That's a bare-bones two-place aerobatic airplane. Fabric covered, noisy as hell, joystick on the floor, with control cables running beside you, sitting in the cockpit. Lisa loved that airplane. Of course—" Now his small smile turned smug. "Of course, I collect vintage sports cars. Which, as you might imagine, turned Lisa on." He broke off, a wayward moment of soft-focused nostalgia. "I have a picture of her in an Aston-Martin I own. If ever a woman and a machine belonged together, she belonged behind the wheel of that car."

Nodding appreciatively, Hastings glanced at his watch. In a half hour, he was due at the Pacific Fund, on Sacramento Street.

"I won't keep you much longer, Mr. Cameron. I know you're busy, and I appreciate your taking the time to—"

"Are you making progress?" Cameron suddenly demanded. Adding: "I'm an officer of the court, as you know, in good standing. So you can answer the question with impunity."

Hastings smothered a smile. Over the years he'd questioned several lawyers. But never had a lawyer told him what he could do—or couldn't do.

Still, the question gave him an opening: "The truth is, Mr. Cameron, we don't have any solid leads. I can tell you, though, that we think it was premeditated murder. So we're looking for connections between the victim and the assailant. We're also looking for motives."

"And?"

"We've got a couple of ideas, but—" He shook his head, waited until he saw interest kindling in the other man's eyes. Then he said, "What about you, Mr. Cameron? Any ideas?"

Cameron rose abruptly to his feet, turned, went to the large window behind his desk that offered a premier vista of San Francisco Bay and the East Bay hills beyond. Seen from the rear, standing instead of sitting, Cameron had the squat, powerful, thick-necked, bullet-headed physique of a linebacker. He stood with head lowered, fists propped on his hips. He held the pose for a full minute, a long time in the lexicon of the rich and famous. Then, abruptly, he turned to face Hastings. He spoke in a calm, flat, carefully modulated voice, as if to give special significance to what he was about to say: "I saw Lisa the evening of Tuesday, October sixth—eight days before she was killed. We had dinner at Masa's, then we went to my place. That night, the last time I saw her, she was plainly preoccupied. Finally I asked her what was wrong. At first she didn't reply. But then she said someone was worrying her. Knowing Lisa, I didn't press her for details. All I said was that, if it was fixable, I most certainly knew people who could fix it for her."

"What did you mean by that, Mr. Cameron?"

The other man frowned, a let's-not-play-games expression. "You know what I mean, Lieutenant. I employ two investigators, full-time. Beyond that, there're private investigators who'll handle anything, for a price."

"She said some*one* was worrying her? Not some*thing*?"

"I told you what she said, Lieutenant." Cameron returned to his desk—and looked pointedly at his watch.

"The information we have suggests that Lisa Franklin regularly saw three affluent older men, more or less in rotation. Were you aware of that?"

Cameron's smile was wry. "Yes, Lieutenant, I'm aware that she saw other men. That's what I've been trying to tell you. One took Lisa on her terms. Period. I understood that. Because, you see, I understood Lisa—and she understood me. We were a perfectly matched pair—amoralists, both of us. We used each other completely. Therefore, we deserved each other completely."

"Did she ever talk about the other men she saw?"

"Not really. That would've been bad manners. But if I'd asked her—which I never did—she wouldn't've troubled to deny their existence. She'd simply have shrugged."

"Of the three men, you were the only one, apparently, that she had more than one telephone number for. The other two, apparently they only gave her their office numbers."

"That's probably because the other two are married. I'm not married, as I told you."

"We're having Lisa Franklin's bank account checked out. A lot of her deposits were for even amounts. Which suggests that she regularly accepted gifts."

"Well," Cameron said, "I can simplify your task for you, Lieutenant. Yes, I gave her money—a thousand dollars or two, every month." He shrugged. "Fair's fair, and beauty is fleeting. It's a perishable commodity, some cynics would say." As he spoke, he rose to his feet behind his desk. "Sorry, Lieutenant. Time's up." And, confirming it, Cameron's intercom chirped once, then twice. A secretary's code.

"One more question." Hastings, too, rose.

"What's that?" Cameron turned toward a coatrack, began rolling down his shirtsleeves, inserting cuff links.

"Where were you from nine to midnight on Wednesday?"

As he slipped into a pinstriped jacket and straightened his tie, Cameron smiled. It was a condescending smile. "Of course, you have to ask that. It goes with the territory."

"Exactly."

"Well, the answer is, I was at home, working late. But there's no one to confirm it, since it was the help's night out."

"Where do you live, Mr. Cameron?"

"On Jackson Street. Near Pierce." The smile twisted mockingly. "About ten minutes from the scene of the crime."

As, still smiling, fatuously now, Cameron gestured Hastings toward the door. The interview had ended.

21 The address for the Pacific Trust was a narrow red-brick town house situated on the crest of Nob Hill, a prestigious location. Across the street, a similar building flew an unfamiliar national flag, signifying a consulate for a foreign country.

"Want me to wait in the car again?" Canelli asked. In the question, Hastings could hear a clear note of reproach.

"I don't want to gang up on these guys," Hastings answered. "This is still the first inning." He checked the time: exactly five-fifteen, precisely on schedule. "This won't take more than an hour. Then you can drop me down at one-oh-one California and take the car home. I'll catch a ride with a black-and-white."

"Right." Amiably resigned to his fate, Canelli nodded. The vintage door of the town house at 1267 Sacramento Street was a gleaming black, with a huge lion's head brass knocker and a discreet brass plaque inscribed simply THE PACIFIC TRUST. Both the knocker and plaque were brightly polished. Were visitors to a place of business expected to use an antique brass knocker? Hastings looked for a bell button, found none, decided to lift the massive knocker and let it drop. Almost immediately, a latch buzzer sounded. He turned the ornamental brass knob and swung the heavy door inward. The entry hall was furnished like an elegant private home: Oriental rugs on the highly polished oak floors, a pair of matching gold silk armchairs, two antique tables, each with a small, expensive-looking ceramic lamp. There were two large paintings, both murky landscapes from another century, both heavily framed in ornate gold leaf. The front door was controlled by a pneumatic closer, and as the latch clicked behind him Hastings saw a tall, spare, conservatively dressed man standing in an open doorway that led off the central hallway.

"Lieutenant Hastings?"

"Yes. Mr. Drake."

"Yes, sir—" Drake gestured Hastings into a large front room off the entry hall to the left. The room was furnished as a library, with a fireplace flanked by two brass-studded leather armchairs. Dominating the room was a long, narrow conference table with ten chairs drawn up, four on each side, one at either end. After inviting Hastings to take one of the leather armchairs, Drake closed the door, stepped to an elaborate electronic control panel, and pushed a series of buttons that armed an alarm system. As Hastings watched, he regretted that he hadn't decided to wear a wire for the day's interrogations. The recordings wouldn't have been admissible but might have interested Friedman.

With the October dusk falling, Drake touched a button that illuminated the room's table lamps, then took the armchair that faced Hastings. Over six feet tall, Drake was a thin, narrow man, precise when he moved, clipped when he talked. His dress was Ivy League: a muted herringbone tweed suit, button-down white shirt, old school tie, burnished brown wing tips with, yes, argyle socks. His long face was defined by a small, pursed mouth, mild blue eyes behind traditional tortoiseshell glasses, a long, pinched nose, a middle-aged neck that was sagging beneath a bony chin and jaw. His hair was brown and sparse, combed to disguise an expanse of bald, shining flesh. His movements were studied: a tall, lean man who moved with the prissy precision of a turn-of-the-century schoolmaster.

"I'd offer you something," Drake said, "but everyone's gone for the day." Like his movements, Drake's speech was dry and precise.

"Thanks—no problem."

"Do you—" Drake moistened pale lips tentatively with the tip of his tongue. "Do you have any idea why she died—who killed her?"

It was the most common question a subject asked—a subject, and also a suspect. If the question was predictable, so was the response: "We're making good progress. But there're still some loose ends."

"You mean you—?" As if he were confused—or frightened—Drake abruptly stopped speaking. Then, in a subdued voice: "You have someone—a suspect? Is that what you mean?" Behind the tortoiseshell glasses, Drake's pale eyes seemed to grow smaller.

"If you don't mind, Mr. Drake, I'd like to ask the questions." This time, Hastings didn't smile. Time was passing.

"Oh. Yes. Certainly." Drake blinked, cleared his throat, forced himself to sit back in the leather armchair. But, almost immediately, he uncrossed his legs, adjusted his trouser creases, recrossed his long, spindly legs. "Please—" He gestured with a bony hand. "Go ahead."

Unlike Victor Cameron, Drake could probably be opened up with one quick, harsh question: "Over the past six months," Hastings said, "how much money did you give to Lisa Franklin?"

"Oh, Jesus—" Drake's head dropped; he touched his high, narrow forehead with the tips of his fingers, hiding his face. "The whole thing, then," he muttered. "You know about it— the whole thing."

"Will you answer the question, please?" Hastings spoke coldly, an effort to disguise the anticipation he felt, seeing Drake so craven, so vulnerable.

"I—" As if he were baffled, Drake lifted his eyes, searched Hastings's face. "I'm sorry, Lieutenant. You said—what—six months?"

"Yes, give or take."

"Well, I—" Once more, Drake's tongue tip circled his pale lips. "I suppose it was five thousand dollars. Something like that."

"And you saw her—what—every week, ten days?"

Forlornly, Drake nodded. Muttering: "Yes. Something like that." Once more, his gaze had fallen, fixed now on the dead embers in the fireplace.

To change the pace, keep the other man off balance, Hastings decided to ask, "What is the Pacific Trust, Mr. Drake?"

"It—it's a foundation. My—my family's foundation."

"And you're the head man."

"Y-yes."

"What's the purpose of the foundation?"

"It makes grants to deserving members of the arts. It's like the Ford Foundation, or the Carnegie. But much smaller, of course."

"You sponsor artists, then. Award them grants."

"Artists and others, too. I didn't mean to say that—"

"How did you meet Lisa Franklin?"

"It was a poetry reading. Afterwards, someone introduced us."

"And you became lovers?"

Once more, one last time, Drake searched his adversary's face, looking for some shred of hope. There was nothing—no way out.

"Answer me, Mr. Drake. *Were* you lovers?"

"Yes. God, yes—" It was both a desperate confession and an inarticulate plea. "But you can't—I can't—" In anguish, he broke off.

"You can't let your wife find out about Lisa Franklin. Is that what you're saying?"

"I—" His eyes left Hastings's face, traversed the large, expensively furnished room, as if to find refuge. "I've never—never strayed, before. Never. I'm fifty-one years old. I've been married for almost thirty years. My family—I don't know whether you realize it, but my family goes back to the Gold Rush. This—" His hand lifted, circled the room, fell nervelessly back into his lap. "This is my family's trust. It was established by my grandfather when I was still very young. My father ran it until his death, ten years ago. He did other things—real estate, investments. But this was always his headquarters. I did other things, too. But—" Suddenly he broke off again, swallowed. "But the point is, if my wife ever found out about Lisa—if there was a public scandal—she'd divorce me. She wouldn't have a choice. And my—my whole life would be over."

"You should've thought about that before you got involved."

"I—I know. And, God, I'd give anything to turn back the clock. *Anything.*"

"How long were you involved with Lisa Franklin?"

"It—it's been a little less than a year. And I—I knew it'd end badly. I knew what she was doing to me. I knew exactly. And I knew exactly what I was doing, too. But I—I couldn't help myself."

"What *was* she doing?"

"She was playing with me—toying with me. Manipulating me. It was a game, with her. Pussy whipping, that's the street-corner expression. *The Blue Angel,* with Marlene Dietrich and Emil Jannings—I don't know whether you ever saw it, but it was a perfect expression of our relationship. Except that the Dietrich character was cheap—a nightclub singer. Lisa was never cheap. Lisa was—" He broke off, forlornly began to shake his head.

"Is that the movie where Marlene Dietrich makes the middle-aged professor do anything she wants, even imitating a chicken crowing?"

Miserably, Drake nodded. "She humiliated him, completely. The film—there's no question—it was a classic, one of the best films ever made. It—it was tragedy. Classic tragedy. It depicted the fall of an otherwise superior human being."

"Sex, you mean. He'd do anything she told him, so long as he could get into her pants."

"Actually, 'lust' is a better word. In the film, it's never clear that they had sex. It was desire—lust—that brought him down."

"And the woman didn't give a damn. For her, it was just a game."

"Exactly."

"Is that what it was for Lisa, Mr. Drake? A game?"

For a moment Drake made no reply, gave no indication that he'd heard. Then, when he began to speak, it was as if he were reading from prepared text, his voice an academic-sounding monotone: "The truth is, I know very little about women. My wife and I had known each other since we were children. We both went to Stanford, which we were expected to do. All during college, we dated. The week after graduation, as expected, we got married. And in due time, as expected, we had a child. So at age fifty, looking in both directions, the view was just exactly as prescribed.

"And then I met Lisa." Marveling, he shook his head. "And I was possessed, that's the only word for it. Ever since yesterday about noon, when I learned that she was dead, I've thought of nothing but her. It—it was as if I were coming out of a very serious illness. And I began to realize that Lisa was the most manipulative, the most diabolical person I've ever known. Everything she did was calculated totally for her own gratification. But, once she got her own way, which she always did, ultimately, she was perfectly contented, like a child at the candy jar."

"What happened when she was crossed?"

"She simply withdrew her favors. That's the option beautiful people have. They simply turn their backs and walk away. And there you are—standing there, lost."

"Did she ever walk away from you, Mr. Drake?"

"No, she didn't. That's something I've thought about, since yesterday. And the truth is that she wasn't deeply enough involved with me to walk away. True, I offered certain things that interested her. But I, myself, didn't interest her. I was her trinket, nothing more. A bauble."

"You knew that, and still you kept on with her—knowing what it could cost you?"

Sadly, he shook his head. "You misunderstand, Lieutenant. I know all that *now*, since yesterday. Call it shock therapy. But when I was involved with her I was blinded. I was willing to take any risk, just to be with her on her terms. That's the nature of compulsion, you see. You're blinded to consequences."

"And now she's dead."

"And now she's dead."

They sat in silence for a moment, each looking away from the other, each lost in thought. Finally, feeling his way, Hastings said, "Suppose—just suppose—that Lisa Franklin had threatened to go public with your relationship. Suppose she threatened to go to your wife."

"Lisa would never have done that. Because, you see, that would have been venal. Lisa was never venal, never sordid."

"In her room, she had some art objects. Paintings, too. Did you give them to her?"

"Yes."

"Did you ever see her room?"

"Only once."

"When you—got together, did you go to a hotel?"

"Usually we came here. The third floor is an apartment."

"Where were you Wednesday night, Mr. Drake? From nine o'clock until midnight?"

"I was home. I watched a video."

"With your wife?"

"Yes."

"Did you know that Lisa Franklin was involved with at least three other men?"

"I—I always suspected. But I never knew, not really."

"Lisa never mentioned other men?"

"No. She never would've done that."

"One of the other men she saw—he's a well-known law-yer—he said Lisa was worried, lately. Uncharacteristically worried. Did you have that impression?"

Drake frowned, considered. Finally: "I'd say, the past month or so, she was sometimes preoccupied. But I don't think she was worried."

"Do you have any idea why she was murdered, Mr. Drake?"

"No. None."

"Was she involved with drugs?"

"Not that I know of. Certainly she never took drugs in my presence."

"Considering her, ah, life-style, I'm wondering whether she could've been killed by a jealous lover. Or—" A pause. "Or a wife."

"I—" Helplessly, the other man spread his hands. "I couldn't say. I can't—" He broke off, swallowed hard, began to shake his head. Once more, his eyes sought the security of the elegantly furnished, gracefully proportioned room, for Walter Drake the center of everything.

Everything, and nothing.

22

As he stopped the cruiser in a loading zone and looked up at the soaring height of the 101 California Building, Canelli shook his head in wonderment. "Jeez, I'm only thirty-four, but I can remember when this was the old Flatiron Building."

"I don't think so," Hastings said. "I don't think the Flatiron Building was here. I think it was at Pine and Market."

"Hmmm—" It was a judiciously noncommittal response.

Then: "Are we going to work the Franklin case tomorrow, Lieutenant? Saturday?"

"Let's see what I get from Clayton Wallis—" He gestured to 101 California. "So far, he's the last known person to see her alive. And let's see when the lab comes up with something on fingerprints."

"Those diary entries . . ." Canelli shook his head again. "Pretty heavy going. What about Janet Collier? Can she figure them out?"

"Maybe there's nothing to figure out, as far as the case is concerned." Hastings got out of the car, said good-bye, walked across the small marble plaza to the building entrance. He signed the after-hours register and took the elevator to the thirty-ninth floor. Palmer and Wallis occupied the entire floor. The reception room was furnished in VIP modern, with one wall devoted to a huge abstract sculpture. The sculpture was metal and soared almost as high as the ceiling. Outsized abstract paintings dominated the other three walls. The reception desk was free form; the desktop contained only a communications console and a single rose in a crystal bud vase. Seated behind the desk, a young, smiling woman was a perfect complement to the decor.

"You're Mr. Hastings."

Not *Lieutenant* Hastings, but *Mister* Hastings.

He nodded, returned the smile. The young woman said something into the phone, then rose gracefully to her feet and opened a door to a short hallway. She led the way to one of two unmarked doors. She opened the door on the right and stood aside.

"Mr. Hastings—Mr. Wallis."

Unlike the reception room, Clayton Wallis's office was furnished entirely in period pieces, most of them European antiques. His desk was a large, claw-footed leather-topped library table with intricately worked brass embellishments. The walls of the office were covered in watered silk. The paintings were traditional, most of them landscapes with a modern flair. One wall of the office was entirely glass, offering a premier view of San Francisco in the foreground, the Golden Gate Bridge in the middle distance, and the Marin County hills in the background.

In his vigorous, meticulously barbered, custom-tailored late forties, Clayton Wallis was the personification of midlife masculine success. Everything was perfect: the deep, resonant voice, the thick, mod-cut brown hair brushed with gray at the temples, the clear blue eyes. The drape of the three-piece suit, the urbane face, the genial affability—all of it had surely been shaped at the best eastern schools. Plainly, Clayton Wallis's forebears were charter members of the privileged classes. His build was perfection: medium height and weight, broad shoulders, a flat stomach. Rounding the desk to shake hands, Wallis moved smoothly, athletically, self-confidently. His handshake was firm but not overbearing.

"Thanks for coming after hours, Lieutenant—" Wallis gestured the detective to a velvet-covered Louis XIV armchair. As he resumed his seat behind the desk Wallis smiled. It was a warm, engaging smile—a confidant's smile. "I'm sure you know how it is, when the—ah—other woman surfaces, so to speak."

"Is that what we're talking about, Mr. Wallis? Was Lisa the other woman?"

"Oh, yes—" Now Wallis spoke heavily, let himself slump slightly. It was another confidant's gesture of trust. "Oh, yes, Lisa was definitely the other woman."

"You're married, then."

"Yes, Lieutenant, I'm married. Happily married, certainly. But these things happen."

These things happen . . . another cliché, another cheap excuse, another vow broken, scratch another marriage.

"How long did you know Lisa Franklin?"

"About a year and a half."

"And you saw her every week or so."

Appreciatively, Wallis smiled. If Victor Cameron was a bully-boy, and Walter Drake was a fidgety schoolmaster, then Clayton Wallis was an executive-suite charmer.

"You do your homework," Wallis said. "How'd you know?"

"Her appointment calendar."

"Ah—" Another appreciative smile. "Of course." Then, casually: "You undoubtedly know, then, that there were other men in her life."

"But you were the last person to see her alive."

"Except, of course," Wallis countered smoothly, "for the murderer."

Hastings debated taking up the challenge but instead decided to shift ground: "You had dinner together at Reggie's Wednesday night. You got to the restaurant about seven o'clock. Correct?"

"We arrived separately. She didn't get there 'til about seven-fifteen." Wallis's patrician mouth upcurved in a wistful smile. "Lisa was always late. It was part of her charm."

"Give me a rundown on Lisa, Mr. Wallis. What kind of a woman was she?"

As if he were deciding whether Hastings merited a confidence, unsmiling now, Wallis studied the detective for a moment before he said, "She was beautiful, as you already know, I'm sure. She was also the most sexually exciting woman I've ever known. She had it all. In bed, she could be bold and inventive and incredibly abandoned one moment, and then she could turn intense, sometimes even combative. She was totally unpredictable. She had no inhibitions. None."

"The perfect mistress, in other words."

"Actually, I never thought of her as a mistress. A mistress is a kept woman—a possession. But that wasn't Lisa. She belonged to nobody but Lisa."

"You gave her money, though."

He shrugged. "One pays to play, Lieutenant. In the parlance of the marketplace, Lisa was dealing from strength—a seller's market, in other words. She made the rules. If you wanted to play, fine. Otherwise, she'd move on."

"Is that the way she put it to you?"

"No. But it was implied. Clearly implied. One could never imagine Lisa without enough money to gratify her every whim. It was part of her charm."

"Did you ever go to her room?"

Wallis nodded. "Twice. But only briefly. Lisa made it quite clear that her home was off limits."

"Did you see her collection of art?"

"Yes, I did. Impressive."

"The pieces were gifts from another admirer."

Unpredictably, Wallis smiled, another confidant's idiom. "If you're trying to disconcert me, Lieutenant, you aren't succeeding. Of course there were other men in her life. But that was part of the challenge, you see. It was a competition, of sorts—who could please Lisa the most."

"Did you ever meet Barbara Estes? Lisa's roommate?"

"No. Never."

"Did she ever talk about Barbara to you?"

"No."

"Then you probably didn't know they were lovers."

"Ah, Lieutenant—" Wallis shook his head; his smile turned mocking. "You'll have to do better than that."

"I'm just repeating what Barbara told me."

"Well, she's lying. Believe me."

"That wasn't my impression."

Wallis shrugged. In his clear blue eyes, the genial sparkle of good fellowship had faded.

"What'd you do Wednesday evening, Mr. Wallis? From nine till midnight, what'd the two of you do?"

"Well, the fact is, it wasn't the *two* of us, for very long."

"How do you mean?"

"I mean that, during dinner, we quarreled. So, midway through the entrée, Lisa got up and left."

"What was the quarrel about?"

"It was personal, Lieutenant."

"Not anymore."

Across the claw-footed antique table, their eyes locked. Then, projecting a condescending contempt, the man of affairs dealing with an inferior, Wallis decided to smile. "Whatever you say, Lieutenant."

"Well?"

"It was about a weekend flying trip we were going to take. I'm a private pilot, and Lisa loved to fly. This weekend—tomorrow—we'd planned to fly up to Ashland. It's a beautiful flight, over the Cascades and down into Oregon. But, Wednesday morning, my wife announced that her mother was coming up over the weekend, from Palm Springs. And her mother, unhappily, has cancer. So, of course, I couldn't leave."

"If it hadn't been for your mother-in-law's visit," Hastings said, "would your wife have minded if you'd gone away for the weekend?"

"Not in the least," Wallis answered promptly. Then, after a moment's calculation: "I want to be honest with you, Lieutenant. It'll save us both a lot of time. So I'll tell you that, after ten years of marriage, my wife and I have arrived at a rapprochement. Which is to say that we act the part of the happily married couple. Whereas, actually, we each go our own ways, except for high-visibility parties and opera openings, things like that."

"So you would have gone to Ashland with Lisa, and your wife might've gone to Acapulco with some guy. Is that what you're saying?"

Wallis nodded. "Exactly."

"And neither of you would ask questions."

"Right."

"But you'd each know what the other was doing."

"Yes."

"Names? Did you know names?"

As if he were vexed at Hastings's naïveté, Wallis frowned. "Of course not. No names. That's the only way it can work, you see. All of us, after all, live duplicitous lives. Love, business, diplomacy—you name it, if everyone suddenly started telling the truth, we'd all self-destruct."

"About what time did Lisa leave Reggie's?" Hastings asked.

"About ten o'clock."

"Did she tell you where she was going?"

"No. She just got up and left the table."

"She had her own car, then."

"I don't know. But I'd think so."

"Does Reggie's have their own parking lot?"

"No. They have valet parking."

"Where did you think Lisa was going after she left you?"

"Home, I assumed."

Hastings shook his head. "No, she didn't go home. She drove out to Baker Beach."

"Yes . . ." Wallis's voice dropped; for the first time, his face registered sadness. "I know that now."

"Do you have any idea why she was killed, Mr. Wallis?"

"None. Absolutely none." His voice was heavy with regret. A ballpoint pen and a pad of unlined white paper lay on the otherwise uncluttered desktop. Wallis picked up the pen and began doodling. His manner had turned brooding.

"We have information that, during the past several weeks, Lisa Franklin was worried about something. Is that true?"

"Not from my perspective it isn't true."

"You're sure?"

Wallis nodded over his pad of paper and the steady movement of his pen. "I'm sure."

"She had no enemies, so far as you knew."

"None."

"What's the nature of your business, Mr. Wallis?"

"We're in venture capital."

"What's that mean, exactly?"

"If someone wants to start a business, we finance it. In exchange, we usually take stock. For the most part we've been involved in Silicon Valley—computers, software. We're also in real estate, to a certain extent." He spoke in a dulled monotone, as if the subject didn't really interest him.

"What time did you leave Reggie's?"

"It was about ten-thirty."

"Did Lisa have a lot to drink, Wednesday night?"

Wallis looked up from his doodling. He frowned, then said, "No more than usual. Lisa drank wine. Usually two or three glasses at dinner, sometimes more."

"So she wasn't drunk when she left Reggie's."

"Not at all."

"Where'd you go, when you left Reggie's?"

"First I went to Rabelais. Then I went home."

"Rabelais—that's the men's club."

Wallis nodded. "Yes."

"Where's it located?"

"On Leavenworth, near Bush Street."

"What time did you leave Rabelais?"

"About eleven-thirty. I just had a couple of drinks."

"And where do you live?"

"On Broadway near Laguna."

"So you got home—when?"

As if to dismiss the relevance of the question, Wallis shrugged indifferently. "About midnight, I suppose."

Hastings nodded, looked away, began to calculate locations, weekday traffic flow, portal-to-portal routes. Conclusion: it would have been possible to drive from Rabelais to Baker Beach in fifteen minutes. Allow five minutes to stalk his victim and pull the trigger, allow another fifteen minutes to drive to Broadway and Laguna—it was a perfect fit.

"Was your wife home when you got there?"

"She was in bed. Asleep, as far as I know."

"Did she know—suspect—that you were out with a woman?"

"I've already told you, Lieutenant: my wife and I have an understanding, no questions asked."

"What's your wife's name, Mr. Wallis?"

"It's Harriet. But—" Wallis looked up from the doodle, fixed Hastings with a narrow, cold stare. "But I'll take it badly, Lieutenant, if you get her involved in this. Do you understand?"

Hastings decided to smile, decided to rise to his feet, decided to speak quietly, concisely: "I think I do understand, Mr. Wallis. You're telling me that you're rich, and you're powerful, and you belong to all the right clubs."

Wallis's only response was an enigmatic smile.

"The thing is, though," Hastings went on, "that Lisa's father is also rich and powerful. And he's just identified his daughter, at the morgue. Do I make myself clear?"

The enigmatic smile froze, then faded.

23

"What we should do," Ann said, "is get away for a weekend. What about Mendocino? What about a week from now—Friday? If we left by four o'clock we could be there by eight or nine. We could try Harbor House. October—the beach can be wonderful this time of year."

But, as she spoke, she could see his face begin to close. She knew they wouldn't be going to Mendocino next weekend.

He'd arrived home more than an hour ago. He'd already

eaten at a fast food place, as he'd said he would. She'd been in the living room when he'd come home. She'd been reading. Earlier in the day, shopping for dinner, she'd picked up a copy of *Beloved*, from the paperback rack at the supermarket. She'd decided to read a chapter before dinner. And, God, she'd gotten hooked, dazzled by Toni Morrison's wizardry. When Frank had called to say he'd be late, don't wait dinner, she'd asked Dan and Billy to cook the dinner, she'd do the dishes. The deal was struck, and she'd continued reading, before dinner and after dinner, with the dirty dishes still in the sink. Now it was nine o'clock, and the dishes still hadn't been washed. Across the living room, Frank was shaking his head.

"This case," he said, "Lisa Franklin, the poor little rich girl. I can't take time off, not now. Not until we put the cuffs on someone."

She put *Beloved* aside, took off her reading glasses. "How much leave time have you got coming, Frank? The truth."

He lowered the *Sports Illustrated* he was reading, folded it closed in his lap—after dog-earing a page. The message: they would talk about next weekend. Then he would return to his magazine. There were, after all, almost two hours left before they got ready for bed. By that time, eleven o'clock, Billy and Dan would have finished their homework, watched TV, brushed their teeth, gone to bed. The ground-floor Victorian flat, her flat long before they'd begun living together, was huge: three bedrooms, a bath and a half, a large kitchen, a dining room, and a living room in front. According to custom, Frank would lock the front door, check the windows, switch off the lights, set the alarm. While she was relieving herself in the half-bathroom, Frank would turn on the local TV news, giving her time to finish at the commode, then go into the bathroom. With the door closed, she would undress, take a quick shower, cream her face, brush her hair, brush her teeth, floss, get into her nightgown, which hung on the door. From the living room, she would hear the TV go off. Leaving the bathroom light on, she would go into the bedroom, turn down the bed—and wait for him.

"The truth is—" Across the living room, he was smiling at her. Whenever he smiled like this, ruefully, almost shyly, she could imagine him as a teenager: big for his age, good-looking, a gifted athlete—but quiet, often withdrawn, always serious.

"The truth is," he repeated, "I've got twenty days' leave time, at least. But that's not the point. With this case hanging fire, I'm stuck."

"I'm not talking about twenty days, Frank. I'm talking about a weekend. Everyone takes weekends off."

"Ann, listen—this case is getting more publicity every day. I can't ask my people to work through a weekend while I—"

"Hey—" It was Billy, age twelve, standing in the hallway arch. Barefooted. Tousle-headed. Fists propped on his hips. Demanding: "Hey, what's the most important export of Indonesia?"

Ann frowned, exchanged a tentative look with Hastings. For almost a decade, she'd taught school: kindergarten at first, currently the fourth grade. Economic geography wasn't part of the fourth-grade curriculum.

"Oil?" she said, directing the question to Hastings. Hesitantly, he nodded. "I think so." She looked at her younger son, saying decisively: "Oil. That's what the Japanese were after in the Second World War. They—"

In the hallway, the telephone warbled.

"Get it, will you, Billy?"

"Hello?" Then, after a moment: "Oh. Hi." As he spoke into the phone, Ann saw Billy turn his back on them. The mannerism, the cadence of his voice, confirmed that his father was calling. Speaking to Hastings, she said softly: "I've got to do the dishes."

"Can I help?"

Smiling, she shook her head. "You don't eat, you don't have to do dishes. Read your *Sports Illustrated*."

He returned the smile, opened the magazine, shifted to a more comfortable position in his armchair. As Billy made room for her in the narrow hallway, he kept his back to her, signifying that he was in private conversation with his father. Tomorrow, Victor Haywood was taking his sons houseboating in the San Joaquin Delta over the weekend. Thus, the necessity to do homework on a Friday night.

In the kitchen, Ann set the stopper in the sink, ran the hot water, added liquid soap. With the dishwasher once again malfunctioning, she would do the dishes by hand, back to basics.

"Sometimes," her mother had often said, "it's a balm for the soul to do good, hard work."

When she'd been fourteen years old, a high school freshman, she'd come home from school early because of a teachers' conference. She'd found her mother on her hands and knees, scrubbing the kitchen's ceramic tile floor. Her mother had been crying: harsh, wracking sobs, torn from deep inside. Reflexively, she'd fallen to her knees beside her mother, put one arm around the heaving shoulders, used her free hand to cradle her mother's tear-streaked face in the hollow of her shoulder—just as, all through childhood, her mother had comforted her. But she hadn't asked why her mother was crying.

She hadn't asked because, intuitively, she'd known.

It was another woman.

Her father, and another woman.

Two years afterward, her mother had been diagnosed with cervical cancer. Only a year later, when Ann was a high school senior, her mother had died.

After the funeral, riding in the funeral parlor's limousine, holding her hand tightly, her father had begun to cry. And it was then, dry-eyed, that she'd accused him. Her mother, that proud, loyal, compassionate woman, fallen to her hands and knees, sobbing because she knew her husband had been unfaithful.

If her father had protested, lied to her as they rode in the limousine from the funeral, it would surely have been over between them. Presents sent by mail at Christmas, calls on birthdays—nothing more.

But her father hadn't lied. He'd told her everything, a confession. He'd asked how long she'd known. And he'd asked her to forgive him. He would make it up to her, he'd promised.

And, yes, he'd tried. She'd had the best of everything: a first-class education, all the money she needed, even a car her last year of college.

But none of it could excise the tiny, corrosive germ of suspicion that, had she not been weakened by unhappiness, her mother would still be alive.

In the sink, only the dirty cooking pots remained. In the hallway, Billy was finished on the phone. From the living room she heard the voice of a TV news commentator.

In one of the pots, Billy and Dan had cooked canned spaghetti and meatballs, the dregs caking the bottom of the pot. She reached for the scouring powder and began scouring.

Her mother had found solace in scrubbing tile.

For her—now—there was only this dirty pot, caked at the bottom with canned spaghetti.

24

"Mom?"

Instantly Janet identified the inflection in her son's voice: Charlie was about to ask a favor, run a con. For the past half hour he'd been on the phone to Roger Sobel, his best friend—and constant co-conspirator.

"Roger's on the phone. He wants to know whether he can go shooting with us tomorrow."

She laid the file folder aside, sighed, shook her had. "It won't work, Charlie. You *know* it won't work. You're in the family, so that's okay. But, technically, no civilians're allowed on the firing range."

"Can't we say he's a cousin?"

"No, Charlie, we can't." She put an edge on her voice. "If there's no one waiting, and he knows you, the rangemaster'll probably let you fire. But it's against regulations."

"Regulations." He snorted.

Watching him turn indignantly away and walk down the hallway to his room, where he'd taken the hallway phone on its long cord run under his bedroom door, she sighed again. If her child were a fifteen-year-old daughter, not a fifteen-year-old son, would it be easier?

Harder?

She was stretched out on the living room sofa—the sofa that badly needed recovering. For more than an hour, doggedly, she'd been reading Lisa Franklin's journals. It was like staring into a clouded pool trying to discover what lay on the bottom: shapes without substance that changed with light and shadow, shifted with mood and perception.

The folder with the photocopied pages lay open on the floor beside the sofa. Last night, in bed, she'd read until one in the morning, reading fast, taking no notes, marking no special passage. Today, in the office, she'd read only a few entries; it was impossible to concentrate in the controlled confusion of the squadroom.

Now, after almost two hours, she was finally finished with the third volume. This time through, she had marked the passages she would show Hastings. She would—

"Mom?"

Once more, a favor.

This time, she kept her eyes cast down on the page she'd just taken from the folder. "Yes?"

"Can Roger come over and stay all night?"

"Tonight?"

"Sure."

"It's after ten."

"But it's Friday night." His voice rose plaintively.

"Can he get a ride?"

"He already asked his dad. And he'll bring a sleeping bag."

"Okay. But this doesn't change anything about the firing range tomorrow. No tricks."

"Sure. Thanks, Mom." And, before he turned away, she received her reward: a small smile, almost a shy smile. A smile, and "thanks," all in less than a minute. Sometimes it took days—weeks.

She'd paper-clipped the pages with the entries she wanted Hastings to read, and she'd already marked two of the entries. Now she marked the remaining four. They were in sequence but were undated. If there was a clue here, in these journals, then it must be here, in these four verses:

The string has run out, the circle has returned to dead center now. Whatever remains must be in repayment. Therefore, write out the roster of victims, contemplate their transgressions, choose one, just one.

And let the game begin.

Yes, the game progresses. Does he suspect? Sex is the vehicle of vengeance, the ultimate universal imperative. Choose the time, choose the place, present the bill.

And watch him squirm, impaled.

These men, so-called, see how they run, slathering dumb as dogs chasing the randy bitch. A carefully calculated twitch of the ass, an over-the-shoulder smile, arch the torso, tender titties offered for critique, and the game begins again—and again.

How incredible that he persists, let it twitch, watch him hop aboard, oblivious.

Oblivious?

Or could it be a riposte, a reverse con?

Does he, too, have an agenda, pick a number, spin the wheel—live or die? Is that what lies feral behind his eyes?

Now he has been stripped defenseless, all his weapons broken at his feet.

They are naked. Yes, naked.

But now, the reducible reduced to the irreducible, sex is not the game.

Leaving only death.

Capitulation, or death.

Which?

Still stretched out on the sofa, she let the sheets of paper fall across her thighs.

What did the fragments signify? What did they reveal?

An angry woman, certainly.

A defiant woman. A fearless, don't-give-a-shit woman.

But, infusing every line, every word, a woman alone.

Boldly alone. Manmade law or natural law, neither had governed Lisa Franklin. Whatever Lisa wanted—a man, a woman, a car, a check—whatever she wanted, she took. Never mind the thanks, never mind the smiles.

Were men the targets, the essential targets?

Or was it nature itself, Lisa against the cosmos?

Frank had at least skimmed the entries. Some of the fragments were erotic. Had he been aroused? Was it possible that they'd both been reading the same fragment at the same time, a sensual experience shared? She leaned back against the arm of the sofa, let her eyes close. When she'd been a young girl, no more than ten, lying in bed, eyes closed, waiting for sleep, she would often imagine she was in psychic contact with a boy. They were, she could feel, thinking of each other at that very moment, sharing the same unformed desires, in mystic communication. Sometimes she thought those presexual fantasies were the only true expressions of love. Simply to be with that one special boy, not even to speak, not even to touch, those had been moments of pre-pubescent magic—a magic that would always remain pure, enshrined in memory.

One special boy, Gerald Faust, must have been much like Frank, when they were both so very young. Every girl in their sixth-grade class, without exception, had been in love with Gerald Faust. He'd been a quiet, serious boy—as Frank certainly had been. Big for his age, always the first chosen for sports, both of them. Not shy, but not outgoing, either. Not loud. Most particularly, not loud, never pushy. But, God, even then, sexy.

Since yesterday, whenever she was alone with her thoughts, Frank had materialized. Frank, standing close to her in the parking garage, almost touching her. Frank, across the table in a funny Chinese restaurant, talking so seriously about his life—about his hopes and dreams, so many of them crushed.

Frank, speaking so hesitantly, confessing that, yes, he wanted to—

Wanted to what?

Rent a hotel room, punch out with Communications, undress her and take her to bed, make love for a few hours, then check back in with Communications, refreshed?

Did he know, could he imagine, how much she wanted him, yearned to caress him, to feel his flesh press against her, feel him press into her?

But not a one-night stand. Never a one-night stand. And never a clandestine affair, lying and cheating, living by their wits, he deceiving the woman he lived with, she concealing part of her life from Charlie.

And yet . . .

25

In the darkened room he lay on his back, eyes closed. It was necessary, he knew, to sleep. It was therefore necessary to breathe regularly, evenly, deeply. Even with the pills, even after the liquor, it was still necessary to control the body, control the mind. Because, without sleep, he was endangered. Without sleep, the mind ran wild. Uncontrolled, the mind became the enemy within.

But, still, the elapsed time counter continued: soon, forty-eight hours would have elapsed. Exactly forty-eight hours.

Two days, in constant company with his thoughts, helpless, possessed. Whatever the images that had flashed on the screen of his consciousness during those hours, he had been forced to confront them. To turn away, close his eyes, only sharpened the images. But to sleep, he must close his eyes. Therefore, to seek the solace of sleep, it was necessary to worsen the pain. It was, in fact, the ultimate instrument of torture, a diabolical inversion. Since earliest memory, when he'd closed his eyes, the pain had lessened. Now, though, he must find escape. But in what? In a blinding light, would that help? Noise? If the darkness of closed eyes and the silence of the bedroom darkness made the agony worse, then, ipso facto, a cacophony and the brightness of the interrogator's light shone in the eyes should make it better.

Was interrogation the only solace?

Confession?

Now, once more, his eyes were open. Was he testing the thesis? Were the images sharper now? Must he therefore sacrifice another night of sleep to find out?

Strangely, no sound accompanied the images. It was a silent movie, running behind his eyes on endless sprockets.

131

It began—and ended—with the blood.

In his planning, he had not considered the blood. Or her head lying in the gravel. Or her eyes, so empty. Or the way her lifeless, inert body had rolled and flopped when he'd dragged it toward the brush.

Rolled, and flopped—and gurgled.

Unaware that it had happened, he realized that his eyes had closed. And now, more vividly, he saw her empty eyes, staring up at the sky.

And then he realized that the images appeared in shades of gray, without color. Meaning that never would he know the color of her eyes.

As long as he'd known her, so intimately, he was unable to remember the color of her eyes. He—

In the next room, beyond his closed bedroom door, he heard the phone ring. And ring. And, finally, stop ringing.

At eleven forty-five on a Friday night, who could be calling? Would it be the police: the lieutenant of Homicide—Hastings—could he be calling? But why? Some new development? A clue, previously overlooked? What had Hastings been thinking, behind that expressionless mask that all detectives must wear?

In the darkened interrogation room, Hastings would speak: "Sit here," he would say, smiling slightly. "Do you mind if we shine this light in your eyes?"

And then it would begin: the endless questions, the cold cop stares, the sidelong smirks between the detectives.

Until, finally, he would blurt it out: *It was the money. It wasn't Lisa. Always, from the first, it was the money.*

26

Friedman glanced at the notes he'd taken on the back of an envelope. Then, settling back in Hastings's visitors' chair, he reflectively unwrapped his Monday morning cigar as he said, "These three high rollers—they'd have had a lot to lose, if Lisa had talked to their wives."

Walter Drake would've had a lot to lose," Hastings answered. "And maybe Clayton Wallis. They're both married. Drake, especially, is *very* married. But Cameron's a bachelor."

After lighting his cigar and performing his ritual with the smoking match, arcing it unerringly into Hastings's wastebasket, Friedman drew on the cigar, then said, "This Lisa kept busy. She had these three fat cats to take care of, plus this C. J., it sounds like, hit or miss. Plus maybe she swung the other way, with her roommate. When'd she find time for relaxation?"

"She kept her diary. And she went to poetry readings."

"These three guys," Friedman mused, "I wonder whether they knew about one another?"

"Cameron and Wallis know each other."

"Did they know she was screwing both of them?"

"Of course. What're you getting at? Jealousy?"

Friedman shrugged, drew on the cigar, exhaled a robust smoke ring. "Greed and jealousy, they're right at the top of the list."

"These guys aren't hot-blooded Latino studs. They're rich. And they're middle-aged, for God's sake, with lots to lose." As he spoke, he irritably destroyed the smoke ring as it sailed across a corner of his desk.

"Well," Friedman said wryly, "so much for motive. What about evidence? Those bloody prints, for instance."

133

"There were only two people in the lab over the weekend. And they—"

Hastings's telephone interrupted, an interoffice call.

"It's Joe McCarville, Lieutenant."

"Joe—?"

"The lab. Sorry."

"Ah—" Hastings nodded across the desk. In anticipation, Friedman raised his eyebrows as Hastings spoke into the phone: "Something?"

"The Lisa Franklin case."

Hastings decided to wait.

"We compared the victim's prints with the prints in blood on the door. And they don't match."

"Ah—" An expression of pleasure this time. Anticipation.

"We're just running the prints now. With this new Japanese computer, it should take about two hours. Hopefully."

"Keep me posted. Me, or Lieutenant Friedman."

"Yessir."

Hastings broke the connection, told Friedman the news.

"I hate to second-guess you," Friedman said, "but when you interviewed Cameron and Drake and Wallis on Friday, it would've been nice if you could've gotten their prints on something. An eight-by-ten glossy of the victim, for instance."

"Except that I left the Hall about three o'clock Friday. Pictures weren't available until six o'clock." As he spoke, Hastings opened the Franklin folder, took out the picture taken at the morgue, and sailed it across the desk. Friedman nodded appreciatively, then said, "Someone who looks like that, and considering her life-style, I'd've thought she would've had pictures of herself at home. You know—a nude, maybe a blowup. T and A stuff. By the way—" A puckish pause, another smoke ring followed by a sly sidelong glance. "How's Janet Collier doing on the case?"

Today, at nine-thirty on a Monday morning, having spent Sunday at the beach with Ann, followed by an impulsive, urgent, perspiration-slick hour of love when they'd returned to an empty flat, Hastings was ready for the question: "Collier's doing fine. No problems. She's a hard worker."

"Does that mean you've conquered your carnal longing?"

"It means," Hastings said, "that she's a good detective. She uses her head. And she works hard." Saying it, he made stern eye contact. Then, firmly shifting ground: "In fact, I'll send her around with those pictures you were talking about."

"These fat cats—how'd they feel about having cops in their reception rooms?"

"That's why I'll send her. I'll call first, tell them I'm sending her by for an identification, a minute in, a minute out. All they've got to do is tell their secretaries she's coming. They'll—" Struck by a sudden thought, he broke off. Then: "The picture of Lisa, showing that, it doesn't make sense. We don't need her identified, and these guys'll know it."

"So?"

"So we'll find a picture in the files—a guy. We'll imply he's involved, no specifics, no names, everything hush-hush. Have they ever seen this guy with Lisa, we'll ask."

Friedman nodded decisively. "Very good. Excellent. And there's a potential plus, which I know you've already factored in."

Hastings decided not to accept the gambit.

"If one of our suspects says, yes, he's seen the guy, then we know he's lying."

"Or she," Hastings said. "Don't forget Barbara Estes."

"Whatever." Friedman rose, flicked an inch-long cigar ash into Hastings's wastebasket. "I've got to get to my In tray. Keep me posted."

As Hastings nodded in reply, his phone rang again, another

135

interoffice call. Friedman flipped a hand and left the office.

"It's Janet Collier, Lieutenant." Her voice, once more, was absolutely neutral, all business.

"Janet—" He tried to keep the pleasure from his voice. "Listen, have you got some time today?"

"Sure."

"Okay. I've got a job for you."

"Now?"

"Now."

"Let's use this one." Hastings pointed to a full-face picture of a Caucasian male in his thirties.

"Right." Janet took the photograph, put it in her folder.

"Get ten eight-by-ten glossies at the photo lab. You take five and I'll take five. Tell the lab you want them immediately. If they stall, I'll talk to them."

"Yessir."

"I'll call Wallis and Cameron and Drake. I'll tell them all we want is an identification, not an interrogation, no big deal. So you just show them the picture, get the prints, get out."

"What if they ask me about the case, how it's going?"

"Tell them we're making progress, but it's too early to go public." He smiled at her, watched her lips stir in reply, saw her eyes kindle. Her eyes were light brown. Like his.

"The standard bullshit, in other words," he said.

In reply, she nodded.

"If they want to talk, though, see what you can find out. And if you finish with them and you've got time—" He wrote on a slip of paper, passed it across the desk. "Barbara Estes, Lisa's roommate, works at Jamison Coffee Company, south of Market. Get her prints, too. I'm going to go over to Page Street, get prints from C. J. Kirk and Jamie Thomas. I want to talk to them, too."

"What about Barbara Estes? Shall I question her?"

He considered, then decided to say, "No, don't question her. Just get in and get out. It's the prints that we want."

Her small, tight smile was wry. "I'm a messenger, in other words."

"Oh, God—is this women's rights?"

"Just an observation, Lieutenant."

"Frank."

"Frank." Coolly.

For a long moment they let their eyes linger together, each speculating—each calculating. When Hastings finally spoke, the words were measured: "The only physical evidence we've got is two good, clear fingerprints on the driver's door—in blood. I just heard from the lab. The prints don't match the victim's. So it's ten to one they match the murderer's." He decided to let the rest of it go pointedly unsaid.

"Ah—" She lowered her gaze, an apology. "I—I'm sorry. I didn't know the victim's were eliminated. I'd just assumed the prints were hers."

"What you'll be doing," Hastings said, "is trying to establish a connection that could make the case."

Her eyes came up. "I already said I'm sorry." Now she was frowning.

He abruptly waved the apology away, saying, "When you're finished, check in with Lieutenant Friedman. I'll do the same. Let's plan on meeting back here at four o'clock."

"Shall I take the glossies to you, once I get the prints?"

"Take them right to the lab. Make them sign for the evidence, though. In Homicide, the chain of evidence is what it's all about."

"Bunco, too." She closed the folder, clicked her pen. The pen, Hastings noticed, was a gold Cross. Was it a present from a lover?

"Nice pen."

"Thanks." As if she knew what he was thinking, she

smiled—a nonprofessional smile. "My mother gave it to me."

"Ah—" He nodded. Repeating: "Ah." Then, unintended: "Good."

27

"Sorry—" Thomas shook his head, handed the photo back to Hastings. "I can't help you."

Handling it carefully, Hastings returned the photograph to the folder discreetly labeled THOMAS, in pencil. "Where's C. J.? I'd like to show one of these to him."

"I haven't seen C. J. all weekend." Thomas pointed to the folder, now lying closed on the cluttered coffee table. "Did he do it?"

"We aren't sure. But we want to talk to him."

"Hmmm." Slouched in a threadbare armchair, one thin leg hooked over the arm, Thomas studied Hastings thoughtfully, as if to decide whether to offer a confidence. Today, barefooted, Thomas wore loose-fitting baggy white trousers and a shapeless shirt. If a rope were holding up his trousers, with his long unkempt sandy hair and a day's stubble of beard, with his too-bright, feverish eyes sunk deep beneath spiky eyebrows, Thomas could have been a down-on-his-luck beachcomber.

"Is C. J. out of town?" Hastings asked.

"Man, I haven't a clue. All I know is, the night after Lisa died—Thursday—it all went crazy around here. Barbara, she got the idea C. J. knew more about Lisa's death than he was telling. And, Christ, she went right over the edge, she really did. C. J., by that time, he'd had too much to drink. I mean, he'd had *way* too much. Plus he, ah, popped a controlled substance or two. So when Barbara started pounding on him, he wasn't too quick with the counterpunch. So then—"

"She *hit* him?"

Thomas raised his bony shoulders and spread his hands in a gesture of wry resignation. "There was blood on the floor, man. What can I say?"

"What basis does she have for thinking C. J. knows something?" As he spoke, Hastings thought of Janet Collier. After she finished with the three men, quickly getting their prints then getting out, Barbara Estes would be next on Janet's list. Should he try to intercept her? Or should he—?

"As far as I know," Thomas was saying, "she had no basis at all. If I had to guess, I'd say maybe Barbara was popping something, too. Plus, she and C. J. don't get along."

"So C. J.'s run off somewhere. Is that what you're saying? He's left town?"

Thomas shook his head. "I think he'll be back, sooner or later. I mean, all his stuff is here. His tapes, CDs—everything. He'd never leave without taking his music." Thomas pointed to the photograph in its folder. "If you want, I'll show it to C. J., give you a call."

Hastings shook his head. "I've got to show it to someone else. But—" He put a business card on the table. "But when C. J. comes back, give me a call."

"Sure."

"I understand," Hastings said, "that Lisa wasn't acting normally during the week before she was murdered. Was that your impression?"

"Hell, I probably didn't even *see* her then. We exchanged maybe ten words a month, Lisa and me. She kept busy."

For a moment Hastings let his gaze linger on the other man. Then, no longer a policeman, now simply curious: "What about you, Jamie? Do you keep busy?"

Thomas's face first grew rigid, self-protective. Then the face began to dissolve, a confession of defeat. "I've done a lot of things, Frank. All the time, I guess I thought I was keeping busy. Now, though, looking back, it doesn't seem to amount to much. That's starting to happen to me—looking back, I mean. I guess that's what middle age is all about. Looking back."

"What kind of things did you do?"

"Oh, I painted a hundred houses or so. And I've fried a few thousand eggs and home fries." He shrugged. "That's about it."

"What about now?"

"Now," Thomas said, speaking heavily, "now, I'm afraid of the ladders. And I'm not as fast as I used to be, cooking short order."

"So you're not employed."

"I work at nights sometimes, cooking."

"Ever get married?"

He grimaced. "Twice. Once when I was twenty, once when I was twenty-five. Both times, it only lasted a year." Looking inward, lost, he broke off. Then, a confession: "It was drugs. Both times, it was drugs, mostly. My twenties—shit—it was all a blue haze. That's all I cared about, that blue haze."

"You and C. J. . . . ." He let it go meaningfully unfinished, probing.

Once more, Thomas grimaced. "C. J., yeah. He's fucked himself up, no question. I see him, it seems like it's the sixties again."

"What kind of a habit does he have?"

"You name it, he'll do it."

"Heroin?"

Thomas shrugged cautiously, looked evasively away.

"I'm not a narc, Jamie. I could care less."

"Yeah—well—let's just say that C. J.'s teetering on the edge."

"He's unemployed. Where does the money come from?"

"Man, I don't have a clue. If he pays for his half the rent, which he does, mostly, that's all I care about."

"What *is* rent, here?"

"It's eight hundred a month. Plus utilities."

"If C. J.'s got any kind of a habit, it's costing him a couple of thousand a month, Jamie. You *know* that."

"Oh, yeah—" Thomas nodded ruefully. "Yeah, I know that."

"Okay, so where's the money come from? What's he do? Rob?"

"I guess," came the slow, considered answer, "that even if I knew, I probably wouldn't tell you." Now the other man's gaze had steadied.

After a long, hard moment of silence that was meant to intimidate, Hastings finally decided to let the question go, back away, shift ground: "How tight were Lisa and Barbara?"

"Aw, come on, Frank—" Thomas unslung his leg from the arm of his chair, rose, walked to the living room's big bay window that looked out on Page Street. "What d'you *want* from me?"

"I want help finding out who killed Lisa Franklin."

"Yeah, well, you won't get anything from me. Because I don't *know* anything."

"You knew that Barbara attacked C. J. because she thought C. J. knew something about the murder. That's more than I knew when I walked in."

"Well—" it was an ironic rejoinder "—then you should thank me, shouldn't you?"

"Come on, Jamie, don't play games. You play games with me, you lose. It's built in."

Thomas made no reply.

"Lisa and Barbara were lovers. Right?"

Reluctantly, moving leadenly, shoulders slumped, eyes defeated, Thomas left the window, returned to the armchair, sat down. "I imagine that, yes, they were lovers. I mean, okay, the bedsprings creaked upstairs. But how tight they were, how the hell should I know? If I had to guess, I'd say Lisa was just enjoying herself—taking what she wanted and leaving the crumbs. That's what she did with guys. Why not women, too?"

"How do you think she died, Jamie? Who do you think killed her?"

"Jesus—" It was a high, plaintive protest. "I don't *know*. I'm *telling* you, I don't—"

"I don't mean names. I'm not talking about names. I'm talking about types."

"Types?"

"A robber, out at Baker Beach? A boyfriend? A girlfriend? Who?"

Now Thomas snorted, pointed to the manila folder. "If I've got to choose, if that's the game, then I pick him."

28

"Did Lieutenant Friedman get in touch with you?" As she spoke, the receptionist handed Hastings his messages. "Or Deputy Chief Bentley?"

"No."

"Well, they've been trying to get you." Millie Ralston looked accusingly at Hastings. She was an efficient, cheerful, robustly proportioned woman in her unattached middle twenties. In only a few months on the job, she'd mastered the art of parrying sexual advances without making enemies.

"I had my pager off."

"How about your radio?"

"That, too, Millie. I was thinking."

"Hmmm."

"What's the chief want?"

"He wants you, Lieutenant. He's got Lieutenant Friedman. And now he wants you. If you hurry, you won't miss much. There's a guy from Washington with them. Good dresser, probably a big shot."

"Here—" Hastings handed over the message slips. "I'll be back."

"The file folder, too?"

He shook his head. "I'll hang on to it." He returned to the bank of three elevators, rode up to the executive offices, on the Hall of Justice's top floor. In order of rank, Deputy Chief Bentley's office was two removed from Chief Dwyer's office. After a brief, businesslike greeting, Bentley's secretary opened the inner door for Hastings.

"Ah, Frank." Seated behind his desk, flanked by three flags, Bentley smiled, gestured Hastings to an empty chair facing the desk as he smoothly performed the introductions: "This is Howard Browne, Frank. Mr. Browne is regional director of the SEC." Then, with only a hint of condescension he added, "The Securities and Exchange Commission."

Browne was a squat, overweight, overdressed man with two double chins and a flaccid handshake. Behind sparkling gold-framed designer glasses, his eyes were quick and shrewd.

"Lieutenant Hastings and Lieutenant Friedman are co-commanders of Homicide." Bentley's smile briefly touched his three visitors. It was a perfunctory, all-purpose smile, only one of Bentley's several job-related assets. A political appointee, not a sworn officer, Bentley was a small, wiry man, a wily, quick-thinking, perceptive opportunist. Like his body, his face was reduced to its essentials: the eyes that seemed never to blink, the mouth that seemed perpetually pursed, the nostrils that seemed permanently pinched, as if to avoid something distasteful. He had never been seen wearing anything but a three-piece suit, conservative tie, and impeccably polished English shoes. A lifelong bachelor in his early fifties, Bentley was totally bald. Bentley had always disapproved of Friedman—who had always despised Bentley. Hastings's status was unclear.

"To get right down to it—" Bentley addressed Hastings, an update: "Mr. Browne tells me that the SEC is, ah, interested in one of the men who figures peripherally in the Lisa Franklin homicide. I wanted you and Pete to get the information firsthand, so we're all using the same playbook."

As he nodded, Hastings stole a look at Friedman. Predictably, Friedman's expression was pained.

Now Bentley settled back in his chair, touching the knot of his tie with one hand while he gestured with the other to the man from the SEC. Browne had the floor and spoke directly to Hastings:

"You realize, of course, that this is all off the record, for your ears only."

"Yes . . . "

"The person we're interested in—*very* interested in, I might say—is Clayton Wallis."

Even without benefit of a stolen look at Friedman, Hastings had decided to make no response. Plainly, this was Browne's show.

"I won't go into the details," Browne continued. "They couldn't possibly have any bearing on your case. But the fact is that we've been investigating Wallis for almost a year in connection with an insider trading deal. And it's just beginning to come together. We've got the trap cocked, and we've got the bait in place. And we've got Wallis coming our way." As if he expected some sign of approval, Browne looked in turn at the two lieutenants. Then: "We've got, ah, a mole, in Wallis's organization, a disaffected employee who got passed over for promotion. That's how we discovered that you'd interrogated Wallis in connection with the Lisa Franklin murder case. So, as soon as I heard about it, I wanted to contact you, warn you off. Because if this person—the mole—is compromised, well . . ." Browne shook his head. "You see what could happen."

Friedman frowned. "I'm afraid I don't follow."

"Well, obviously, we don't want Wallis stirred up. If he starts looking over his shoulder, and if he finds out that this mole is leaking information, then we've got a problem."

Friedman continued to frown. "So, in effect, you're asking us to lay back, subordinate our investigation to yours."

"Not at all. We're simply—"

"What Mr. Browne is saying, Pete," Bentley interrupted smoothly, "is that he'd appreciate it if we held back until the SEC files charges."

"Files charges and impounds records," Browne prompted. On cue, Bentley nodded. Plainly, the discussion was polarizing: two working policemen on one side, two administrators opposing them. "It's the records we need," Browne explained.

"How long will it take," Hastings asked, "to get the records? So far, it's taken a year. How much longer?"

"That's hard to say."

"A month?"

"Possibly."

Hastings shifted his gaze to Bentley. It was an appeal for a decision, for leadership. Bentley returned his gaze but said nothing, revealed nothing. At that moment, Hastings wondered, where was Janet? Had she gotten Wallis's fingerprints on the photograph? If she'd seen Wallis, would Browne's snitch know?

"As far as we can determine," Hastings said, "Clayton Wallis was the last person to see Lisa Franklin alive. Furthermore, he had a sexual relationship with her. And he gave her money. Regularly."

"However," Bentley temporized, "he's alibied for the time the murder actually took place."

"He's alibied by his wife," Hastings retorted.

"Which, really," Friedman interjected, "is no alibi at all."

145

Thoughtfully, Bentley looked at each of the three men in turn. Finally he spoke directly to Howard Browne: "What I'd like to do is review this case internally. Meanwhile, why don't you get a better fix on when you're actually going to bring charges against Wallis. Then, say in a day or two, we can get together again, probably make a determination."

"Will you stipulate, though, that your people will stay away from Wallis until we get together again?"

Bentley looked inquiringly at Friedman and Hastings in turn. In unison, both men shrugged. Assistant Chief Bentley was on his own. Concealing his exasperation, Bentley nodded to Browne. "Deal."

Immediately, Browne rose to his feet, perfunctorily said his good-byes, and was about to turn toward the door when Friedman said, "Mr. Browne, are you aware that Lisa Franklin's father has a seat on the New York Stock Exchange?"

Browne's only response was an involuntary blink.

29

"Jesus—" Hastings looked at the coffee and double Danish Friedman had just brought from the cafeteria line in the basement of the Hall of Justice. "It's only been a couple of hours since lunch."

"This is a low-cal Danish."

"Bullshit. What d'you weigh? Two-forty? More?"

"No comment." Friedman bit into the Danish, chewed appreciatively. Then, glowering: "That prissy-ass Bentley. 'Review the case internally,' he says. What the hell's that mean?"

"You know, the only time you ever lose your cool is when you have to deal with supervisors. Do you realize that?"

"There's something about Bentley's face, his expression—" Grimly, Friedman shook his head.

"Look on the bright side. Think how dull it'd be if you didn't have guys like Bentley to kick around."

"How's Janet Collier doing with those pictures?"

"I haven't heard from her. I got Thomas's prints. But C. J. Kirk is missing. I didn't get a chance to tell you."

"Missing? As in skipped town?"

"I don't think he's skipped. Thomas didn't seem to think it was so unusual that he'd disappear for a few days. Maybe he's drugged out. I've ordered a stakeout."

"This case—" Friedman shook his head. "It's like—like—" He searched for the words. Finally: "It's like water. No substance. Put your hand in, try to stir something up. But when you take your hand away, nothing's changed."

Resigned, Hastings nodded, sipped his coffee. Was it his third cup today? One more cup and he'd reached his limit.

"Everything points to premeditation," Friedman said. "Somebody knew she was going to be at Baker Beach. He—"

"Not necessarily. He could've followed her when she walked out on Wallis at Reggie's. She got in her car and he followed. He could've been a complete stranger. Maybe he's a serial killer. He drives around looking for a certain kind of woman. Young, brunette, beautiful. He could've—"

Friedman groaned. "Don't say 'serial killer.' Part of the definition of a serial killer, as you might recall, is no known motive, nothing to connect the murderer to the victim. Nothing except what's in the killer's brain. Which, by definition, is all screwed up."

"Go back to premeditation," Hastings said. "How do you figure premeditation?"

"I figure Lisa knew her killer. Which is why he could park real close to her car. He got out, got into her car. Then he shot her. He brought a gun to kill her, and that's what he did. However—" Friedman bit again into the Danish, washed it down "—premeditation implies motive. Which, in this case, we don't have."

"Didn't we talk about jealousy? What about a jealous wife?"

"To me," Friedman pronounced, "it just doesn't *feel* like jealousy. Still—" He finished the Danish, finished the coffee, searched for his paper napkin, fallen on the floor.

"Here—" Hastings handed over his own napkin. "I haven't used it."

"Ah. Thanks." Friedman wiped his mouth, dropped the wadded-up napkin in his Styrofoam cup. "Our next move, I figure, is that we've got to interrogate Clayton Wallis's wife. Then we—"

"Why do you say that?"

"Say what?"

"That we've got to interrogate Wallis's wife? Christ, weren't you listening to Bentley?"

"Bentley says we should keep away from Wallis's office, because of the snitch. He didn't say anything about Mrs. Wallis. And, since she's Wallis's only alibi for the time of the murder, it's only natural to—"

"You know damn well that if Bentley thought about it, he'd've told us to lay off the wife. You *know* that."

"You may be right. The point is, he *didn't* think about it."

"Listen, Pete, you—"

"The point is, we've got the moral high ground here. Which is why Bentley'll never call us on this."

"You're bugging the brass again. You realize that, don't you? You've got a problem with authority figures. And it's getting worse. They give you an order, right away you start figuring how to duck around it, make the brass look bad."

"I've got a problem with jerks."

"What's this moral high ground? What's that mean?"

"It means," Friedman said loftily, "that, in the natural order of things, murder has priority over theft. Think about it."

"Hmmm."

"Let's get back to Mrs. Wallis. Let's assume that, in fact, Wallis killed Lisa. Let's assume Lisa was blackmailing him. 'Give me a few hundred thousand dollars,' she could've said, 'or I'll spill the beans about us to your wife.' The wife, naturally, would call up her lawyer. In the divorce, the wife would get many millions. So Wallis decides to kill Lisa. He doesn't have a choice. So then—"

"Except that he was home with his wife, when Lisa was killed."

Friedman raised a professorial forefinger. "Not necessarily. It would've been close, but the way I read the time frame on Wallis, he'd've had time to leave Rabelais, kill Lisa, and still get home before midnight."

"If that's what happened, then some sand from Baker Beach would be on the floor of Wallis's car, from his shoes."

"Forget about sand," Friedman said. "Those bloody fingerprints—" Sagely, he nodded as he pushed back his chair. "We get a match on that, we've got a case."

"Except that the way this case is going, we'll be—" At his belt, Hastings's pager beeped. He unclipped the pager, read the message: *All prints in lab. Collier.* Smiling, he handed over the pager to Friedman. The other man read the message, nodded approvingly.

"This Janet, she gets the job done."

Taking back his pager, Hastings looked squarely at Friedman. "You really think I should see Mrs. Wallis?"

Gravely, Friedman nodded. "I really do."

"Okay, then—" Resigned, Hastings nodded. "I'll do it. Maybe—" As the spontaneous thought surfaced, he broke off, considered, finally decided to complete it: "Maybe I should take Collier along. For the woman's point of view."

For a moment Friedman made no reply. Then, meaningfully: "That's up to you, Frank."

Between the two men, another silence settled. Until, finally, Hastings nodded. "I'll think about it."

"Good." Friedman rose, picked up his empty cup and plate. "Good. You think about it."

30

"We'd like to see Mrs. Clayton Wallis. My name is Frank Hastings. This is Janet Collier."

"Is Mrs. Wallis expecting you?"

"I called about an hour ago."

Seated behind a formidable reception desk that was really a command center, the uniformed security guard tapped at his computer keyboard, waited for a response on the screen. Behind the desk, five TV monitors were glowing. In one of them, Hastings saw himself, full face. At his side, Janet was looking at him. Was she aware that she was on the screen? Did she know what was revealed in her eyes, in the attentive tilt of her head as she looked up into his face?

"Mrs. Wallis is on the top floor," the security man said, tapping a final computer command. Adding: "The whole top floor." He gestured to a bank of three elevators. "Take the elevator on the left. The other two only go to the twenty-sixth floor."

"Thanks." As Hastings turned with Collier to the elevators he touched the small of her back. Her spine was deeply cleft, a strong, vital line, vibrant to his touch.

But immediately she moved ahead of him, away from his hand. Almost imperceptibly she was squaring her shoulders, raising her chin as she led the way to the elevators.

The lobby was lavishly furnished, a combination of antique

and modern. Oriental rugs were spread on the marble floor, modern paintings contrasted with artfully displayed period furniture.

"Places like this remind me of my humble origins," Janet said, stroking the marbled wall inside the elevator.

Hastings smiled, moved a half step closer, looked down at her as he said, "Me, too. Some things never change."

Once more, subtly, she moved away, saying, "This is the top of the world, you know. The fanciest apartment building on Nob Hill, which is the fanciest address in one of the fanciest cities in the world."

The elevator had stopped; the doors were sliding silently open. Facing them, a woman stood in the foyer that opened directly on the elevator. The furniture in the small foyer, the clothing the woman wore, everything enhanced an aura of affluent elegance, neither exaggerated nor understated. The woman was dressed casually in slacks, a simply cut silk blouse, and low-heeled leather walking shoes. Her age, Hastings calculated, would be the late thirties. Her tawny blond shoulder-length hair was meticulously styled, not too elegant, not too casual. The lines of her body were Thoroughbred lean; the contours of her face were *Town and Country* aristocratic. Her hazel eyes were calm, marginally haughty. It was inevitable, Hastings realized, that Clayton Wallis would have married a woman like this, his most dramatic possession, nothing but the absolute best.

Her name was Harriet. When the introductions were completed, she turned and led the way down a short hallway to the glass-walled living room that offered the choice San Francisco view: a panorama that began at the Golden Gate and swept across the cobalt blue of San Francisco Bay to the hills of Berkeley. On a warm, clear day in October, the waters of the bay were festooned with tiny picture-postcard white sails. The wind today was light. Seeking out the best breezes, the sailboats were clustered in a crescent from the Golden Gate to the waters off Alcatraz, where the wind picked up velocity as it came through the narrows.

Harriet Wallis gestured them to a white leather sofa. She waited politely for them to seat themselves before she took a matching chair. Then she crossed her legs and calmly waited for Hastings to begin.

"We're with the homicide squad, Mrs. Wallis." As he said it, Hastings sensed Janet's pleased reaction. *We,* he'd said. Not *I.*

"Last Wednesday night, roughly between ten o'clock and midnight, a young woman named Lisa Franklin was murdered. It happened at Baker Beach, in the Presidio. Beginning the next day, when the body was discovered, we began talking to everyone who knew her, trying to piece together what happened—what Lisa Franklin did that could've gotten her killed." Watching Harriet Wallis's face for some hint of a reaction, a flicker of recognition at the victim's name, Hastings momentarily broke off. But except for a subtle tightness around her mouth and nostrils, there was nothing.

"We're also trying to reconstruct the victim's movements during the time before she died." He paused again, this time for emphasis. Then: "And we discovered that, Wednesday night, Lisa Franklin had dinner with your husband at a restaurant called Reggie's. Apparently they had an argument, and Lisa Franklin left the restaurant alone. Your husband left about ten o'clock. He went to his club—Rabelais—and had a drink or two. Then he came here—home. That would've been about eleven-thirty, maybe midnight."

Still her expression remained rigid, revealing nothing. Hastings covertly shifted his gaze to Janet, a suggestion that she participate.

"Were you here when your husband came home Wednesday night, Mrs. Wallis?" Janet spoke quietly, firmly.

After a long moment of silence, staring coldly at the other

woman, Harriet Wallis said, "Have you already spoken to my husband?" Her speech matched her demeanor: elegant and aloof, the patrician dealing with an irksome inferior.

Janet nodded calmly. "Yes, we have." Imperceptibly Hastings shook his head. Especially in the first phases of an interrogation, it was never advisable to answer a subject's question. Success depended on intimidation, keeping the initiative.

"Then my husband told you that I was here when he came home. I'd gone out earlier, to a meeting of the Opera Association."

"And what time did you come home, Mrs. Wallis?"

"I got home a little after eleven."

"Are you sure?" Hastings asked.

She turned her attention to him and nodded coolly. "The eleven o'clock news had just come on."

"So you were here only for a half hour, give or take, when Mr. Wallis came home."

She nodded.

"How did your husband seem, when he came home?"

Harriet Wallis suddenly rose, went to the room's glass wall, stood looking out across the city. Her whole body was taut; her hands were rigid at her sides, straight down, fists tightly clenched. It was an acting-school evocation of anger rigidly suppressed.

When Harriet finally turned to face them again, her eyes were blazing. Choked with fury, her voice fell to a low contralto: "Are you telling me that you're accusing my husband of murdering this—this woman? Is that what this is all about?"

"We've already told you what this is all about, Mrs. Wallis," Hastings said. "We're investigating the death of—"

"If I said he didn't come home until one o'clock, what would you do then? Would you arrest him? Is that it?"

"You didn't answer the question. I asked you how—"

"I know what you asked me. You asked how Clay acted,

153

when he came home. What am I supposed to say? Am I supposed to say he acted like he'd just killed a woman?" As she said it, her speech roughened, suddenly lost its elegance. Her face, too, had hardened, no longer as composed, no longer the aloof Elizabeth Arden ideal. Angered, some women became more exciting, more desirable. Others were coarsened. Like every strong emotion, anger could illuminate the dark corners of the soul.

Had Harriet come to this penthouse that seemed to suit her so comfortably after a life of privilege: good schools, expensive country clubs, the best of everything?

Or had she come up the hard way, clawing for every handhold, spreading her legs when the price was right? Was the socialite's persona more fiction than fact, a survival technique?

"Were you aware," Janet said, "that you husband was seeing someone? Regularly?"

As if she were stalking prey, Harriet Wallis focused her anger on the other woman, still seated.

"When I hear that a man is *seeing* someone," Harriet said, once more dropping her voice, "that means to me that they're having sex. Is that what you're saying? Because if you are, then—"

"Nobody said anything about having sex, Mrs. Wallis." Looking up into the face of the woman standing over her now, Janet Collier spoke calmly, steadily.

Hastings cleared his throat, saying, "We have two separate statements that say your husband and Lisa Franklin met approximately twice each month, regularly. Whether they had sex or not isn't why we're here. We're—"

"Jesus, I'd hate to have your job, poking around, looking for dirt."

Hastings decided to make no reply. Picking up on the cue, Janet also remained silent, watching and waiting.

"Did you talk with Clay about all this?" As she spoke, Harriet Wallis returned to her chair and sat down—hard. But now her fury seemed to subside, replaced by an alertness, a hard-edged calculation.

"We talked to Mr. Wallis on Friday." Making his own calculations, Hastings watched for a reaction. Then: "Did he tell you that we talked to him?"

Instead of replying, she rose once more from the chair, went again to the window, stood looking out. Now, though, the woman's movements were controlled, deliberate. Hastings turned again to Janet. Her eyes were alive with suppressed excitement. Like Hastings, she sensed a shift of mood in their quarry. The next moments could be crucial.

This time, when Harriet turned to face the two detectives sitting side by side on the white leather sofa, she was no longer furiously defiant. Instead, her voice was low, grimly resigned: "I can see where you're going with this. You'll talk to Clay, then me, then go back to Clay. Whipsawing, isn't that the word for it? Playing one suspect off against the other, until you trick them into saying what you want to hear. Isn't that what this is all about?" Contemptuously she looked from Janet to Hastings, then back to Janet. "*Isn't* it?"

"No one said anything about suspects, Mrs. Wallis," Janet said softly. "That was your word." It was a perfectly placed barb.

But Harriet Wallis took no notice. Now it was bitterness, not anger, not defiance, that made her say, "I'll try to make it simple for you. Is that what you want to hear?"

Hastings nodded but said nothing. Taking her cue from him, Janet did the same.

Still standing in front of the window, looking down at them, the woman said, "Clay *did* come home last Wednesday. And it *was* just a little after eleven, no more than twenty minutes after. I know, because we watched the last part of the news together for a few minutes. And—" Now, no longer combative, she dropped her eyes. "And, yes, he seemed jumpy, ill at ease. But it wasn't anything dramatic. It was just that he seemed tense, the way he can get when there's a big deal on, and something's hanging fire. So—" She gestured, perhaps a tentative overture. "So that's all I can tell you about last Wednesday."

"Did you go to bed right after the news?" Hastings asked.

"I went to bed. Clay stayed up. He—" She hesitated. "He mixed a drink, I guess. Our bedrooms are on the floor below, so that's just a guess. But—"

"Bedrooms?" Janet interrupted.

Harriet Wallis looked at the other woman for a long, inscrutable moment. Then, bitterly resigned, she nodded. "Right. Separate bedrooms. Which brings us to Lisa Franklin, I suppose."

Silence.

As she began to speak, the woman was once more walking toward them. This time, though, there was no hostility. There was only resignation: "Clay and I were both married twice before, so there weren't many stars in our eyes when we decided to get married. He needed someone like me, and I needed someone like him." She paused, as if she were reflecting on what she'd just said. "And it worked, too. Probably because Clay and I have always been honest with each other. Right from the start, even before we got married, he made it clear that he expected to have affairs on the side. He's one of those insatiable men. Whatever he wants, he takes. Most successful businessmen are like that, at least the ones I know. Most politicians, too. They're insatiable—the dominant male."

"So what you're saying," Janet said, "is that he had women on the side—and you had men."

Once more seated, Harriet Wallis shrugged as she traced a design on the arm of her chair with a carmine-tipped forefinger. Like her body, the woman's hands were long and graceful, a study in perfection.

Taking the shrug as an admission of infidelity, Hastings said, "So you knew about his affair with Lisa Franklin."

Her reply was muted, as if her thoughts were elsewhere. "I didn't know her by name. I'd never met her, never seen her, to my knowledge. I just knew there was someone."

"How did you know?" Janet asked.

As if to explain something that should have been self-evident, the woman shrugged again, impatiently spread her hands. "By the hours he kept—by the number of weekend business trips, so-called, that he took. And by the way he acted, with me."

Janet queried Hastings with a quick glance. It was, Hastings knew, a request for more latitude, a gamble, or a bluff. He decided to grant the unspoken request.

Turning to face Harriet Wallis, Janet began diffidently, almost apologetically: "You're married to a man who's very, very wealthy. And you know he plays around with other women. Now—" Carefully framing what would come next, Janet momentarily broke off. Then: "Now, a lot of women in your position would hire a private detective to get pictures. And names. And dates. Then they'd call a divorce lawyer."

"And they'd be rich. Is that what you're saying?" With the question, Harriet Wallis's bitterness returned. The bitterness, and the brittleness, too.

Janet made no response.

"The answer to the question," came the reply, "is that, last time around, my second marriage, yes, I called the detectives. Then, yes, I called the lawyers. But—" A final pause. "But he hired detectives, and lawyers. Very good lawyers. So when I finally walked out of the courtroom, I had a lot more money than I went in with." The depth of her sigh expressed it all: the futility, and the waste. And, most of all, the humiliation. "But I had a whole lot less pride."

In response, gravely, Janet nodded. Yes, she understood. Woman to woman, she understood.

31

"You want to drive?"

"Sure." Janet plucked the keys from Hastings's outstretched palm. They were approaching the cruiser from the driver's side. Should she round the car, unlock the passenger's door for him? If they were equal in rank, in this position, she wouldn't open the offside door. But, as her superior, he rated the few extra steps, yet another privilege of rank.

Frank Hastings . . .

A policeman . . . a lieutenant . . .

And a man.

A man who, God help her, she wanted to touch, to draw close, to feel hard against her.

Meaning that she must now walk directly to the driver's door, open the door, get into the car, quickly slide over to unlock his door.

"So," he was saying as he settled into the passenger's seat, "what d'you think?"

"I think Harriet Wallis is a pretty angry lady. Controlled, but angry. I don't think she realizes how angry she is."

"Do you think she was telling the truth?"

"I think she was telling the truth about Wednesday night. But when she was talking about her husband, what he was worried about, I think she was holding something back."

"He's being investigated by the SEC. She might've known that but didn't want to tell us."

"If he goes to jail for securities fraud . . ." She let it go speculatively unfinished.

"There goes her meal ticket," he finished.

"God, what a marriage. One long armed truce."

"I wonder if she fools around?" he mused.

"She'd almost have to fool around."

"Why do you say that?"

"How else could she keep her self-respect?"

"Jesus . . ." In wonderment, Hastings shook his head. "The battle of the sexes. Is that what it comes down to: screwing around on the side, to keep the score even?"

"For a lot of people, that's it." Still she sat behind the steering wheel, eyes straight ahead. As a silence settled between them, she felt him shift slightly on the seat. His next question, she sensed, would be personal, not professional:

"Your husband—what was he like?"

Still looking straight ahead, she smiled faintly. "He was dull. Very, very dull. But, God, he was good-looking. Very, very good-looking. Mostly, though, he was twenty-one—and I was eighteen. And we couldn't keep our hands off each other. So we got married. We thought we were in love."

"And you had a child immediately."

"I was nineteen when I got pregnant. When I was five months along, I found out that Richard—my husband—was playing around. And the son of a bitch didn't even have the grace to deny it. He—"

Across the street, the security gate guarding the garage of Clayton Wallis's building was rolling up. A bright red Japanese sports-styled car was coming up the ramp, turning right. A woman was alone in the car—

—Harriet Wallis, driving intently, quickly gathering speed, cut in front of a pickup truck that had to brake sharply.

"Hey—" Instinctively Janet's hand went to the cruiser's ignition. "Hey, there she is. Harriet, in a hurry."

"Where?" Hastings was dropping his head, moving close to her, to look out the driver's window.

"That red car." She twisted the ignition key, brought their engine to life. "What d'you think?"

But the next moment the red car disappeared around the first corner. A line of traffic was stopping beside them, boxing them into their parking space.

159

Still leaning across her, their heads close, Frank snorted amiably, saying, "She's probably going to buy cat food." Now he smiled at her—God, that slow, half-shy smile. Determinedly she drew away—and waited for him to do the same, as, still smiling, he leaned back against his door, neutral corners.

"She didn't look like she was buying cat food. She looked like she was in a hurry. And she looked worried."

"Did you make her plates?"

"No."

He shrugged. "She'll be back."

"Sure. But where's she *going* in such a hurry?"

He made no reply, instead asking, "When you took those pictures around to Wallis and Cameron and Drake, how'd they act?"

"Wallis was the only one who took any time with me. I did him first."

"How'd it go with Wallis? How'd he act?"

"Very cool, I'd say. Very much in control."

"Do you think he was suspicious?"

"I'm not sure. At the time, I thought he was—you know—coming on to me. And maybe he was. He's that kind of a man, just like his wife said. Still—" She frowned, searching for the words. "Still, there was something there, I can't put my finger on it. Maybe he was too cool, maybe that was it."

"What about the other two, Cameron and Drake? How'd they strike you?"

"I got nothing from Cameron. All the time I was there, maybe five minutes, he was on two phones, giving orders to a couple of secretaries, wheeling and dealing. He took one look at the picture and that was it. He's a powerhouse—a street fighter, really. I can see how he'd excite a woman like Lisa. If she wanted to go for broke, he'd be right with her."

"What about Drake?"

"Ah—Drake." Warming to the subject, she smiled, turned

to face Hastings. Should she say it, take the risk of familiarity, just one of the squadroom guys?

Yes, she would say it. "Drake," she repeated, "that prissy-ass. Talk about variety, Lisa sure had it in her men."

In response, immediately, Hastings's smile widened. "I know. I thought the same thing. Wallis and Cameron, that's a fit. They're both rich, and they live high. But Drake—who would've thought it?"

"Then there's C. J., too. And don't forget Barbara."

Reflectively, Hastings nodded. "Right . . ."

"It's strange, you know—" Framing the thought, she paused. "I suppose it's a cliché, but I feel like I've really gotten involved with Lisa Franklin's life, reading her journals. Have you gotten into them?"

"No," Hastings admitted, "I haven't, not really. I read a couple of entries, which I didn't understand. Then I skimmed the rest, and that was it." He smiled—deep into her eyes. "That's when I decided to unload them on you."

Resisting the temptation to return the smile, she said, "I've read them through three times. The first time through, I didn't think there was any particular order. There're three books, you know. And there's no real indication which one was written first, which last. They weren't numbered or dated. But, gradually, I got it sorted out, at least to my satisfaction. Because there *is* a progression, starting with her recollections of childhood. And, God, it's fascinating. The more I read, the better I knew her."

"So what d'you think?"

"I think she was a poor little rich girl, an only child raised by nannies. Her parents hated each other. When they weren't using Lisa as a weapon against each other, they ignored her. Absolutely ignored her. And she was certainly a pretty, bright, vivacious little girl—for all the good it did her."

"So she grew up hating everyone."

Janet nodded. "She was a very complex lady who was loaded

with aggressions. These people we're dealing with on this case, C. J. and Wallis and Cameron and Drake—and Barbara, too— they all represent the different facets of Lisa's personality, that's my theory. C. J. is her lost, confused, childlike side. Wallis represents greed, the 'me first' side, which is also child-like, really. Cameron, well, I suppose he was more of the same. Or maybe she and Cameron understood each other com-pletely because they were both utterly ruthless. Drake— well—there was certainly a poetic, creative aspect of Lisa. Or maybe—" She smiled at the wayward thought. "Maybe she just felt sorry for him, because he's such a wimp. Everyone has a softer side. Even Lisa Franklin."

"Okay—that leaves Barbara."

"Yeah, well, Barbara and I didn't exchange more than a few words today, so I'm sticking my neck out. But you told me Jamie Thomas said Lisa was a modern-day courtesan. Which, I guess, translates into a high-price hooker. And a lot of hook-ers really hate men. Meaning that they get off with women, not men. So I'm guessing that the only relationship Lisa really cared about was the one she had with Barbara."

"You could be right," Hastings said thoughtfully.

"I don't think she would've lived with someone, shared that much of herself with another person, if the relationship didn't mean something."

"Lesbians . . ." Bemused, Hastings was shaking his head. "I can't get a handle on them. I never guess right. My God, I just heard that Marlene Dietrich was gay."

"I read that article. It also said she had affairs with General Eisenhower and General Patton, during the war. And she had a daughter and a husband, too."

"So she was bisexual."

"Like Lisa." She let the smile linger. God, was he really so innocent, such a straight arrow?

"So, what *about* Barbara?" he pressed. "How'd she strike you?"

"She struck me as a very smart, very determined, very no-frills lady."

He nodded agreement, then said, "I keep getting hung up on motive. We're all assuming it was premeditated murder. But where's the motive? Jealousy? An irate lover?" Skeptically, he shook his head. "That's a crime of passion—a demented lover, something like that. But, of all these people, C. J.'s the only one who might be out of control. And that's drugs, not jealousy."

"When we get back to the Hall, I'd like to show you a few of Lisa's journal entries. They were probably made a month or two before she was killed. And they suggest that she had a grievance against someone. She—" Impatiently, Janet shook her head. "No, that's not right. It seemed like she was *targeting* someone, laying a trap for him."

" 'Targeting'? 'Him'?"

She shrugged. "Him—her—"

"Victor Cameron said she seemed worried about something the week before she died. He said—" At his belt, Hastings's pager beeped. She watched him unclasp the pager, read the message. "It's Friedman," he said. He picked up the cellular phone, punched out a number, waited for the connection. Then: "Pete." While he listened, she could see a shadow of disappointment in his face—followed, rapidly, by a quickening of interest, then anticipation. "Okay, we'll get right over there. We've got a picture. Who's on stakeout?" A pause, listening. "We should be there in ten, fifteen minutes."

Janet brought the engine to life, checking the mirrors as Hastings spoke again into the phone: "Right. I'll get back to you." As he cradled the phone he spoke to her. "Page Street, near Pierce. Code two." As she pulled out into traffic, he opened his window, clapped the magnetic red flasher on the roof, saying, "It's C. J. He's just showed up at his place."

"Ah—" Feeling an adrenaline rush beginning, the real essence of the job, she pressed hard on the accelerator, swung the cruiser sharply into the oncoming traffic lane. "What else did Lieutenant Friedman say?"

"He said that he just heard from the lab, on the four pictures you got. The prints were great, they said, very clear. But there wasn't a match with those bloody prints."

"Crap."

32

"He fits the description," Welch replied. "And he used a key, went right into the lower flat."

Hastings nodded, pushed away from Welch's car. "Okay. Good. You wait here. Who's in back?"

"Ernie Talbot. We went to the Academy together."

"Okay." Hastings pointed to the surveillance radio lying on the front seat beside Welch. "Tell Talbot we're going inside."

"Yessir."

With Janet walking beside him as they crossed the street, Hastings reflexively unbuttoned his jacket and loosened his revolver in its spring holster. Taking the cue, Janet unfastened the flap of her oversize leather handbag, shifted the envelope with the picture to her left hand, slipped her right hand into the purse, with its concealed four-inch revolver. Her eyes were steady, her stride firm. Whatever might happen, she would be ready.

On the second ring, James Thomas opened the door to them.

"Hey, Frank—back so soon." As he spoke, Thomas looked at Janet, smiled, waited for an introduction. Hastings obliged, then said, "We want to talk to C. J., Jamie." As he spoke, he moved forward expectantly. Unpredictably, Thomas did not yield the doorway, saying instead, "Yeah, well, C. J.'s not exactly up to speed, you might say. He's— I guess he had a pretty rough weekend."

"That's no problem." Hastings pointed to the envelope. "I just want him to eyeball this picture, the one I showed you."

"Hey," came a voice from inside. "Hey, is that the cops? Lieutenant Hasty Something? Is that him?"

Muttering a mild obscenity, Thomas stepped back, making way. Hastings thanked him, walked down the hallway and into the living room. C. J. Kirk was sprawled on the lumpy sofa, feet flopped on the floor, one arm hanging loose, knuckles down.

"The name is Hastings, C. J. Lieutenant Frank Hastings. This is Inspector Janet Collier. She's got something to show you."

"Ah . . ." With an effort, Kirk lifted his head, focused on the woman. "Ah—hey—" Kirk nodded bleary approval. "A lady detective. A foxy-looking lady detective. Beautiful lady detectives, a beautiful lady murdered. It's very—very—" Baffled, he shook his head. Then, lighting up: "It's very beautiful. It's very—"

"Sit up straight," Janet snapped. "I've got something I want you to look at. An identification."

" 'Sit up straight,' " he mimicked, a mumbling mockery. "*Now!*"

Muttering like a child roused from sleep, fretfully, he levered himself straighter, gathered his feet closer. His vague, watery eyes were focused on Janet, who slipped the photograph out of its envelope, carefully handed it over.

"Have you ever seen this man before?"

Kirk took the photo in both hands, blinked, stared at it, blinked again. Finally: "I'm not sure. Why? Who is he? Is he—was he—another gentleman friend of Lisa's?" Now he smirked. But, like Kirk's other affectations, the smirk was inconclusive, unconvincing. "Is that the word? 'Friend'?"

"Do you recognize him?"

"No. Never saw him before."

"Okay—" She held out her hand, for the picture.

"Ah—ah—" Playfully, he moved the picture out of her reach. "Say 'please.' "

"Give me that picture, asshole. *Now.*"

"Hey—wow—the lady bites."

"*Give* it to me."

"Ah—Jesus—" Leering, he surrendered the picture. "You're pretty tough, hey?" Answering his own question, he nodded. "You should meet Barbara, upstairs. She's pretty tough, too. Maybe we could arrange a fight, just you two girls."

"I've already met Barbara." Handling it carefully, she slipped the photo into the envelope.

"So what d'you think? You're about the same weight. So how about three rounds, no holds barred?" At the thought, his eyes kindled lasciviously. "Yeah—three rounds. How about it? I'll hold your coat, give you a rubdown between rounds. What d'you—"

"Where were you all weekend, C. J.?" Hastings broke in.

Visibly perplexed, confused, Kirk frowned, blinked, finally refocused, this time on Hastings. "What?"

"This weekend—you weren't home. Where were you?"

"Why?"

"I'm asking the questions, C. J. I ask, you answer." As he spoke, Hastings looked toward the living room archway, where James Thomas stood, arms folded, leaning against the wall. Watching the spectacle, Thomas appeared resigned, long-suffering. Once again Hastings was struck by the similarity of the two roommates, both burned-out cases, the older one resigned, the younger one still flailing away, making waves.

"Okay, Jamie—" Hastings moved his head toward the back of the house. "We can handle it from here. Thanks."

Diffidently, Thomas raised his bony shoulders, said something unintelligible, disappeared down the hallway.

"Hey," Kirk protested. "Hey, come on—don't shove people around. Jamie, he lives here, you know. He—" Suddenly Kirk guffawed, dropped his chin on his chest, began to shake his head, muttering, "What is it, all this shit? People coming and going, shoving other people around, what's it all about? Living or dying, what's it take? Make one little mistake, say something wrong, and then there she was, dead. Isn't that what happened?" Suddenly Kirk raised his head, confronting the other man. In his drawn, sallow face, a mask of misery, Kirk's sunken eyes were ablaze, a fevered, futile flame. "Isn't that what you said? Didn't you say that Lisa—that she—" The words were lost in a backwash of confusion; the feverish flame flickered, quickly died. It was, Hastings realized, the metaphor for C. J.'s life, a chronicle of waste and confusion. In his whole life, had C. J. ever won one?

"We were talking about the weekend," Hastings said. "We want to know where you were this weekend."

"I didn't go anyplace. I was right here, all weekend."

"That's not what Jamie says."

Kirk blinked, frowned, pursed his lips. Then: "How would he know where I was?"

"He'd know because he was here. And he says—"

"Oh. You mean *here. Right* here." Kirk pointed a forefinger down at the floor. The finger, Hastings noticed, was crooked, had once been broken.

Hastings nodded. "That's what I mean."

"Oh. Well, no, I wasn't *here* all weekend. But I was in San Francisco, I thought that's what you meant. I was partying, mostly."

"What were you celebrating?" Janet asked.

Kirk studied her for a moment. Then he frowned, as if he were baffled. "Celebrating? Is that what I said?"

"You said 'partying.' People party when they're happy—when they've got something to celebrate." She watched his face for a reaction, but there was nothing.

"That's happy partying. But there's sad partying, too." Kirk shook his head. "I can't remember happy partying. Ever."

The two detectives exchanged a quick glance before Hastings decided to say, "The night Lisa died—last Wednesday night—where were you, that night?"

"I already told you that, when you told me she died."

"No, you didn't, C. J. I didn't ask you, and you didn't tell me."

"Hmmm." It was a suspicious-sounding monosyllable.

"Do you have a car?"

"No. I used to have one. No more, though."

"So how'd you get around, partying over the weekend?"

He shrugged. "Different ways. It depended."

"Let's talk about Wednesday night. The night Lisa died. What'd you do, that night?"

"*Wednesday night*—" It was an aggrieved exclamation on a rising falsetto, an inarticulate protest. "Man, how can I tell about Wednesday night? It's—man—it's been forever, since Wednesday. My brain, it's going to explode, from all that's happened, all this shit. I'm going to—"

"I want you to answer the question, C. J. Never mind about your brain. I want you to—"

"Never mind about my *brain*? Is that what you're telling me? Never *mind*? You're telling me to—" Suddenly Kirk broke off, looked incredulously at Hastings, a hysterical confrontation. "I'm going crazy, and you're telling me to never *mind*?"

"Why're you going crazy, C. J.?" Janet asked the question softly, soothingly. "Were you in love with Lisa? Is that what you're telling us?"

"Love—" Once more, Kirk's voice skipped to a hysterical

falsetto. "Jesus, love. Is that what we're talking about? Love? I thought it was death we were talking about. Isn't that it? Death and taxes, isn't that it, what it's all about? Taxes, and money. Forget about love. Tell me about money. Tell me about—"

"Okay," Janet interrupted deftly, "let's talk about money, if you want to." She still spoke soothingly: the big sister now, the sympathetic listener. It was, Hastings realized, the old good cop/bad cop game. But, so far, Janet was taking both parts.

"What *about* money?" she pressed. "What's bugging you so bad about money?"

"Nothing's bugging me," he flared, suddenly defiant, eyes wide and wild. "What're you trying to do? You trying to— to—" Now, confused, his anger collapsed, he blinked, broke off, lapsed into a sullen silence, muttering something unintelligible. Janet looked at Hastings, a mute question. Did he have the game plan?

Hastings, too, spoke softly, a gentle reminder, nothing more: "C. J., I want to go back to Wednesday night. I want you to tell me what you did, Wednesday. Where were you? Were you—"

"You can't ask that," Kirk mumbled. "When Lisa died— where I was, then—you can't ask me that." Now, another transformation, Kirk had turned transparently crafty, his eyes narrowed by guile, his mouth twisted derisively. "Because I don't have a lawyer. And if I don't have a lawyer, then I don't have to talk to you. And you know that. Both of you." As if he were lecturing two misbehaving children, Kirk waggled his forefinger at them. "*Both* of you," he repeated.

Resigned, Hastings rose, signaled to Janet that the interrogation was finished, dead end.

Leaning side by side against the cruiser, they stared thoughtfully across the street at the Page Street building. In the ground-floor flat, Jamie Thomas stood in the bay window of the living room. Gesticulating, he was talking to someone in the room, doubtless C. J. Kirk.

"So what d'you think?" Hastings asked.

"I think," Janet answered, "that he's one very screwed-up guy who's got something pretty heavy on his mind."

"Whatever he's on, it must be pretty good stuff. He's obviously high as hell. But the whole time, he was ahead of us." As he spoke, Hastings looked at Tim Welch's car, parked close by. In the approved stakeout manner, Welch was slumped down low in the driver's seat, offering almost no silhouette. Overhead, at five o'clock, the sky was darkening.

"Listen—" Hastings pointed to the envelope with the picture inside. "Where's your car? At the Hall?"

She nodded.

"Okay. Tell Welch to drive you downtown. I want you to take that picture to the lab. I want you to breathe down their necks until they pull a comparison. I'll call ahead and set it up. I'll cover for Welch here, until he gets back. Then I'm going to go by Walter Drake's house. Maybe I'll get lucky, and his wife'll be there."

"Ah—" She looked at him—and smiled. Instantly his perceptions shifted, his moorings loosened. Her smile—what was its meaning?

"Ah," she repeated, "the old betrayed wife game."

"We've got to get some more balls in the air. The bloody fingerprints aren't looking like much. It'll probably turn out they were left by the first beat cop on the scene. As usual."

"Isn't that kind of a dirty trick, though—blowing the whistle on Drake to his wife? I mean, it's not like he's a hot suspect."

"Janet—" Playfully patronizing, he smiled, a brief moment of sidewalk intimacy. "Dirty tricks are what police work is all about. Didn't they teach you that in Bunco?"

"But doesn't Drake have an alibi for Wednesday night?"

"He says he was at home with his wife. But it wouldn't be

the first time a wife lied to protect her husband in a situation like this. She sees her meal ticket threatened, she'll lie. Then she holds it over him, that she lied." He shrugged. "Husbands and wives, it's a guessing game. Speaking of which, there's always the jealous wife angle."

"Mrs. Walter Drake—" Also playfully patronizing, she shook her head. "She's a Pacific Heights matron, Frank. Besides, Walter Drake doesn't strike me as a guy who's capable of arousing a whole lot of jealousy in the female breast. The guy's a nerd."

"Okay, then, turn it around again. Whether he's a nerd or not, maybe he was terrified that his wife would find out about Lisa. Maybe Lisa threatened to go to his wife. And if that happened to him—if there was a divorce, and a scandal—it'd ruin his standing in society. And that's his whole world. That's *him*. He's a blueblood. Period. End of the story."

"Personally," she said, "I'll put my money on C. J. I think there was something between him and Lisa—something we're missing. That's my theory."

"Are we going back to her journal?"

"I'm going to highlight some passages for you, see what you think."

"Okay. But meanwhile . . ." He touched the envelope. Then, unaware that he'd meant to do it, his hand was on her shoulder. In appearance, it was no more than a comradely gesture. But, as if he were powerless to exert his own free will, his hand was lingering on her shoulder, subtly drawing her closer, as if they would surely kiss each other in the softly gathering dusk on Page Street.

Willingly, eagerly kiss each other.

Helplessly, passionately kiss each other.

But, even as their eyes acknowledged what had happened, acknowledged what surely would have happened in a different place, at a different time—yet now they were drawing back. It was another lost moment between them.

33 "Yes, I read about the murder."
Fiona Drake nodded attentively.
She was a small, prim, plain woman in her early fifties. Her graying hair was cut in the conservative style of an earlier era. The flesh of her face was beginning to wrinkle; her mouth was circled by countless small creases. Except for pale lipstick, she wore no visible makeup. She was dressed in a plain skirt, a shirtwaist blouse, and a gray wool cardigan sweater buttoned around a narrow torso. Her single concession to current dress code was a pair of spotless white tennis shoes. Behind rimless glasses, her gray eyes were narrowly focused, fixed watchfully on Hastings. Sitting on a silk damask love seat, knees together, hands clasped in her lap, an evocation of good girls' schools, she personified the matured society matron, infinitely secure in the elegantly furnished living room of her million-dollar turn-of-the-century town house, Watching her, Hastings wondered whether Fiona Drake had ever sweated, or farted, or enjoyed a belly laugh.

"Since Lisa Franklin died," Hastings said, "we've been checking out everyone who knew her, everyone whose name we found in her address book." According to plan, he looked at her expectantly, as if he were politely awaiting confirmation that, yes, she had been acquainted with Lisa Franklin.

She frowned, plainly puzzled. "Address book? You found my name in her address book?"

"Well—" He spread his hands, a disclaimer. "I think the actual listing read 'Walter Drake.' I'd have to check, to make sure. But I assumed—" As if he, too, were puzzled, he frowned, broke off.

"Was there a phone number?"

"Yes. Only a phone number, if I remember correctly. No address. I think—" He made a show of searching his pockets until he finally found his spiral-bound notebook. He flipped through the first few pages, found Walter Drake's office number. "Yes, here it is." Innocently, he recited the number.

In the few moments that followed, without shifting her position on the love seat, Fiona Drake entered an altered state, as if she were immobilized by some force from within. Her face went rigid. In her lap, her clasped hands were knuckle-white. In her throat the ligaments were drawn taut. The musculature of her face was suddenly so shrunken that she might almost have been mummified. Finally, with great effort, she spoke. Her voice was hardly more than a whisper:

"Have you come to humiliate me, Lieutenant? Is that why you're here?"

He decided to make no reply.

"That's my husband's number, at his office. It's not our number, here."

"Ah—" He nodded. "Yes, I see."

"What kind of a detective are you, Lieutenant, if you didn't know that?"

"Mrs. Drake. I don't want to—"

"My husband had a—a fling with this woman, and you found out about it. And now you've come here to torment me, make me look cheap. Is that what they pay you to do, Lieutenant?"

"I've come here to investigate a murder, Mrs. Drake. All I've got is a phone number, and I'm trying to—"

"Have you talked to Walter?"

"I—ah—don't think I should get into that. I mean, whatever problems you and your husband have, that's one thing. All I'm interested in is—"

"Oh." It was a venomous retort, half choked in her throat. "Oh, I see. You're like all the other cheap character assassins. You and the *National Inquirer*, you're all alike. You deal in innuendo, isn't that right? You make allegations, but you don't reveal your sources. You—"

"Look, Mrs. Drake—" Abandoning the pretense of bumbling innocence, he spoke harshly now, the policeman taking charge: "I came here primarily to ask one very simple question."

"Oh?" Behind the rimless glasses, her pale eyes snapped furiously. But her finishing school posture remained rigidly unchanged, as if she were bound by invisible chains that she hadn't the strength to struggle against. "And what's that?"

"Were you home, here, last Wednesday night?"

"As a matter of fact, I was." She spoke quickly, decisively, self-defensively.

Too quickly?

Too decisively?

Most people, Hastings knew, had to pause for thought, trying to remember what they'd done on a given day, a given date.

"And your husband—was he here, too?"

"Yes." This time, she spoke as if the answer had been torn from her by torture.

"You're sure?"

As if she couldn't trust herself to reply, she said nothing. Watching her, Hastings realized that Fiona Drake was on the ragged edge and could lose control. If it happened, would he profit? Lose? Break even? What were the odds? How could he—?

"Marriage . . ." She could have been pronouncing an obscenity. But now her voice had dropped to a lower note, as if bitterness had overcome her flare of anger. "You're twenty, and you marry a stranger you've known all your life. You do it because everyone you know is doing it—because people you don't even like *expect* you to do it. And then you're suddenly fifty. And you realize that you could be chained to this man for another thirty years. And you realize how stupid you were, thirty years before. Because he's still a stranger—a dull, lifeless, dishonest stranger who's hopelessly addicted to his petty little deceits. And you realize that, surprise, your whole life is nothing but a collection of old newspaper clippings. You at the debutantes' ball. You standing beside this stranger, in your wedding picture. And, later, faded pictures of the two of you, doing the accepted things together. And then, suddenly, you—" A dry, cruel sob wracked her narrow body. But, even while she was blinking desperately against the tears, she remained as before: sitting immobilized on the elegant silk damask love seat.

Without calculation, perhaps only out of curiosity, Hastings said, "Do you have any children, Mrs. Drake?"

For a long moment she sat as before, now staring straight ahead, far beyond Hastings. Then, very softly, she said, "We had a child—a boy named Eric. But he was drowned in a boating accident, when he was eight years old. His life preserver wasn't properly snapped. And so now—" She drew a long, shallow breath. "Now I only have Walter. Just Walter."

34

From the kitchen he heard the rattle of cooking utensils. Jamie, making dinner. Whatever happened, blow off the top of a mountain, discover a rattlesnake under the covers, Jamie would still cook dinner.

Snakes and skyscrapers, mountaintops exploding on volcanic islands—to himself, C. J. smiled, drank from his wineglass, a small, civilized sip, no more. Then, carefully, he went to the front window, drew back the curtain a cautious half

175

inch. Yes, he was still there: the detective, keeping watch. They were about the same age, the two of them: he, peering out; the cop, peering in.

Peering?

No, not peering.

But if not peering, then what? Was it worth the effort, that 'what'? Now, today, Monday the nineteenth day of October, almost seven o'clock, with darkness already fallen, how could he tell? The lieutenant, that quiet, watchful man, therefore dangerous, where was he, now? And the woman, dark haired, the tits and the ass of a high-priced hooker, but with bold, hostile eyes—what had she discovered, today?

Slowly he released the curtain, let it fall back in place.

When times get tough, the tough get going. It was his father's favorite saying. His father: that small, sad man. That frightened, foolish failure. That fraud, mouthing words without meaning.

And yet—now, with darkness offering the beginning of concealment—he must get going. Tough or not, they'd given him this one last chance.

He returned to the coffee table, placed his glass on a magazine so as not to mark the wood. Now, relieved of the glass, he stood motionless, listening. Yes, there was still the sound of pots and pans. Meaning that, yes, he could enter the hallway—as he was doing now. As he'd already known, Jamie's door was still half open. And, yes, Jamie's keys were on the dresser top, along with his wallet and loose change. Quickly he entered the bedroom, plucking the keys from the dresser top. Seconds later, with the keys in his pocket, safe, he was once more in the hallway. The door to his room was closed. He opened the door, entered the room, closed the door. He took the single straight-backed chair to the closet. This, he knew, was the test. Grasping the door frame with both hands, he put one foot on the chair. Then, heaving, he was standing on the chair.

The tough get going . . .

Freeing his right hand from the door frame, an act of faith, an occasion for prayer, Hail Mary, full of grace, he was reaching far back on the top shelf. Yes, faith rewarded, thank you blessed Mother, he touched the rolled-up sweatshirt. Moments later he was unrolling the sweatshirt on the floor of the closet—

—exposing the money: the paper miracle fanned out against the dingy gray of the sweatshirt, four bundles of fifties and hundreds, each secured by a red rubber band.

Four bundles? Only four? It had been five bundles at first. Signifying that, slips, some of the money was gone.

Spent? Or gone?

No. Not gone. Spent. Either lost, or spent. But, still, gone money could be spent. Just as, flip the coin, spent money could be gone.

Now, as he'd planned, he was sitting on the floor in front of the open closet door. He was slipping off one of the thick red rubber bands. He was unlacing his shoes. He was stuffing in the money, a handful in each shoe, carefully smoothed down. Could he do it, cram his feet into the shoes? Yes—*yes.*

But some of the bundle was still left—plus the other three bundles, still intact. For this, though, he was prepared. The hunting jacket he'd bought, with the huge pockets—two bundles went into the inside pockets, and then the rest of the third bundle. Leaving the last bundle, which would go back into the sweatshirt. But, now, he could toss the sweatshirt up on the closet shelf, saving him from teetering on the chair.

With the closet door closed, with the chair in place beside the bureau, wearing the jacket now, pockets bulging, he stood in the bedroom doorway, one last look. Then he switched off the light, closed the door.

One last look . . .

Was he sobbing?

Would Jamie hear?

He stood for a moment with head bowed. Deep breathing,

177

the cure for anxiety: long, deep, slow breaths. Until, finally, he could raise his head, clear his throat, call down the hallway: "I'm going across the street to the store. Need anything?"

"No. Nothing."

"Okay. Back in a minute."

He walked to the front door, turned the knob. Moments later he was outside, on the sidewalk. Yes, there he was: the detective parked across the street, carefully looking casually away, pretending not to see, not to notice.

Each of them, pretending not to notice.

He waited for one car to pass, then waited for another car—and another. Then, careful to stroll casually, buttoning the jacket closed as he walked, an actor pretending to be someone else, anyone else, he was crossing the street. He was inside the store. It was a small neighborhood grocery store. Paul's Market, was that the name? After three years in the neighborhood, why couldn't he remember?

Behind the counter, Paul—Pete?—looked up from a newspaper printed in a foreign language. He was a large, dark, unfriendly man, a Semitic. His forearms were matted with thick black hair. His eyes were like smooth black pebbles. In the rear of the store, a door led to a parking area shared by four stores.

"My car's back there. Is the door open?"

Paul—Pete—nodded.

"Thanks. I'll be back. I just need to get something from the car."

Without comment, the other man went back to his newspaper, licking a large, flat thumb as he turned a page, irritably batted it flat.

There were four cars in the parking lot—Jamie's battered white Ford sedan, and three others. On the second try, the key worked in the driver's door. He was inside the Ford. The key was in the ignition—the engine had started. It was now only necessary for him to move the gear selector to *R,* back out of the parking space. In minutes, then, he would be on Stanyan, safe from capture.

Why, then, was he unable to move his arms? Why this sudden helplessness, his arms weighted down, one arm in his lap, one on the seat, like large, lifeless sausages? Was it fear that had immobilized him? Stalked by a snake, some small mammals were helpless. Hypnotized by fear, they awaited their fate: fangs filled with poison, sinking into soft, furry bodies.

And yet he felt no fear.

He felt only fascination as, very slowly, his right arm was lifting, as if it were suspended by some invisible thread that was tightening, tightening. Until, finally, he was able to touch the gear selector, put the car in motion, slowly moving.

Soon, he would discover whether it was possible to escape them: Hastings, with his predator's eyes—

—and Lisa, with her dead eyes.

35

She watched him as he brought his car to a stop next to hers and then sat motionless behind the wheel. He was driving his silver Mercedes, the 380-SL. He was casually dressed: a soft leather jacket, no tie. Somehow he seemed uncomfortable. He was staring straight ahead, toward the skyline of downtown San Francisco, outlined now in lights. They were parked at Vista Point, a favorite spot for tourists. Even in darkness a tour bus was arriving, parking, disgorging the tourists with their cameras and children and polyester clothing and elaborate hairdos and shrill, strident voices. She'd arrived fifteen minutes ago.

She'd confirmed that, yes, they could see Baker Beach, across the Golden Gate narrows.

Somehow it had seemed essential that they meet here, within sight of Baker Beach. Lisa Franklin, R.I.P. At the thought, she winced. R.I.P., the abbreviation for *Rest In Peace,* chiseled on the stone markers of rough frontier graves, where life had been so hard, so violent—so cheap.

So cheap . . .

God, so obscenely cheap. How much had the bullet cost that ended Lisa's life? A dollar? Less?

Still watching him, she realized that he would never turn his head to look at her. He was, after all, a superior person. Even on the phone he'd kept his persona intact, playing out the part, running the string to the end.

The end . . . and beyond.

But she, too, was playing out a part.

Slowly, deliberately, she swung open the door and stepped out of the car. For this performance she'd chosen her clothes with great care: the androgynous avenger, stalking her prey, closing in. And, God, she could feel it beginning: the surge of power, the anger—the inevitability. He was here because she had commanded him to come. He had surrendered.

Surrendered?

So easily?

Soon she would know. Finally, she would know.

As she reached for the Mercedes' door handle, she remembered: *Fingerprints. Evidence.* She made a fist, knocked on the window. For a moment he didn't respond, didn't move. Then, slowly, he leaned across, tripped the door latch, pushed the door open. She slipped inside, left the door ajar.

"I don't have much time." His voice was absolutely level, without expression. He continued to stare straight ahead, across the darkening San Francisco Bay to the city beyond, where lights were glowing. Over the waters of the bay, the first pale tendrils of fog were materializing, intruding through the narrows. On the Golden Gate Bridge, orderly columns of lights were moving: headlights coming north, taillights moving south.

"This won't take long," she said.

He said nothing, gave no sign that he'd heard.

"But I want you to look at me when I tell you. That's what this is all about. You've got to look at me. Do you understand?"

Still no response.

"*Look* at me, goddammit. *Look.*"

Still gripping the steering wheel, he slowly turned his head until their eyes met. "You don't have to tell me," he said. "I know why we're here."

"I don't think you do."

"It's because of Lisa. Because of what she did, before she died. What she knew, and what she did."

"Ah . . ." She felt an unreasoning rush of relief, an irrational surge of gratitude.

But in the next moment she felt the emptiness—and then the first wrench of fear. Because, in his eyes, she saw the danger: the stalker, watching and waiting.

Meaning that, somehow, she must frighten him—as he was frightening her. She must meet his gaze, and she must speak as he spoke, quiet as death:

"You only made it worse when you killed her. Because now you've got me. I know what she knew. And I know how she died. Do you understand?"

He was shaking his head. He spoke patiently, precisely: "You don't know how she died. Because it wasn't me. I didn't kill Lisa."

"God, how you lie. Your whole life, it's one enormous lie." As she said it, she felt fury rising—finally rising. She could kill him now. He knew she could kill him.

But why, then, was he smiling? Why was he speaking so smugly, so confidently. "If my life's a lie," he said, "then your life's a lie, too. You understand that, don't you? You understand that we're connected. From now on, we're connected."

"You son of a bitch, we'll never be connected. *Never.*"

Almost imperceptibly, the smile widened. Then he nodded.

Meaning that, yes, he accepted the terms. With his small, inscrutable smile in place, he was conceding defeat.

Meaning, that, yes, they were connected.

Meaning that this, then, was what Lisa had known. But how long had she known it?

How long, before she died?

36

"What I don't understand," Billy said, "is why they stick with the guy. Nobody on the whole team likes him. Plus he's crazy. Everybody *knows* he's crazy."

"He also happens to lead the American League in RBIs." As Dan spoke he gestured to the bowl of rice for another helping. It was Uncle Ben's rice, Dan's favorite.

"But he's been arrested—what—?" Billy turned to Hastings. "How many times, Frank?"

"Hey," Dan said. "Rice, please."

Sighing a little brother's aggrieved sigh, still with his eyes on Hastings, Billy passed the bowl.

"I think three times," Hastings said. "Mostly for vehicular violations."

"He was carrying a gun, though," Ann said.

Hastings nodded agreement but added, "It wasn't loaded, though, even though it was concealed—under the seat. He got off with a slap on the wrist."

"Well," Billy said, "I still think they should trade him. They could get two pitchers for him. Maybe three."

Hastings helped himself to a second helping of chicken wings as Ann turned to Dan, her eldest. They began discussing the weekend to come, both of them reluctantly turning to a previous conversation that must be settled. Dan, a high school junior, planned to go snorkeling for abalone on the coast north of Fort Bragg. It was a conversation that had begun earlier in the meal, delicate mother-son negotiations that were slowly focusing on the central question of whether Dan could take Ann's car for the weekend. So far, for eight teenagers, there was only one car. The implied conclusion: if Dan couldn't use Ann's car, the trip would be a bust.

But Dan, sixteen, had just gotten his driver's license. And sections of the coastal highway north of Fort Bragg were no more than two lanes clinging precariously to the edge of steep, rocky cliffs that fell directly into the surf below.

It was inevitable, Hastings knew, that Billy, the volatile one, would get involved: "But Mom's got to take me to soccer practice next Saturday."

"Jesus," Dan said, focusing his frustration on his younger brother. "Take a bus."

"There's two transfers, on the bus. And you have to wait an hour on Saturdays. Every transfer." Vehemently Billy shook his head. "No, sir. If I have to take a bus, I won't go. And then I won't be able to play in the game Wednesday. That's the rule."

"Oh, that's bullshit, and you know it. You—"

"Besides," Billy said, "that's dangerous, that road. That time we went to Stinson Beach, there was that car that went over the cliff. It—"

"Ah—Jesus—" Deeply aggrieved, Dan turned to his mother. "Do I have to listen to this?"

Rather than reply, Ann looked at Hastings, a tentative overture. He moved his head subtly aside; he would rather not get involved. But then, again subtly, he nodded. Yes, he would take Billy to soccer practice next Saturday, But, no, he had no opinion on the wisdom of Dan's driving the coast highway.

There was a pause as, separately, the two Haywood brothers glanced speculatively at Hastings, each one making his own calculations. Finally Ann ended the episode, announcing that she would talk to Victor Haywood, the boys' father. Then a final decision would be made. Soon after, the dinner ended. Hastings helped clear the table, then went into the living room. He glanced at the TV log, saw nothing of interest. From the kitchen at the rear of the spacious ground-floor flat he heard angry voices: Dan and Billy, arguing again, counterpointed by the clatter of the dishes they were washing. Hastings sank down into his favorite chair. He loosened his shoes, slipped them off, wriggled his toes, gratefully sighed. It was, he knew, a Japanese custom to take off one's shoes immediately on entering the house. Score another one for the Japanese.

He sighed again, closed his eyes, let his head rest on the chair back. The time was about seven-thirty. In her tiny sewing room, so-called, behind the kitchen, Ann would be working on a new lesson plan for her fourth graders. In an hour, give or take, she would join him in the living room. Almost certainly they would talk about Billy and Dan and abalone fishing. And—yes—about Victor Haywood, the society psychiatrist who, after all, helped support his sons.

Child support . . .

Divorce . . .

He and Ann and Janet; all of them were casualties, statistics. "The fifty percenters," someone had recently written. Meaning that, for every two marriages in America, one ended in divorce. Neither he nor Ann nor Janet had remarried. Their spouses, though, had each gotten married again: Carolyn, who'd married her tennis partner. Victor, with his hairpiece and his Porsche, had married one of his patients, a divorcée

184

who'd just had her second facelift. And, finally, Janet's ex-husband, with his salesman's smile and his weight lifter's biceps, had married a manicurist.

Of them all, Janet was the only one who slept alone.

Now, at least, Janet slept alone.

Her son, Charlie, was fifteen, only a year younger than Dan. Janet had divorced Charlie's father when Charlie was only two. Meaning that, for thirteen years, Janet had been without a man. Not without sex, not without occasional affairs, she'd told him that. But, always, Charlie had come first. *He's had one weekend uncle,* Janet had once said. *No more.*

And yet, God, when he touched her—just a touch, not a kiss—he could feel her responding, a deep, primitive tremor of desire. He knew, most certainly knew—most certainly could feel—that once they were alone, anywhere, anytime, they would come together, flesh against flesh, seeking, straining, finally fulfilled.

Just as he knew that tonight, in bed with Ann, the two of them making love, he would think of Janet.

Just as Janet, lying alone, would think of him.

37

Tomorrow . . .

Now there was only tomorrow. The years, the months, the weeks—finally the days, then the hours, all gone.

And, finally, the minutes would fade away until only seconds remained.

Lisa . . .

In the moments before the endless void descended, would it

be her face he'd see? In the procession marching through eternity, would she look back and see him join the procession? Would she smile? Even knowing that he was her executioner, knowing that it had all happened for nothing, a greedy whim, would she smile?

38

From the back of the flat came the sounds of the Haywoods: Dan, talking on the extension in the kitchen. Billy, playing his TV too loud. Ann, ordering Billy to turn the TV down, close his door, so she could concentrate on her lesson plan.

At headquarters, Janet would still be waiting for the fingerprint report from the lab, ramrodding it through.

At home, Friedman would probably be doing as Hastings was doing: sitting in his living room, shoes off, dinner still heavy in his stomach.

As he picked up the TV wand, Hastings heard Dan calling from the kitchen: "Hey, Frank. Call waiting."

"Right." Hastings went to the phone, picked up the ballpoint pen that was always by the notebook beside the living room extension. In the year he'd lived here, his only nonnegotiable demand was that there always be pad and pen beside the phone.

"Yes."

"Frank, it's Janet."

And, instantly, he knew: the bloody prints.

"It's C. J.," she said. "Ten points, three fingers."

"Where are you? The lab?"

"Yes."

"Have you called anyone else? The stakeout?"

"I thought I should call you first."

"All right. You stay put. I'll get back to you."

"Are you going to pick him up?"

"Of course."

"I want in, Frank. When we pick him up, I want to be there."

"Listen, Janet. I've got to—"

"I've earned it, Frank. This one I've earned."

He sighed—loudly enough for her to hear. Then: "You're sure about the match? Absolutely sure? You don't want Friedman or me to sign on with you?"

"I've already got it in writing from Lieutenant Pietrie." In her voice he could plainly hear resentment. Hard-nosed resentment. Once more, the contradiction surfaced: Janet, so desirable, so wonderfully formed, yet so determined, so goddam stubborn sometimes.

"Okay. You stay put. I'll get back to you."

"Promise?"

"Promise."

"How long, about?"

"Janet . . ." It was a warning, a chain-of-command reminder of rank.

"Sorry."

"You stay at the lab." He broke the connection, called Friedman's home phone.

"It's Frank, Pete."

"Ah . . ." The single exclamation said it all: Friedman, too, sensed that the prey was in sight. "Just a second." In the background, the sounds of television subsided. "Okay."

"We've got a ten-point fingerprint match in the blood on Lisa's car. Inside, on the driver's side. It's C. J. Kirk."

"Is he staked out?"

"Front and back. Welch and Talbot."

"Who's vouching for the fingerprint match?"

"Janet's got it in writing from Pietrie."

"And, therefore, Janet wants in."

"Pete—"

"She's entitled, what the hell. But if you go in after him, leave her on the sidewalk."

"I've gone in with her before—that waiter who killed those five guys. She was fine."

"All I want to do—all I'm concerned about—is that we get this guy downtown with zero fuss. That's my whole concern."

Hastings took time to consider. Then: "I already told her she could come in. But if there's going to be a problem . . ." He let it go unfinished.

"There's no problem. Just get the cuffs on the guy and give me a call. I'll meet you downtown. Okay?"

"Okay."

As Hastings broke the connection and waited for the line to clear he saw Billy coming down the hallway. Whenever action was imminent, Billy invariably materialized, avidly listening in. At these times Hastings realized that, yes, Billy admired him. And he realized that, yes, Billy's admiration mattered. A lot.

"You got to go out?" Billy asked.

"Yes, probably. Just a minute—" About to punch out the number for police Communications, he was startled when the phone came alive in his hand. Watching his face, Billy giggled.

"It's Canelli, Lieutenant. I'm catching till midnight."

"What's happening?"

"Well, jeez, I just heard from Welch out on Page Street. It looks like they lost C. J. Kirk."

"*What?*"

"Yeah. See, Welch said he saw C. J. come out of the house about an hour ago. C. J. went across the street to one of those little mom and pop grocery stores, like he was going to buy a quart of milk, or something. Well, it was one of those decisions you've got to make on stakeout. Lose, lose is what I call it. I mean, if Welch went right into the store after the subject, then he blows it. But if he—"

"Canelli, cut it short. We just got a fingerprint matchup on him—that blood on the door. The guy's a murderer." As he said it, Hastings looked down at Billy. Yes, the boy's eyes were round, his mouth was open, marveling. Unconsciously, the boy had drawn closer.

"Jesus . . ." Canelli's voice was chastened.

"So what're the details?"

"Well, like I said, the subject went into the store and Welch decided to stay outside. He decided to give it five minutes, by his watch. Then he went across the street to the store. No C. J. It turns out there's a back door that leads to a parking lot in the rear. Welch took a few minutes to see whether he could turn up anything on the street, then he called in. That was maybe forty-five minutes ago, something like that. I decided not to call you right away, since you're off the board. Naturally, I didn't know about the fingerprint match."

Hastings looked at his watch: a few minutes after eight o'clock. If Kirk had been running for an hour, he could already be out of town.

"Did you check the DMV computer?" Hastings asked.

"Yes, sir. No car's registered to him."

"Shit." As he said it, he exchanged a look with Billy, followed by a shrug. Then, into the phone: "Okay. You work up a description of him and get it out on the air."

"Yessir."

"Give me the lab." As he waited, he smiled down at Billy, whose expression was rapt. "Problems," Hastings explained. "One of our guys got—"

"Forensics," a voice said. "Pietrie."

"Yeah—Dave, this is Frank. Inspector Collier—Janet Collier. Is she there?"

"Right here, Frank. Just a second." A moment later, Janet came on the line.

"Kirk's on the loose," Hastings said. "It looks like he's running."

"When?"

"Almost an hour ago, now. And he doesn't have a car, so an APB's no goddam good."

"Shit."

Hastings smiled. "You still want in?"

"You know I do."

"Okay. I'm going over to Kirk's place, see if I can pick up the trail. I'll meet you there. If my car is empty at the curb, I'll be inside the house, talking to Jamie Thomas. You stay outside, if we're talking. Jamie and I went to the same high school, he thinks we're buddies. I may be able to get some mileage from that. Got it?"

"Yessir."

He hesitated, then decided to say, "This could be a late night, Janet. What about Charlie?"

"I'll see you at Page Street, Frank. And thanks. Thanks very much." She broke the connection.

"I hope you understand, Jamie, that everything I've been telling you is off the record. *Everything*."

"But—Jesus—" Helplessly Jamie Thomas shook his head. His eyes were blank, disbelieving. "You're saying, what you're telling me, is that you're going after C. J. for Lisa's murder."

"Jamie—" Hastings let the single word linger until Thomas raised his eyes, focusing on Hastings. "Does that surprise you? My God, you already told me that Barbara thinks he did it."

"Yeah—that's Barbara. But, Jesus, this is me. Barbara, she's—you get to know her, get a peep behind that velvet-macho lesbian façade of hers—you see she's pretty strange. But this—" Once again, dejectedly, he shook his head.

"So you don't think he could've done it?"

Thomas spoke slowly, cautiously: "C. J. is strung out on

drugs, that's no news. And I guess that, this last year, it's gotten worse—to the point that once or twice there, I was thinking C. J. could've bent the law."

"How do you mean, 'bent the law'? Robbery, like that?"

"Yeah." Deeply resigned, Thomas sighed, nodded. The network of lines that creased his face, a pattern of defeat, seemed to deepen. His washed-out eyes wandered helplessly away. "Yeah. Like that."

"Does he own a gun?"

"I don't know, Frank." The reply had the exhausted resonance of absolute truth. Jamie Thomas was too discouraged to lie.

"If you were me, where would you look for him, Jamie? Has he got a girlfriend? Parents? Who does he hang out with?"

"C. J. hangs out with anyone who'll give him a fix, as far as I can tell. People like C. J., they don't have friends."

"What's he on?"

"I never asked, Frank—never wanted to know."

"Take a guess. Cocaine? Heroin?"

"If I had to guess, I'd say crack, maybe. I never noticed any needle marks."

"Did you look?"

"No, man. It's like I said—*noticed*. There's a difference. Right?" As he spoke, a pathetic flare of pique that quickly faded, Thomas leaned forward on the sofa, took a half-full waterglass of white wine from the coffee table, gulped down most of the wine that remained. During the twenty minutes they'd been talking, Thomas had already replenished the glass twice. The pale eyes were irresolute now, losing focus.

"C. J. doesn't have a car," Hastings said.

"Naw, man. Cars aren't for people like C. J." Thomas smiled, a rueful twisting of his colorless lips. Watching the other man, Hastings wondered for the first time whether Thomas was sick, chronically ill.

Suddenly aware that talking about junkies' behavior was an

exercise in futility, Hastings abruptly rose. "I'm going to take a look in C. J.'s room." As Thomas gathered himself also to rise, Hastings raised an authoritative hand, a command. "No. You stay put." Obediently, Thomas fell back in the sofa, slack-shouldered, head bobbing forward on his chest.

Hastings went quickly into the hallway, tried the door to Kirk's room. The door swung easily inward, latched but not locked. He found the light switch, turned on the overhead light, vintage turn-of-the-century pressed glass. The room was small: a single bed, a chipped bureau, a small desk, and a single chair. The room's only window looked out on an air-shaft. Hastings closed the hallway door and went immediately to the airshaft. He opened the lower sash of the window. In the light from the room he was able to see the graveled oblong at the base of the shaft. Nothing. He closed the window, went to the desk, methodically went through the drawers. No gun, no drug paraphernalia, no correspondence. Nothing. The bureau was next. And the bed: under the bed, under the mattress. Strip off the bedclothes and shake them out. Still nothing. He went to the room's only closet. Dust and shoes and a nylon flight bag and odd bits of clothing littered the closet floor. He knelt down, felt inside every shoe, every boot. Opening the flight bag he found only two dogeared paperback science fiction novels, a jar of Vaseline, a tube of toothpaste, a blue bandanna handkerchief, and one leather glove. The top shelf of the closet was all that remained. Standing on tiptoe, he was able to sweep the shelf with a forearm, tumbling clothing to the floor—

—clothing, and money: fifties and hundred-dollar bills, thousands of dollars, rubber banded, concealed in a rolled-up sweatshirt, lying now on the floor.

The next moment, there was an instant's disconnect from his sworn duty. Three words, only three: *Who would know?*

Except for C. J. Kirk, running, who would ever know?

Running?

Running away from thousands of dollars? Did it make sense?

He stepped over the money, went again to the window, carefully scanned the airshaft: sheer sides rising to the roof, with ladder rungs attached. If a burglar wanted in, this was the way. He closed the window, checked the catch. Then he switched on the surveillance radio clipped to his belt, put the earpiece in place, spoke into the tiny surveillance microphone:

"Janet?"

"Yessir," came the prompt reply.

"Are there any lights in Barbara's place?"

"No."

"Well, ring her bell anyhow. If she's there, upstairs, tell her to stay put. We'll talk to her later."

"Right."

"Have you got seals with you? Two seals?"

"Yessir."

"All right. Bring them into C. J. Kirk's place. Don't knock. Just open the door and come in."

"Right."

"Come in," Hastings said. "Close the door."

The bed was between Janet and the money that was still on the floor. Hastings stood at the foot of the bed, mutely looking down at the money. Instinctively, Janet came to stand beside him, looked down.

"Wow," she breathed. "C. J.'s?"

"I'm assuming so."

She made no reply. Her function, she knew, was to witness a colleague laying hands on something of great value. Together, they would verify the count. In unison, both detectives slipped on the rubber gloves they always carried.

"All set?" Hastings dropped to his knees beside the money.

"All set." Standing, she moved closer. She was wearing a

windbreaker, twill slacks, and hiking boots. Her dark, thick hair was long, caught in a ponytail. Her left leg and thigh were close beside Hastings's right shoulder, so close that he could circle her legs with one arm. He could draw her close, hold her with both arms, bring her down on the floor with him, an erotic tackle.

He blinked, cleared his throat, focused his attention on the money. At the same time Janet moved subtly away. Yes, she knew what he was thinking, what he was feeling. And yes, she felt it, too.

Was she, too, remembering the last time they'd been together in a strange bedroom, sitting side by side on the suspect's bed less than five minutes after the suspect had blown his head apart while Hastings had watched helplessly?

He cleared his throat again, grasped the sweatshirt again, shook out the last of the money, dozens of bills, most of them hundreds, all of them old. As he stacked the hundreds and fifties, he asked, "Is anyone out front?"

"Yes. Welch."

"Give him a call. Tell him to keep his eyes open. Don't tell him about the money. Just tell him C. J. could be coming back."

"Right."

As Janet made the call, Hastings began counting, stacking the bills in thousand-dollar piles. The total: eleven thousand three hundred fifty dollars. When Janet finished talking and stowed her radio, Hastings ordered her to verify the count. He moved to his left on his knees, making room for her. Now, both of them were kneeling, their shoulders almost touching. As, yes, Hastings was aware that his genitals were tightening. Had it been a mistake, letting her in? Professionally, the answer was clearly no. She'd earned her way in.

But personally . . . ?

As she counted, he decided to rise, step back, watch her face, absorbed in the count. Her fingers, he realized, were short, almost stubby. But they moved deftly, decisively. Just as Janet, too, moved decisively.

When she'd finished the count, still on her knees, Janet looked up at him, expectantly.

"What'd you get?" he asked.

"Eleven thousand three hundred fifty."

He nodded. "Right." He looked at her windbreaker, with its large patch pockets, zipped closed. "You carry it." He smiled down at her. "I'll ride shotgun."

Without returning the smile she divided the money into two large stacks, one stack for each pocket. Then she rose, zipped the pockets closed, patted them in a gesture of finality, looked at him expectantly. What next? her expression read.

"Is Barbara home?"

She shook her head. "She didn't answer the doorbell. And there're no lights showing." She patted a pocket again. "What is it? Drug money?"

"Christ, how should I know?" In vexation, he shook his head. "I don't see C. J. as a pusher, though." He waved a hand around the room. "Look at this place. There's nothing here."

"Could it be a payoff, for killing Lisa?"

Squeezing the flesh below his chin, a persistent habit when he was puzzled, he looked at her thoughtfully. "I like that better than drug money."

"Maybe when he split, he just forgot this. Maybe he's carrying most of it with him."

"Or maybe he didn't really split. All we really know is that he went out the back door of a grocery store and disappeared. That could mean anything."

"Any known haunts? Friends?"

He shook his head. "Nothing."

"And no car." Suddenly she smiled, her dark eyes coming quickly, spontaneously alight. "God, whoever heard of chasing anyone if he isn't driving a car? What d'we do, put out an APB for a scrawny guy riding a city bus?"

As he answered her quick, pixy smile, he realized that, unconsciously, he'd moved a half step closer to her—

—just as a tap sounded on the bedroom door.

"Frank?"

It was Thomas, in the hallway.

"Come in."

The door swung open; Thomas stood in the doorway. His stance was uncertain, his eyes muzzy as he gazed uncertainly around the disheveled room.

"Something?" Hastings asked, making it an official question.

"Well—" Thomas ventured, "Well, I was just in my bedroom, I had to get some Kleenex. And my car keys weren't on the dresser. That's where I always leave them, on the dresser, in a bowl. So I thought I should—"

"C. J.," Hastings interrupted curtly. "Is that what you're saying—C. J.'s got your car?"

"Well, sure. Who else?"

39

Matching the speed of her car to his, she braked, slowed, finally came to a stop, double-parked, a half block behind him. Was he about to park? Yes, he'd found a place, was beginning to maneuver: clumsy, erratic lurches. She released the hand brake, sent her car moving slowly ahead. She must wait for a break in the oncoming traffic before she could drive around him, hopeful that he wouldn't see her, wouldn't recognize the car. Then, quickly, she must find a parking space.

The traffic cleared, just enough to let her pass. But there

were no parking spaces. A bus stop or a fireplug, that was the choice. She couldn't risk searching farther for a space and losing him. She pulled into the bus stop, checked the rearview mirror. Yes, he was still maneuvering, trying to park the big white American sedan. She switched off her engine, set the brake, killed the headlights. Now, for as long as it took, she must wait. She drew a long, deep, tremulous breath, momentarily closing her eyes. Another deep breath—and another. Yogis, she knew, practiced deep breathing, a discipline that soothed the emotions, therefore the mind, therefore the body.

But it wasn't working. Not here, not now, not for her. At the center of herself, deep down, she felt the trembling begin, at first only an almost imperceptible quivering. But then— now— the spasms were spreading, gathering strength, soon to engulf her, render her helpless. "Anxiety attack," her therapist would call it. "Take this pill. Breathe deeply. Try to relax."

Try not to panic, not now. Because panic could immobilize her, could therefore save him from death.

40

"I keep wondering about motive," Janet said. "What would make him do it, a wimp like that?"

"When we know where the eleven thousand came from," Hastings answered, "I think we'll have the motive. That's my feeling. And the kind of guy he is, I think he'll crack wide open. All we've got to do is keep him away from lawyers for a few hours until his last fix wears off, and we've got him."

"That's something else I wonder about," she said. "With a

drug habit, why would he leave that much money behind?"

"Someone like C. J.," Hastings said, "if you're looking for a motive, for rational behavior, you're wasting your time. Besides, we already agreed: he might not be running. He could be at a goddam double feature." He pointed through the windshield, toward 1830 Page Street. "He could show up any time, whistling."

"But he stole Thomas's car. He wouldn't do that if he was going to the movies."

He shrugged. "It's like I said: druggies, it's a waste of time trying to figure why they do things."

"Still . . ." She turned in the seat, looking back up the street. Every time she did it, shifted her body, Hastings was acutely aware of the movement, as if he was sensitized to her. At the thought, he smiled. *Sensitized,* was that the word for pure, raw sexual desire? Was he—?

"He's already denied being at Baker Beach," she was saying. "So we've got him cold with those fingerprints."

"Maybe." He yawned, checked the time. It was nine-thirty, three hours after Kirk had disappeared and more than an hour since the APB had gone out on Jamie Thomas's aging Ford Victoria. "Check the net, will you?"

She nodded, called Welch in front, Talbot in back. Both men came in loud and clear on surveillance channel B. Then, suddenly, the primary radio crackled to life: "Inspectors Eleven."

Hastings fumbled with the cruiser's dash, finally found the microphone, hung in a nonregulation position.

"Inspectors Eleven."

"Yessir. Lieutenant Hastings?" It was Communications, one of a dozen communicators working the citywide net.

"That's right. I'm Hastings."

"Well, sir, I was instructed to patch you through to Inspector Canelli, in Homicide."

"Fine. Do it." As he waited for the patch-through, he exchanged a look of expectation with the woman beside him, seated behind the cruiser's steering wheel.

"Lieutenant?" It was Canelli's voice.

"Yes. Something?"

"That Ford Victoria—Thomas's car. It just turned up."

"Ah . . ." As he spoke, Hastings was smiling into Janet's eyes, letting the anticipation show, something they could share—*would* share. She was ready with her notebook open, holding it to catch the faint light from a streetlight, ready to write.

"It's at six forty-five Valencia. That's between Seventeenth and Eighteenth. There's a two-man black-and-white at the scene. The Ford's empty and the door's unlocked."

Seventeenth Street and Valencia . . . It was only two blocks from Valencia Gardens, a block-square housing project that was ruled by drug hustlers, pimps, and some of the toughest, most dangerous youth gangs in San Francisco. On the city's crime charts, only Hunter's Point was rated more dangerous than the few blocks surrounding Valencia Gardens.

"Is there anyone who can catch for you, Canelli?"

"Marsten's here."

"All right. Put Marsten up on the board. You're only ten minutes from the scene, and I could be twenty minutes, at least. So you get to the scene and take over. Tell the black-and-white to use surveillance channel B."

"Surveillance B. Yessir."

"Tell them to keep a low profile. Park a block away, whatever. Do the rest on foot, if possible."

"Yessir."

"But be careful. Bring a couple of shotguns, one for me."

"Yessir. I'm on my way."

With Canelli's first words, Janet had brought the cruiser's engine to life as she relayed the information to Welch and

199

Talbot. Hastings reached under the dash again, found the magnetized red blinker, switched it on, stuck it to the car's roof. "Okay—" He fastened his seat belt, gestured straight ahead. "Do it. Code Two."

She nodded, gripped the wheel with her small, determined hands, swung out into traffic, engine roaring, tires squealing. Looking at her, Hastings saw her tuck her chin in, bow her neck. In hot pursuit, Hastings realized, Janet would go all out.

Ahead, at the busy Gough Street intersection, a traffic light was turning red. Without asking permission, she hit the siren once, then twice. She braked hard, twisted the wheel to the right, then to the left. The cruiser slewed, recovered, broke free. Deftly, Janet steered with the break, bringing the cruiser back into line as cars scattered in the intersection.

"Jesus. Take it easy. Canelli'll be there, you know. And don't use that siren anywhere near the scene." It was an order, not a request.

"Yes—sir." But she couldn't resist a quick, mischievous over-the-shoulder smile.

"There—" Hastings pointed to the white car, parked across the street on the same side. "See it?"

"Yes."

"Drive past, slow. Let's find Canelli."

Janet moved her head to her left. "There he is, in that Plymouth."

They were drawing abreast of Thomas's battered white Ford. Across the street, his eyes on them, Canelli nodded almost imperceptibly. Hastings returned the nod, gestured to a parking place, just ahead. "Park there. Then you stay put, on the radio. I'll see what Canelli says." When the car was parked, hands in the pockets of his suede jacket, whistling, Hastings strode slowly to the white Ford, glanced inside as he passed. Predictably, the car's interior was a shambles: littered with empty fast food containers, newspapers, discarded bits of clothing, soft drink cans—and, incongruously, a baby's seat, in the rear.

Still whistling, Hastings crossed the two northbound lanes of Valencia, waited on the center divider for the southbound traffic to clear, then angled across to Canelli's Plymouth. On cue, Canelli swung the door open. Hastings slid inside, noting with approval that the cruiser's interior courtesy light had been disconnected.

"Where's the black-and-white?"

"Around the corner," Canelli said. "When I got here, I told them to get out of sight but be ready. I mean, this neighborhood, uniforms don't make it, on stakeout." He looked across the street at Hastings's cruiser. "Who's that? Janet Collier?"

"Right. She's worked her ass off on this thing."

"Yeah—and what an ass."

Hastings was aware of a sudden proprietary flare. Was it job related?

Or sex related, simple male jealousy?

"How long've you been here?" Hastings asked.

"About ten minutes, no more. You made good time."

"Collier's a tiger behind the wheel."

"Hmmm. I bet." Then: "Jesus, I bet I've seen a half dozen drug buys, since the uniforms split. Maybe a dozen." Shaking his head, Canelli looked out on the dimly lit, nearly deserted sidewalks. Four- and five-story buildings lined both sides of the street, most of them decaying apartment buildings with commercial space at ground level, no trees, no amenities. Many of the storefronts were boarded up; the rest were protected by expanding metal grills.

Hastings switched on his surveillance radio, verified that he was transmitting on channel B. He called for a check-in, got Janet first, then Charlie Black, a corporal riding in the black-

and-white. Hastings described the suspect and summarized the case.

"We've got to figure he's armed and dangerous," Hastings concluded. "On the other hand, there's no history of violence, and no indication that, if he *is* armed, it's anything but an ordinary pistol. So let's take it one step at a time. Corporal Black, I'm going to get a couple of inspectors, to help out."

"Yessir."

Hastings made the call to Communications, then spoke to Canelli: "Have you got a cellular phone in this unit?"

Canelli shook his head. "Sorry. I wanted a unit with a phone, but the only one available was leaking brake fluid."

"Okay—stay put." Hastings got out of the Plymouth, crossed the street again, coming up behind Collier, still seated in their cruiser. Beyond the cruiser, three young black men were approaching from the opposite direction. They walked shoulder to shoulder, taking up the whole sidewalk as they passed beneath a streetlight, one of only a few streetlights in the neighborhood that hadn't been broken out. They wore black warmup jackets, black jeans, and air cushion athletic shoes, the standard uniform of black street gangs. They came from the direction of Valencia Gardens.

And they were looking for trouble.

With ten feet still separating him from the rear of the cruiser, the same distance that separated the three black youths from the front of the car, Hastings zipped the suede jacket open as he moved to his left, giving ground. One of the blacks nudged another. His companion snickered, said something inaudible. Palpably, the imminence of violence heightened. With five feet still separating him from the cruiser, Hastings stepped off the curb, into the gutter. In the same movement he slipped his right hand inside the open jacket. Close to the cruiser, one of the youths looked inside the car, saw Collier, still behind the wheel, eyes front, pretending indifference.

"Hey, what's this we got here?"

With his left hand, Hastings produced his leather shield case, shield exposed. His right hand rested on the walnut grip of the .38 Smith and Wesson holstered at his belt on the left side, for a cross-body draw. He spoke evenly, conversationally: "Okay, guys, keep moving." He raised the shield to shoulder height.

"Hey—wow—look at that." One youth nudged his companion. "It's the man himself, big shiny badge and all." He turned to Hastings, asked mock-innocently: "You got a gun, to go with the badge?"

"You've got thirty seconds, asshole. Then you're on your way to jail. Your choice."

"Hey—man—he's tough, this guy."

"Come on, Eddie—" One youth turned away, began walking down the block, hands in his pockets, head bobbing rhythmically, already looking for simpler pleasures. "Fuck him." The second youth followed the first.

"Go with your buddies, Eddie," Hastings said. "Do yourself a favor."

"How 'bout you show me your piece," Eddie said. "How 'bout that? Show me the piece, then I'll go. See, I'm kind of a gun collector, you might say."

"You're running out of time. I warned you."

"Hey, Eddie, come *on*. Stay loose."

"Aw, shit—" Angrily, Eddie turned away, broke into a run, caught up with his companions. He feinted, hit one of them with a solid left on the upper arm. His moves, Hastings realized, showed some training, some potential. Was this the next Ali—another Tyson?

He folded his shield case, buttoned it in his jacket pocket, slipped into the cruiser.

"Nice kids," Janet commented.

"I'd hate to tangle with any one of them, let alone three."

She smiled. Hastings picked up the cellular phone, got James Thomas's number, punched it out. Waiting for the connection, he checked the time: five minutes after ten.

"Hello?"

"Jamie, this is Frank."

"Ah . . ." The single word expressed both apprehension and titillation. This, Thomas knew, was business. Police business.

"We've found your car. It's on Valencia, between Seventeenth and Eighteenth. It's empty. No C. J."

"Is the car okay? No problem?"

"Did you expect a problem?"

"With C. J. driving? Are you kidding?"

"Are you familiar with Seventeenth and Valencia, Jamie?"

"Well, sure. I mean, I know where it is. Was that the question?"

"It's one of the most dangerous neighborhoods in the city. The Valencia housing project—any direction, there's a drug deal a minute."

"Ah—yeah—gottcha."

"Have you any idea where C. J. could be, around here?"

"I suppose," Thomas said, "that he's making a deal with his pusher, wouldn't you say? You know, fueling up for the trip out of town."

Looking thoughtfully at Janet's face in profile as she scanned the dark, dangerous street, Hastings considered, finally decided to say: "We found eleven thousand dollars in C. J.'s room. That's why the room's sealed. Do you have any idea where C. J. would get money like that?"

"No. None."

"But you don't sound surprised, that he'd have that much money."

"Who's to say? Druggies, you never know what to expect. You know that."

"Do you think he'd leave eleven thousand dollars behind, if he'd decided to run?"

"Well," Thomas said thoughtfully, "that'd depend, I guess, on why he was leaving town."

Privately, Hastings smiled. Thomas was smooth. "Okay, Jamie. We'll be in touch. If you hear from C. J., call Inspector Canelli, at the Inspectors' Bureau. I left you a card."

"Right. I put it next to the phone."

Hastings thanked him and was about to break the connection when Thomas asked, "Do you really think he killed Lisa, Frank?"

"Yes, Jamie. I really think he killed her."

"Crap." The line went dead.

"I know a couple of crack houses around here," Janet said. "One's right around the corner."

Hastings considered. "Okay, let's drive by, look them over."

"Right." She brought the engine to life while Hastings updated the surveillance net.

41

"There—" Janet pointed across Seventeenth Street. "That stucco building."

Following her gesture, Hastings saw a plain-fronted three-story building that had probably been built in the fifties. Cheaply constructed of plywood and covered by wire mesh that had been stuccoed over, the building might originally have been intended for subsidized low-rent housing, a step up from the nearby projects. Now, though, the windows told the story. Some of the windows were broken, others were covered haphazardly by anything that would keep the tenants safe from hostile eyes: splintered venetian blinds, bedsheets, even newspaper taped to the glass. As Janet pulled into a fortuitous parking place and killed the cruiser's headlights and engine, Hastings saw two hesitant white males entering the building, which Hastings judged to contain six apartments, two to each floor, front and back. On the sidewalk outside the building a handful of black teenagers were standing idly, eyeing the action. It was odds-on, Hastings knew, that the teenagers' air of idleness was a fake. They were probably lookouts, working for a hundred-dollar bill. If a rival gang should drive by, Uzis blazing, the lookouts would be the first to go down.

"It sure looks like a crack house," Hastings said. "How old's your information?"

"About two months. Narco borrowed me for a couple of nights. I was supposed to get inside and plant three or four bugs. We were made, though, before it came my turn. It was a real fiasco."

"Any idea how many crack houses there are around here?"

"Three, four within a two-block radius. At least."

"Let's get out of here," he said. "For sure, we've already been made. Let's get back to his car. Sooner or later, he'll go back to it. We stake it out, we'll find him."

"You're sure you don't want me to go inside, take a look?" She gestured to the crack house. "It's not like we're trying to make a buy, nothing heavy."

"Jesus, Janet—" Wonderingly, he looked her over. "You're tougher than you look, aren't you?" Then, after a moment's good-humored thought, he decided to risk saying it: "You've got brass balls."

It had been a mistake. Her instant reaction was a flare of anger. "I hate that, Frank. I really hate that."

"Aw—sorry. I—" The surveillance radio at Hastings's belt beeped. "Wait—" He raised an apologetic hand to Janet as he put in the earpiece, switched on the radio, finally found the tiny microphone at the end of its long micro cord.

"Lieutenant?" It was Canelli.

"Yes. What?" As he spoke, he nodded to Janet: she should switch on her radio, channel B.

"Well," Canelli said, "one of the sector cars just came by. I checked in with the Mission station when I first got here, so they've been driving by, a wink and a nod, you know. I gave them the Ford but told them to stay clear, don't make waves. But now, this round, the sector guy stopped and said there was a white Caucasian male just shot on Eighteenth, around the corner and down from Valencia. That'd be toward Mission. There's a crack house there. I don't know the address, but there'll be units on the scene. You want me to check it out? Benson and Fiori are here now, all filled in on Kirk. So I could—"

"No, you stay put." Hastings nodded to Collier, gestured for her to get under way. "We'll check it out, then get back to you. This could be a long night."

"There . . ." Hastings pointed ahead. Strobes blinking, an ambulance and two sector cars blocked the eastbound traffic on Eighteenth.

Collier nodded. "Right."

"You may as well double-park. Everybody else is." As he spoke, Hastings took out his ID plaque, clipped it to his jacket. As the cruiser came to a stop, he swung the door open. During the three-minute drive to the scene, following Janet's flare of temper, they hadn't spoken. When he had the chance to do it properly, he would apologize.

Now, though, he was on the sidewalk, striding through a

sullen circle of bystanders, almost all of them black, almost all of them young, almost all of them men. In this demographic grouping, the leading cause of death was homicide. Black-on-black homicide.

The body lay in a dark, narrow service way between two houses, one of them a derelict apartment building, one a run-down private house, its doors and windows heavily barred.

"Here . . ." Walking beside him, Collier nudged his arm with the flashlight she'd remembered to bring from the car.

"Thanks." He turned to the attending medics, a black woman and a white man: "Is he dead?"

"Yessir," the woman answered. "Shot in the back, looks like two shots."

Ordering two uniformed officers and the medics to stand clear, Hastings gestured for Collier to follow him as he entered the service way. With no air circulating here, the smell of garbage and stale urine was overpowering. And now there was the odor of blood, together with the smell of feces released by the dead body. The only sound was the furtive, furry scurrying of rats, caught in the flashlight's beam. Then the circle of light steadied on the man lying facedown on the concrete, just inside the alleyway. Even before he advanced the last two steps to kneel down beside the body, Hastings knew that it was C. J. Kirk.

He rose and nodded to Collier, who nodded in return. Hastings stepped back, turned, gestured for the two uniformed men to join him.

"What've you got? Any witnesses?" Hastings spoke to a black corporal whose face was vaguely familiar. "I'm Frank Hastings."

The corporal nodded. "Yessir, I know. I'm Jack Higgins. That's Andy Strauss." He gestured to his partner, a slightly built white man who hardly looked more than twenty-one. How long, Hastings wondered, had it been since Strauss had graduated from the Academy? The young officer was standing beside a black boy who was certainly no more than twelve, perhaps even younger. The stance of the policeman suggested that, really, the youth was being detained. Hastings acknowledged the introductions, then waited expectantly. Beside him, Janet took out her notebook, asked for the flashlight.

"This kid," Higgins said, "he's all we got. Odds on, he saw the whole thing. We got here—" Higgins consulted his watch "—it was exactly fifteen minutes ago. We were just around the corner on a domestic dispute when we got the call. So it wasn't more than two minutes before we got here. And this kid—his man is Dennis Best—he was still standing with his mouth open and his eyes popping. Andy, he was smart enough to scoop the kid up before the locals got to him, shut him up. In fact, I'm thinking why doesn't Andy put the kid in the car, sit in the back with him?"

Hastings nodded. "Good idea." He watched Higgins give the order, watched Strauss and the boy walk to the sector car, watched Higgins as he returned to stand in the mouth of the alleyway. Higgins was a big, heavily built man who moved smoothly, lightly, with an athlete's deft economy. Idly, Hastings wondered whether the big man had ever played football. At his weight, at least two-fifty, he might have been a coach's dream come true.

"So what'd the kid say?" Hastings asked.

Higgins pointed to the three-story apartment building that adjoined the alleyway. "That's mostly a crack house. Dennis says the victim came out of there maybe a half hour ago. He said the guy stood in front of the place on the sidewalk for a little while. Except that kids, you know, don't have much sense of time. But, anyhow, according to Dennis, the guy finally started walking—but only until he was about here—" He gestured to the sidewalk at the mouth of the alleyway. "So then—" Higgins pointed up the block toward Valencia "—

Dennis says that a car starts up. No lights, the kid says. It
starts up and comes even with the victim."

"Where was Dennis?"

"He was across the street. Almost directly across."

"So he'd've had a look at the driver."

Higgins nodded. "True. But there's not much light on this
block."

"So *did* Dennis eyeball the driver?"

"Well," Higgins said, "that's not clear, Lieutenant. I mean,
we didn't want to put words in the kid's mouth. Basically, once
the medics said it was a homicide, we figured we'd just secure
the area—sit tight and wait for you guys."

Approvingly, Hastings nodded. He stood silently for a moment, thoughtfully eyeing what had once been C. J. Kirk.

C. J. Kirk—certainly a druggie, probably a murderer.

C. J. Kirk—probably carrying drugs enough to have sent
him to prison. And probably money, too—unexplained money.

Finally Hastings looked up, saying to Higgins, "Call your
watch commander, my authority. I want two cars here, to
protect the scene. Two cars, four officers. You and Strauss,
plus two others. Get the goddam crowd dispersed. Then start
looking for cartridge casings and asking questions. Sure as
hell, somebody besides Dennis knows something. If you have
to squeeze them, do it. But not too hard. We might be talking
about something a lot bigger than just this homicide. I don't
want the DA throwing witnesses back at us. Understood?"

"Yessir."

"And if you find any shell casings, don't put your prints on
them. That's important."

"Yessir. What about Dennis?"

"We'll take charge of him." Hastings turned to Janet. "You
take Dennis to our car. Sweet-talk him. Whatever it takes."

Janet nodded. "Yessir."

"All right, let's do it." As he watched the man and woman

turn away, Hastings switched on the surveillance radio. Would it carry to Canelli, several blocks away?

Yes—Canelli answered on the first call.

"It's Kirk," Hastings said. "Dead. Shot outside a crack house."

"You know," Canelli answered, "I had a feeling. I really did."

"You've got two of our guys and two uniforms staking out the Ford. Right?"

"Right."

"Okay—dismiss the two uniforms. Leave Fiori there. Bring Benson over here, it's just around the corner. You and Benson come in your unit."

"Yessir."

"I want you for the officer of record on Kirk. So you make the phone calls, set it up."

"Ahhh . . ." In the response, Hastings could clearly hear Canelli's pleasure at receiving the order. According to regulations, only sergeants or above were authorized to sign off homicides.

"So what d'you think?" Canelli asked.

"Canelli—" Hastings let the mild exasperation come through. "Jesus, you're only around the corner. Do we have to talk about it on the radio?"

Standing beside his cruiser, Hastings tapped on the windshield. Inside the car, in the front seat with Dennis Best beside her, frowning at the interruption, Collier looked up quickly. She had the car's stowable computer in her hand, obviously explaining how the computer worked. In pantomime, Hastings queried her: was she making progress? Could he help? How much longer? In reply, she lifted her chin, almost imperceptibly shaking her head, then shrugging. It was a request for more time. Hastings nodded, turned, walked to Canelli's car. Leaning against the cruiser, Hastings glanced at his watch: eleven-thirty. Ten minutes ago, with both the coroner's van and the police lab's van on the scene, he'd ordered the block barricaded. Now the block was almost eerily deserted. A pair of portable floodlights shone down on the body of C. J. Kirk, lying facedown in a pool of blood that was beginning to congeal at the edges. Soon the ME and the technicians would finish their work. Only then would Hastings and Canelli be free to move the body, conduct a body search.

As if the thought had activated the action, the ME was signing the release form, handing the clipboard to Canelli for countersignature. After Canelli had signed, the ME took the clipboard, nodded cheerfully to Hastings, and walked to his car. Canelli spoke briefly to the waiting forensics technician, then turned to Hastings as the tech withdrew. Nodding as he drew on his rubber gloves, Hastings advanced to the body with Canelli at his side. Bottom to top, Kirk was wearing scuffed running shoes, jeans, and a loose-fitting, thigh-length jacket, brown in color, and now marred by two bullet holes and a spreading stain. His hair, in death as in life, was long and tangled and dirty, somehow the symbol of a short, wasted life.

Hastings moved to the left of the body, gesturing for Canelli to stand to the right.

"I wonder," Canelli said, "whether somebody robbed him?"

"I don't think so. Higgins—that black corporal—he was just around the corner when he got the call." Gritting his teeth, holding his breath against the stench, Hastings knelt, lifted the victim's oversized jacket. Yes, it was still there: Kirk's wallet, in the left hip pocket of the dead man's jeans. Gingerly Hastings freed the wallet. Standing with Canelli beside him, both men with their backs turned toward the sidewalk, Hastings opened the bulging wallet.

"Hey," Canelli breathed. "What've we got here?"

"What we've got here," Hastings said, "is a wad of fifties

and hundreds, the same as in his bedroom. Here—" He handed the money to Canelli. "Count it. Keep your back turned."

As Canelli counted, Hastings examined the remaining contents of the dead man's wallet. There was nothing but miscellaneous scraps of paper. No ID, no driver's license, no credit cards. Nothing.

"I make it three thousand three hundred fifty dollars," Canelli said. "Here—" Surrepetitiously he handed the money to Hastings, for verification. At the same time, Canelli produced a clear plastic evidence bag, holding it open. Once sealed and signed, this bag would be added to the others, most containing sweepings from the crime scene. Sweepings, but no shell casings.

"Right." Hastings dropped the money in the bag, which Canelli immediately sealed. With a smaller bag open, Canelli was waiting for Hastings to examine the contents of the wallet. A business card for a "We Deliver" pizza parlor with "Rickey" and a phone number written on the back went into the bag, followed by another card for a bail bondsman, followed by three more business cards for restaurants—followed by a folded-over picture of an Irish setter that had been clipped from a magazine. Seeing the picture, Canelli chuckled ruefully. "Jeez, you never know, do you?"

Hastings pointed to the open evidence bag. "Get that card with 'Rickey' on it. I want the phone number."

"Right." Canelli produced the card, waited for Hastings to copy down the number, returned the card to the bag. Before consigning the empty wallet to the maw of the plastic bag, remembering that some wallets had hidden compartments for a key or folded-up emergency money, Hastings meticulously turned the wallet inside out—and found a small bit of folded-over paper containing another phone number. He copied down the number, dropped the empty wallet and the slip of paper into the bag, rose to his feet, looked across the body at Canelli.

"Ready?"

Canelli carefully put the two bags aside, one sealed, one unsealed. "Which way?"

"Toward me." Bracing himself, Hastings leaned across the body, gripped Kirk's jacket with both hands. Canelli swallowed, nodded reluctantly. He was ready.

"*Now.*" Hastings heaved, then quickly stepped back as the body seemed momentarily to balance on its left side before it flopped over, one arm flailing, one leg crossing over the other leg at the ankles. Kirk, now a gelatinous, inert sack of flesh and fluid, lay on his back, staring up into the night sky. His full-cut jacket was buttoned to the chin. It was a brown canvas hunter's jacket that might have been bought at a surplus store. The jacket featured several outsize pockets, inside and out. A large circular bloodstain was centered on Kirk's chest. It would be impossible to unbutton the jacket without touching the blood.

"Should I—" Canelli swallowed, gestured diffidently to the blood-soaked jacket.

Hastings's smile was grimly ironic. "Rank hath its privileges, Canelli."

Canelli's answering smile was rueful. "Yeah. Times like this, I think I should take a shot at that sergeant's exam." On his knees, he squared himself with the body, set himself, swallowed again, began unbuttoning the jacket. When the job was finished, still on his knees, he leaned backward from the body, holding his blood-smeared, rubber-gloved hands clear of himself.

"Okay—my turn." With thumb and forefinger, gingerly taking care to avoid contact with the blood, Hastings folded the jacket back to expose the bloody torso.

"Hey—" Canelli whistled softly. "Jesus, look at that."

Both of the jacket's inside pockets were stuffed with bills—fifties and hundreds, with only the ends showing above the pockets. The money was smeared with blood.

42

"You don't think that's a dirty trick?" Reproachfully, Collier shook her head. "Leaving Canelli and Benson to count thousands of dollars in bloody money?"

"I'll tell you what I told Canelli: 'Rank hath its privileges.' "

"Hmmm."

They were standing in the middle of Eighteenth Street, both of them alternately looking at Hastings's cruiser, where Jack Higgins was taking his turn with Dennis Best. At twenty minutes after midnight, the twelve-year-old was plainly enjoying center stage, experimenting with the angles, looking for an edge.

"So what d'you think?" Hastings asked, gesturing to the boy. "How much does he know?"

"He saw the shooting," Collier answered, "no question. But that's about it. He lives on Shotwell. He was hanging out on Valencia with some friends, probably looking for loose hubcaps, something like that. He was on his way home, and he'd stopped by that dumpster, there—" She pointed. "He was looking over here—" She gestured to the crack house. "And, yes, I think he was watching when Kirk came down the stairs to the sidewalk. And he saw the car—" Her hand swung toward the intersection of Eighteenth and Valencia. "It was parked with the lights out, one person behind the wheel. As soon as Kirk appeared, the car's engine started, Dennis says. It was going down toward Mission, as Kirk began walking up toward Valencia. They met here—" she gestured to the alleyway "—directly across from where Dennis was standing. He says the driver stopped the car and leaned across the seat to say something to Kirk, who stopped walking and turned to the car. Then, almost immediately, as if he were spooked, the victim turned away from the car. There were two shots—one, two, like that. So then the driver sat up behind the wheel again and drove off. He went to Mission, driving slowly, Dennis says, no rush, and turned right and disappeared."

"What about the driver? Anything? You said 'he.' "

She shook her head. "Nothing. Dennis just saw a shadow—a profile, inside the car. I took him over that two or three times, and there's absolutely no possibility of an identification that'd hold up."

"Black? White? Man? Woman?"

"Nothing," she insisted. "Absolutely nothing."

"Great." Hands thrust deep in his pockets, irritably, Hastings kicked at a food wrapper lying on the pavement.

"For twenty bucks, of course, this kid'd sing any tune we want, as long as it doesn't get him in trouble on the street. But you said you wanted me to find out what really happened." As she spoke, she looked expectantly back over Hastings's shoulder. It was Canelli, tentatively approaching. His hands, Hastings saw, were bare, ungloved. When Hastings acknowledged him with a nod, Canelli spoke wonderingly: "Jeez, Lieutenant, that guy had two pockets in that goddam field jacket stuffed with money. Not to mention the drugs he was packing."

"How much money?"

"Counting what we found in his wallet, it comes to twenty-seven thousand four hundred dollars and change."

For a long moment the three detectives stood thoughtfully together, each looking off in a different direction. Finally Hastings spoke to Canelli. "Anything else on him?"

Canelli shook his head. "Two sets of keys, and some loose change—and a switchblade knife. I'm sending that to the lab. The rest of it, I'll take to Property. Personally."

"Have someone with you," Hastings said, "as witness. And get two signatures from Property before you turn over the money. If there aren't two people on duty, they've got to get someone out of bed. Clear?"

"Yessir, that's clear."

"Okay—do it." As he spoke, dismissing Canelli, Hastings opened his notebook to the last page and gave it to Janet Collier. "Those're phone numbers Kirk had in his wallet. Check them out."

"Yessir." She took the notebook, looked at it, and was about to turn toward the cruiser and its radio when she stopped, turned back to Hastings. "That second number—not 'Rickey,' but the other one—I think I remember that. I think it's connected to the Franklin case."

Hastings was aware of a visceral lift, a rising tremor of excitement. The two murders—the money—the phone number concealed so carefully in the wallet. Were they connected?

"Well, then—" Hastings nodded to the cruiser. "—you'd better get to work."

As if she suspected that the remark was made condescendingly, she let her gaze linger with his for a moment, her eyes almost imperceptibly narrowed. Then, following orders, she walked to the cruiser.

"Jeez," Canelli breathed as he watched her stride toward the car, "look at that ass, will you?" It was an awed tribute, softly spoken, wistfully reflective.

Hastings pointed toward the body. "Any surprises, besides the money?"

"Not so far, Lieutenant. It looks like he was leaving the crack house and had just gotten to the alley when the car came abreast of him, on the same side of the street. The way I figure, the driver said something to him. He turns his back, maybe to run, and he gets shot. He took two right in the center of the back, which is pretty good shooting, when you think about it."

"I'll bet there were twenty people walking around on this

block when the shots were fired. But nobody's talking. We don't even have a guess on the make of the car—domestic, Japanese. Nothing. We don't know anything about the driver, either. Sex—color—nothing there, either. What was he doing here? How'd he know Kirk was going to be here? *Did* he know? What was the goddam motive?" Frustrated, Hastings angrily shook his head. "It sure as hell wasn't robbery. So what's left, for Christ's sake?"

"If we knew what he was doing with all that money," Canelli said, "we'd be a lot farther along. If he was dealing drugs then—"

Vehemently Hastings shook his head. "Kirk wasn't a dealer. He didn't have the balls. He was a user. Period."

"Yeah, well—" Discouraged, Canelli shook his head. Then, as Janet Collier came toward them, he brightened. Reading the look, Hastings turned to face Collier. In her face he could clearly see excitement, eye-sparkling anticipation.

"The Rickey number," she said, "that was a pay phone down on the Embarcadero. But the other number—" She broke off, then took a half step closer, dropped her voice. She was about to share something of great importance, an offering: "The other one, it's like I thought—it's the private unlisted number for Clayton Wallis, at his office. His goddam hotline."

"Jesus . . ." Hastings spoke softly. "Are you sure?"

"I'm sure."

Hastings looked at his watch: almost one o'clock. At the Hall, in Homicide, there was probably only one man: Donahue, catching. At this hour, Friedman would certainly be asleep. Canelli, the officer of record at the murder scene, therefore the primary link in the chain of evidence in a capital case, would be tied down for another hour, at least.

He turned first to Canelli. "This could change a lot of things. So make goddam sure everything goes right here. Make sure nobody cuts any corners. Leave two men on the scene, and tell them to keep the tapes up until I get back here, even if it's all night. Got it?"

Canelli nodded gravely. "Yessir. Where'll you be?"

"I'll be trying to run Clayton Wallis down."

"Me, too?" Collier asked.

Unable to resist the temptation, Hastings looked at her solemnly for a moment, as if he were trying to make up his mind. Then, gravely, he nodded. "You, too."

43

"I'm sorry, Lieutenant—" Clayton Wallis shook his head. "I simply don't understand. This C. J. Kirk, you say that when he was murdered he had my phone number in his wallet. And on the strength of that—" Bemused, Wallis raised both hands in a graceful gesture of amiable puzzlement that seemed meant to encompass the three of them sitting together in Wallis's small, book-lined, leather-and-antiques study just off the entry hall of the Wallis penthouse. Dressed in a maroon silk robe, Wallis had met the elevator himself. Then, as now, he projected a kind of genial, long-suffering puzzlement.

"On the strength of that," Wallis continued, "a slip of paper, you get me up at one o'clock in the morning to ask me where I've been all evening." As if he were trying to solve some obscure problem, Wallis frowned, his expression incredulous. Speaking to Hastings, he said, "Is that right? Or am I missing something?"

"In my line of work," Hastings said, "we look for connections. We've got you connected to Lisa, and we've always had

Lisa and C. J. connected to each other. And now we've got Kirk connected to you. We've also got a lot of money—tens of thousands in old bills, found on Kirk's body. Right now, that money is the big mystery. I figure, though, that eventually we'll be able to explain the money. And when we do, I figure we'll have a motive."

"And so here you are, at one o'clock, trying to determine where I was tonight." Wallis spoke casually, condescendingly, as if he were almost enjoying their little game.

"Where *were* you, Mr. Wallis?" Collier asked. With the two men seated in deep leather armchairs, she'd chosen to stand, symbolically leaning against the door, as if to block their victim's flight.

"It so happens," Wallis said, "that my wife and I went to a movie tonight. We went to the Vogue, and we saw the director's cut of *Blade Runner,* which happens to be one of my favorite films." As if he were toying with her, he let a moment pass before he said, "It also happened that when we were leaving the theater we met Phil and Lillian Toll, in the lobby. We had drinks together, at Harry's, on Fillmore. We didn't get home until about eleven-thirty. So—" He smiled at the woman, amiably spread his hands. "So I'm afraid you'll have to look elsewhere, for your murderer."

Collier returned the smile, saying mock-sweetly, "Personally, Mr. Wallis, I never thought you killed C. J. Kirk. I mean—" She shook her head. "I mean, you down on Valencia Street—no. Never. It just doesn't fit."

"Well—" Wallis matched her mocking smile. "Well, that's a relief."

"The money, though—" Watching his face, she let the words linger. Then: "If we can tie you to the money we found on Kirk tonight, then that's something else. Wouldn't you agree?"

Almost imperceptibly, Wallis's smile slipped, then immediately steadied. He made no response.

"What I'm thinking," she explained, "is that you and money go together. So I figure C. J. got that money from you."

"Well, Detective Collier, I'm afraid—"

"That's *Inspector,*" she interrupted. "In San Francisco, detectives are called inspectors. No one knows why." She smiled at him.

Wallis returned the smile, playing the man-woman game now. "I'm afraid your logic is flawed, Inspector. You—"

"Earlier today," Collier interrupted, "when I came to your office with that eight-by-ten glossy, for identification, what I really wanted was a specimen of your fingerprints." Once more, mock-sweetly, she smiled. She said softly, "You probably didn't realize that at the time." She waited for a response that didn't come, then continued: "You see, we had some good, clear prints of whoever murdered Lisa Franklin." She paused: a delicately timed interval, perhaps a moment too long, in Hastings's opinion. Then she said, "Your fingerprints, in fact, were remarkably clear, on that photo."

"But they didn't match the murderer's prints." As if he was enjoying their little game, Wallis kept his small, smug smile in place.

Amiably, she nodded. "Correct. But the point is—the reason I'm telling you all this—is that, tomorrow morning, bright and early, the fingerprint lab downtown is going to start working on all that money we found on C. J. And I have a feeling, Mr. Wallis, that we're going to be able to establish, without question, that you handled the money—while you were counting it out to give it to C. J."

Instantly the smile disappeared. Wallis's clear blue eyes glinted with a cold, furious fire. "You're bluffing. Money—paper—doesn't take fingerprints. Photos—glossy surfaces—that's one thing. But—"

"I'm afraid," Hastings said, "that your information is out of date, Mr. Wallis. It's hard getting prints off money, particularly if the paper is old. But it can be done. Definitely, it can be done."

Suddenly Wallis rose and walked to a small carved walnut desk. In the cloisterlike antiquity of the library, the only incongruous note was a console phone on an end table beside the desk. For a long moment Wallis stood leaning over the desk, both hands flat on the richly tooled leather desktop. He was staring at the telephone. Hastings caught Collier's eye and nodded approval. She'd done a good job.

The moment held between them, an affirmation, something of significance, shared. Then, in unison, they turned to look at Wallis, still standing bent over the desk.

When he began to speak, still at the desk, turned away, Wallis's voice was so soft that it was almost inaudible.

"It's strange, how events play out. It's now one-thirty in the morning of Tuesday, October twentieth. Twelve hours ago, I was the undisputed lord of everything I surveyed. And then, surprise, I was served with a subpoena by the United States attorney. And now, in the dead of night, here you are—" As he spoke, he turned to face them squarely, leaning back against the edge of the desk in his maroon silk robe, hands gripping the edge of the desk behind him. In the short time since he'd turned away from them, Wallis's whole persona had changed. His shoulders were slumped, no longer squared; his whole body had gone slack. When he'd turned away, he'd been a winner, one man among millions. Now, facing them, Clayton Wallis was trapped in the body of a loser. His face, too, had gone slack. His features gone soft, no more than a pulp remained of his once dynamic aura of command.

"Here you are," Wallis repeated, "come to accuse me of murder. Perhaps you've even come to arrest me. That's what the Feds'll do, probably tomorrow. They'll take me downtown and lock me up. And then my lawyers will get me released. But not before the reporters find out that Clayton Wallis was arrested."

"The SEC," Hastings said.

Wallis smiled; it was a wan, exhausted smile. "You knew, then. You knew about the SEC."

Hastings made no reply. He had instinctively risen from his chair, as if to remain seated would be bad manners. Janet, too, had come away from the door and was facing Clayton Wallis.

"Well," Wallis said, "I didn't kill C. J. Kirk." As he spoke, Wallis nodded politely to Janet, who gravely returned the nod. "As you surmised, Inspector, Valencia Street isn't for me. However—" The final pause, followed by the final plunge: "However, as you also surmised, I did handle the money Kirk was carrying."

"It was a payoff," Hastings said. "You hired him to kill Lisa. That's where he got the money."

In silence, reflectively, Wallis gazed at him. Then, with an effort, he pushed himself away from the desk and returned to his armchair. The two detectives remained standing, looking down at the suspect. Hastings saw Janet Collier's hand move to the flap of her saddle-leather shoulder bag, which was unfastened. Wallis began speaking in a low, precise monotone, as if he were about to explain a complex sequence of very important details.

"As I'm sure you know, for me, Lisa was an addiction. There's no other word for it. The more I got of her, the more I wanted. I knew she saw other men, I knew she was sexually involved with them. But I didn't care. I knew she'd never change, so I didn't try. Instead, all day long—all night long—I tried to think of ways to please her, titillate her. And I began to realize that the only way I could hold her interest was to tell her about myself—specifically, about my business deals, the coups I pulled off, the money I made, my strategies. I think it had something to do with Lisa's childhood, her relationship with her father, who's a player on Wall Street. Call it the Electra complex: she wanted her father, sexually, but he rejected her. So she looked for her father everywhere else, es-

223

pecially in bed with older men. But, at another level, a deeper level, she hated men. A love-hate relationship, in other words. Accounting, I suppose, for her relationship with Barbara Estes." In an expression of numbed regret, Wallis slowly shook his head.

Then, as if to shift ground, he began speaking more concisely. "About three months ago, I heard through sources that the SEC was looking into my affairs, with a possible view to prosecuting me for insider trading. I wasn't particularly concerned about the problem—then. I knew I was vulnerable, but I was confident they couldn't find the skeletons they were looking for.

"I told Lisa about the SEC—" He spoke as if he were making a confession, nothing held back, all hope forsaken. "I knew it was exactly the kind of thing that would fascinate her—and I was right. Living on the edge, that's what Lisa was all about. Legal or illegal, she'd try anything once—sometimes more than once. So, incrementally, I told her what I'd done, and what the SEC could do to me, if they found out. In a sense, I was showing off for her. I—Christ—I even embellished it, because I knew it would turn her on."

"Did you tell her where the skeletons were?" Hastings asked.

Head bowed, Wallis nodded. "It developed very slowly, a morsel at a time, to keep her interested, keep her coming back for more. But that was the net effect."

"And then," Collier said, "she began blackmailing you."

Slowly, Wallis raised his head to look at her in mute wonderment. "How'd you know?"

"I read her journals. Three times."

His mouth twisted into a rueful, bitter smile. "Her journals—yeah, I should've known."

"So she *did* blackmail you," Hastings said.

Once more, numbly, Wallis nodded.

"That was—when—two or three months ago?"

"Yes."

"And that was the end of your love affair, when she started blackmailing you."

As if to confess some shameful weakness, Wallis shook his head. "Wrong, Lieutenant. The worse the blackmail demands got, the more I wanted her. And the more she wanted me, sexually. We'd—it was as if we'd gone from lovers to sexual antagonists, and in the process everything was supercharged. We couldn't keep our hands off each other. Except that there was no more softness. Excitement, yes. God, yes. Incredible excitement. Sometimes she came at me with her fists. I'd have to—to subdue her, before we could make love. Once, the next day, she had bruises. Actual bruises. But, a few days later, we were at it again. 'Rough love,' that's the street name for it."

"She'd finally found the ultimate turn-on," Collier said. She watched Wallis for a reaction. When none came, she said, "Or maybe death was what it was all about, for her."

"How about it, Mr. Wallis?" Hastings asked softly. "Did she want to die? Did she ask for it?"

Looking up, Wallis searched Hastings's face before, almost stammering, he said, "I—I don't understand. Do you think I killed her? Is that what you think?"

"You had the opportunity. And now it turns out you had a motive. Plus, you fought. Physically."

Wallis made no response. Instead, watchfully now, plainly making a gambler's decision, bet the stack and turn the card, he looked from Hastings to Collier, then back to Hastings. For the moment, Wallis would remain silent.

"Did you actually pay Lisa blackmail money?" Janet asked.

"I paid her about twenty-five thousand dollars."

"Considering the stakes, that's not much money."

"It was only a token payment—a down payment. I suppose, subconsciously, I wanted to keep contact with her, spread the

225

payments out. And, in fact—" Wallis smiled wanly. "In fact, that night, when I gave her the twenty-five thousand, we made love."

"Rough love?" Hastings asked.

"No," Wallis replied. "That night wasn't rough. Exciting. Very exciting. But not rough."

"When did you make that first payment?"

"About two months ago."

"I don't remember seeing a twenty-five-thousand-dollar deposit in her account two months ago."

Wallis shrugged, said nothing. Then, incongruously, he yawned.

"So you deny killing Lisa," Collier said.

The suspect nodded.

"Answer the question, Mr. Wallis," Hastings ordered. "Don't just nod."

"No, I didn't kill Lisa." It was a wooden response, almost inaudible. In his brass-studded leather armchair, Wallis sat with his body slack, his head bowed. Hastings decided to return to the companion chair; Collier returned to her previous position, leaning against the door.

"And you have no idea who might've killed her."

Wallis raised his head to meet Hastings's gaze. Asking quizzically: "Do you want me to guess? Is that what you want?"

Watching him, speculating, balancing the training manuals against real life, Hastings nodded. "Yes."

Wallis smiled. It was a gambler's smile, bet another stack, the last one. Turn another card.

The last card?

Finally, quietly defiant, speaking smugly, superciliously, Wallis said, "Actually, Lieutenant, I don't have to guess. I know who killed her. I know who killed Lisa, and I think I know who killed Kirk, tonight."

In the silence that followed, Hastings struggled to repress the excitement that he knew must show in his face—the excitement, and, yes, the uncertainty, the inability to anticipate, therefore to control the interrogation. The homicide inspector's workplace was the city's sidewalks and alleyways. On Eighteenth and Valencia, he was working familiar territory.

But here, in the library of a Nob Hill penthouse, interrogating an industrialist who could manipulate fortunes the way a spoiled child played with his toys, he was in alien territory. Meaning that, for now, he must ask, not demand: "Tell us what you think, Mr. Wallis."

"Somehow," Wallis was saying, "both C. J. Kirk and Barbara Estes found out that Lisa was blackmailing me. I don't know when they found out. I don't know how, or why. Maybe Lisa wanted insurance, if I should try to kill her. Or maybe Lisa thought C. J. would be useful to her. As I say, I simply don't know. Only Barbara would know now. But, in any case, after Lisa was killed, both Kirk and Barbara came to me, separately, and demanded money." As if to calculate the effect of his words, Wallis broke off, glanced sidelong at each of them in turn. Sensing that Collier was about to speak, Hastings caught her eye, surreptitiously shook his head. Whether he was lying or telling the truth, Wallis was playing their game now, coming to them. Silence, Hastings had learned, could be the interrogator's best tool. Silence, and patience.

Silence and a bland, utterly blank expression.

"First it was Kirk," Wallis was saying. "He called me the day after Lisa was killed. I'd just heard she'd been killed, no more than fifteen minutes before he called. And—Jesus—he called on my private line, at the office. I knew, of course, where he'd gotten the number. Lisa. It had to have been Lisa. Or, conceivably, Barbara, although I didn't know that at the time."

"Did you know about Barbara?" Hastings asked. "Did you know she and Lisa—" He broke off. Did Wallis know that Lisa and Barbara were lovers? If Wallis didn't know, was it smart to tell him?

As if to respond to the unasked question, Wallis sadly shook his head. Or was it exhaustion, not sorrow, that burdened his response so heavily?

"No, Lieutenant, I didn't know then that they were—" He broke off, once more shook his head. He couldn't say it, couldn't pronounce the words.

"Okay—" Hastings lifted a hand. "Sorry. Go ahead. What'd Kirk say, when he called?"

"He said he wanted a meeting. Immediately. That same day."

"That was Thursday. The day after she died."

Wallis nodded. "We met at the Embarcadero underground station, that afternoon. And he told me an incredible story. He—" As if the memory of the meeting still confounded him, Wallis broke off, took a moment to collect himself. "He said—admitted—that he'd killed Lisa. He said it perfectly matter-of-factly, utterly calm, as if he were telling me that he'd had to have a pet put away. It was incredible. Really incredible. He—"

"But *why?*" Collier burst out, unable to contain herself. Repeating incredulously: "*Why?*"

"He said he did it for money." A momentary pause. "My money."

Now it was Hastings's turn to blurt out a question: "Your money?"

"He said, in effect, that he knew Lisa was blackmailing me, so he took her off my back. And, of course—" Wallis's mouth twisted in a bitter smile. "—of course, he demanded money. For services rendered."

"And did you give him money?"

As if it was a negligible point, Wallis nodded. "I gave him forty thousand dollars, the next day. Of course, I knew it'd all go for drugs. And I knew that, in itself, it was a risk. The drugs, I mean. I knew he could get high and tell someone about the SEC's case. But I doubted that he had the same kind of critical information that Lisa had. I was sure of it, in fact."

"Let's get back to Kirk," Hastings said. "Assuming it's true that he told you he decided to do you a favor, up front, without any money exchanging hands, then my question is, how the hell could you ever go along with it? You say that you paid him forty thousand, a kind of tip, for services rendered. But, my God, you're a successful businessman. Surely you must've known that you'd be incriminating yourself, giving money to the man who'd just murdered a woman who could ruin you."

"And whether or not it was smart," Janet joined in, "this man killed your lover. Are you asking us to believe that you *rewarded* him?" Slowly, definitively, she shook her head. "It just doesn't make sense."

"I'm not trying to make sense out of it," Wallis retorted. "I'm just telling you what happened."

"Okay—" Interrupting their dialogue, Hastings raised his hand, a traffic cop's gesture. "Let's forget about what makes sense. Let's get back to what you say actually happened. You say Kirk killed Lisa last Wednesday. Then, the next day, the two of you met at the Embarcadero underground station, at which time you agreed to pay him forty thousand dollars. Right?"

Now looking casually away, as if he'd lost interest in the dialogue, Wallis nodded. Then, incongruously, he began rotating his head, as if he suffered from an athletic injury. The effect was to suggest that he was preoccupied, indifferent to what might happen next.

"And at that time," Hastings continued, "Kirk told you— confessed to you, in effect—that he'd murdered Lisa Franklin."

"Lieutenant . . ." Wallis's tone was long-suffering, mock bored. "I know where you're going with this. You're trying to set me up for withholding evidence. Or collusion to commit murder. Or both. And if you want to play that game, if you're sure that's what you want, then—" He pointed to the high-tech phone. "Then I'll call my lawyers—plural—and your guys and my guys can fight it all out in court. Is that what you want? Or would you rather get through this, off the record, lay it all out, see what the options are?" Wallis gestured again to the phone. "It's your choice. Frankly, I don't give a shit. You're worried about who killed who, and why. But you're talking about two street kids, essentially, who got in over their heads. That's all they were: urchins, really. Oh, yes, I know—" Like Hastings, Wallis raised his hand, palm turned out. "I know, Lisa's father has a seat at the big board. But, in the grand scheme of things, she was a street kid trying to bluff her way through, just like C. J. Kirk. They were both lost—both of them self-destructing."

"You just got through telling us that you were obsessed with Lisa," Collier said.

Wallis looked at her but chose not to reply.

"You and C. J. and Barbara—" Hastings said. "You were all involved with Lisa."

A brief spasm of bitterness distorted Wallis's face, but he said nothing.

"Who killed C. J. Kirk tonight?" Hastings asked.

"I think Barbara killed him."

Instinctively, impassively, Hastings and Collier each sought the other's gaze, a mute exchange that expressed doubt, and hope, and caution, and a burst of headlong excitement, instantly suppressed. Finally, looking again at Wallis, Hastings spoke in a dead level voice: "What makes you say that?"

"She had plans to blackmail me for hundreds of thousands of dollars. Barbara, you see, knew everything that Lisa knew, about my affairs. Kirk had only bits and pieces. He could never have hurt me. But he could've hurt Barbara."

"How?" Collier asked.

230

"Barbara was sure that Kirk had killed Lisa. I don't know whether she had actual proof. I never wanted to know. But Barbara was absolutely certain that Kirk was guilty. She was also sure that, if you suspected Kirk, and took him downtown, and questioned him, then he'd break down and tell everything he knew—including what he knew about my problems with the SEC."

"Did she tell you this?" Hastings asked.

Wallis nodded. "She told me today. We met at Vista Point, in Sausalito. She laid it all out for me." Wallis considered, then admitted, "Barbara's no fool. She's very shrewd. And she's ruthless, too. Absolutely cold-blooded."

"So you think she killed Kirk to protect you."

"I think she killed him to protect her golden goose." Wallis smiled faintly. "Me."

Once more, Hastings exchanged a long, speculative look with Collier. Both of them, he knew, were preoccupied with the same questions: When the stakeout at Page Street had been set up, about six P.M., had Barbara been nearby, perhaps hidden in her car? Had she then followed C. J., when he'd escaped the stakeout? Had she followed Kirk to Valencia Street and killed him? When the word went out that C. J. had been killed, the stakeout at Page Street had been lifted. Barbara could have returned home without being seen a half hour after she'd killed Kirk.

Aware of the lengthening silence, Hastings nodded to Collier. Did she have any wrap-up questions?

"The fact is, Mr. Wallis," she said, "that you—only you—profited from these murders. Isn't that so?"

For a long moment Wallis made no reply. But finally, speaking in a low, exhausted monotone, he said, "As of this afternoon, when the SEC came, there's no more profit, not for anyone, least of all me. I'll be ruined. As for Lisa—" He moved his head in a complicated pattern that seemed without point or purpose, neither an affirmation nor a denial. "As for Lisa," he repeated, "she was meant to die young. Because without youth, she'd have nothing. You see that, don't you?"

Hastings made no reply but instead signaled Janet that it was time to go—

—time to begin the search for Barbara Estes.

44

"The way I see it," Hastings said, "here I am, it's almost two-thirty in the morning, and I'm about to risk my neck for the taxpayers. The least you can do, I figure, is answer the phone."

"My advice," Friedman said, "is not to risk your neck for the taxpayers. That's the first rule. Risk, that's what we've got subordinates for."

In the darkened interior of his cruiser, sitting beside Collier, Hastings smiled, pressed the cellular phone closer to his ear.

"You want me to get out of bed and come down there?" Friedman asked. "I will."

"I just want to lay it out for you. see what you think."

"Fine." Friedman stifled a yawn.

"Apparently she was out all evening. Anyhow, her place was dark, and she didn't answer the door. So let's assume she returned home about midnight, which would make sense. I mean, the stakeout was off, by then. So let's assume she's home."

"Assume? That's all we're doing? Assuming?"

Ignoring this latest Friedmanism, he went on: "There's an

outside stairway that connects the two flats and goes down to the basement. That's the only way out, back there."

"What about the roof?"

"The building's attached on both sides, so that's a possibility. And there's access to the roof from inside—a lightwell, with ladder rungs."

"Are you going to cover the roof?"

"It's two-thirty in the morning. I'd have to wake up the neighbors, go through their place. What d'you think?"

"If Wallis is right," Friedman said, "then this lady is the prime suspect in a very high profile murder case. Plus, if she took C. J. Kirk out tonight, we have to assume that she's armed and dangerous. All of which is to say that we should spare no horses on this one. In fact, the more I talk, the more I think I should pull on my pants and drive over there."

"Great. Put your pants on." As he spoke, Hastings looked at Collier—and winked. She did not respond.

"Is Canelli there? Is he going in with you?"

"He's doing the Kirk homicide."

"On the record?"

"On the record. He's at Property, right now. Kirk was carrying twenty-seven thousand dollars."

"So it's—what—you and Janet Collier, that'll go in? Is that what I'm hearing?"

"That's what you're hearing."

"Listen, Frank—Janet's done a good job on this one. Looks aside, she's first-class. I even bought Captain Frazer a lunch the other day, sounding him out on getting her away from Bunco. But if Barbara Estes has a gun, and if you're going in after her, well, I don't think Collier's ready for that kind of duty. I'm sorry. I know you're the outside man. But you called me up, and we talked. And that's the way I feel about it."

"So what's your idea?" The question, Hastings realized, was more harshly put than he'd intended.

If he'd taken note of Hastings's displeasure, Friedman gave no sign. Instead, speaking mildly, Friedman said, "Barbara has a nine-to-five job. Right?"

"Right. Jamison's Coffee Company."

"Okay. So now it's two-thirty. In a few hours, she'll leave for work, assuming that she plans to keep to her normal routine. So we double the stakeout in back, and we cover the roof. Then we sit tight, wait for her to come to us. We take her on the sidewalk, on her way to her car, whatever."

"What if she isn't in there? It's possible, you know." As he said it, Hastings looked once more across the street at 1832 Page Street. First Lisa Franklin, dead. Now, tonight, C. J. Kirk, dead. Could he have prevented Kirk's death? Could he have saved C. J.? Was it possible that—?

"Obviously," Friedman was saying, "it would help to know whether she's in there. What about a car? Does she have a car?"

"I don't know. As soon as we talked to Wallis, I called DMV. But the computers were down. They're still down. Five A.M., that's the estimate."

"Well, then," Friedman said, "how about this: you get the roof covered. Then you ring your old buddy Jamie Thomas's doorbell, and you ask him very quietly whether he thinks Barbara's upstairs. Then you ask him what kind of a car she drives. If he says that he thinks she's upstairs, and if you can find her car parked nearby, all we have to do is wait till she comes out, tomorrow morning." There was a tentative pause. Then: "How's that sound?"

"It sounds like it makes sense," Hastings admitted.

"Keep me posted."

"Right."

45

The images danced, the faces diverged, converged, finally faded into the black of night. The only sounds were the rumble of the Ford's engine and the rhythmic thudding of a single heartbeat: C. J., fleeing. And the sirens, shrieking.

C. J., out of the car, his mouth agape, arms flung wide, eyes glowing like live coals against the white of his face, caught in the glare of the headlights.

C. J., soundlessly screaming. Running. Tripping. Falling facedown, fingers crooked, clawing at the broken concrete of the street, red with rivulets of blood shining in the darkness.

If he opened his eyes, the images disappeared. And the sounds, too, were diminishing. All the sounds but one: a faint rustle of movement, a scraping. And another sound: paper, perhaps, ripping.

Eyes open now, Thomas turned his head on the pillow, focused on the open bedroom door.

Yes, he could hear it plainly now. In the hallway, someone—something—was moving.

C. J.?

The police?

Had they let C. J. enter the house? Would they take him here—now? Lisa had been killed with a gun. Meaning that, surely, C. J. carried the gun.

Yes, Jamie, I really think he killed her.

In the hours since Hastings had called, the words had reverberated, stifling everything else, all thought, all reason.

No, not the words. Just the one word: *murder.*

And the other word: *murderer.*

Would the police kill C. J., put him out of his misery, as if he were a rabid dog? Was that the plan: run him to ground here, away from prying eyes, then kill him with a bullet to the brain, finally rest in peace, C. J.?

Hastings: that quiet, serious man—would he deliver the coup de grace?

Hastings, the executioner. In high school, who could have guessed?

Without realizing that he meant to do it, he'd slipped out of bed and was standing in front of his open bedroom door. To his bare feet, the floor was uncomfortably cold. He wore only his shorts.

As he drew closer to the hallway, he could hear another sound: a door, slowly opening. Was it C. J.'s door? Yes, the particular pattern of squeaks was unmistakable. Accounting, then, for the sound of tearing, ripping. C. J. had returned and cut away the police seal on his door.

Standing in the hallway now, Thomas turned cautiously to face the second bedroom. Three years—it had been three years, since Kirk had called. "I saw your note on the bulletin board at Colby's," he'd said. "For a roommate."

Even then, on the phone, he'd heard the flawed cadence in C. J.'s voice, the chronic uncertainty. But the rent had been due, and the landlord was unforgiving. And the—

From inside Kirk's bedroom, light outlined the door, now closed. The police. It was surely the police, returned: Hastings and the woman, ransacking C. J.'s room, searching for something they'd missed earlier.

But to enter the house without permission, search without a warrant—now it was the police, breaking the law.

At the thought, the sudden indignity of the intrusion, Thomas stepped forward, switched on the hallway light. Buoyed by a wayward flicker of outrage at the intrusion, he knocked at the bedroom door.

Instantly the room went dark. A moment passed. Then, slowly, the door came open—

—revealing the outline of a familiar figure. It was Barbara, crouched over the pistol she held in her right hand.

"Jesus—" Thomas stepped back, struck the hallway wall with his shoulder. "Jesus. Wh—?"

"Shut up—" It was a low, fierce whisper. Then, beckoning furiously with the pistol: "Get in here. Turn off the light, and get in here. Close the door."

"Wh—wh—?"

"Get—in—here—Jamie. Now. Right now. Then close the fucking door."

Obeying, he advanced—one step, two steps. As if to ward off evil, he raised his right hand before the pistol, in supplication. In the bedroom together, lights on, she would be less menacing. He was inside the bedroom, closing the door, facing her as his fingers found the switch, turned on the overhead light.

God, was it her? Barbara Estes, usually so cold, so controlled, now with eyes blazing, her whole body possessed by fury—was this really her? Which one was real? It was as if the pistol she held trained on the center of his chest had become a part of her: cold steel animated by the rage that transformed her.

This stranger, his executioner.

The voice, too, was a stranger's: uninflected now, yet incredibly menacing, the essence of evil incarnate.

"He killed her," she said. "Clayton Wallis gave him the money to kill Lisa. Wallis told me, admitted it. A few thousand dollars, that's all it took. He—Christ—the bastard, all he could see was dope, enough crack for life, that's what he saw when he took the money. And—" Now she smiled; the smile of a skull, facial skin stretched taut, teeth clenched, bared: Barbara Estes, transformed. "And that's what he got—crack enough to last until he died."

"You—did you—" His throat closed on the words.

Slowly, with infinite malice, she nodded. "Tonight. Two,

three hours ago. It was on Valencia—the police'll think it was because of drugs. When the gun fired, and I saw him fall, the whole world opened up, came alive. I—Christ—I executed him. Can you understand that, understand what it means, to kill someone like him?"

"It means you're a murderer, that's what it means."

Now a rage of contempt tore at her face. "Someone like you, you'd never know what it means. You're incapable of feeling. You could never know what Lisa and I had. You and C. J.—degenerates—how could you know?"

Degenerates . . .

The accusation stung so sharply that the edge of his terror was dulled. Without conscious thought, he swept the devastated room with a gesture of indictment, accusing her.

"What're you looking for, Barbara? The money this guy paid C. J.? Is that it? You and C. J.—what's the difference between you? You're both after the money."

"The difference is that he's dead. And I'm alive."

"Yeah, well, I've got news for you, Barbara. The money isn't here."

Once more, fury focused the blaze in her eyes, fixated on him. The eyes, the muzzle of the gun, there was nothing else.

"You know where it is. You know, and you'll tell me, Jamie. Now. Right now."

"If there was any money, the police have it. You saw the seal. They came earlier, and searched. C. J. was already gone." He paused for a moment, watching her. Then, moving his head toward the street: "They're probably out there now, Barbara. Watching the house."

Almost imperceptibly, the muzzle of the pistol dropped. As—yes—her eyes shifted toward the street. But her voice was harsh: "Bullshit. I've been here for hours. And—"

"How'd you get down here? The doors—they're both locked."

"The airshaft, asshole." She spoke contemptuously.

"Have you figured out what to tell the police, about the seal on the door? They'll know I didn't do it."

No longer crouched, she was standing straight now; she held the automatic lowered along her right side. In her eyes, he could see the suggestion of uncertainty. Finally she said, "That lieutenant from your high school—did you talk to him, tell him what he wanted to know?"

"I talked to him."

"Did he tell you what he's thinking?"

He hesitated, looked aside, considered. Then: "He told me some of it, yeah."

"When? What time was he here, tonight?"

"About eight o'clock, maybe a little later."

"They were after C. J.," she said. "Not me. C. J." As she spoke, her eyes lost focus. The pistol was no longer menacing. He could see some of the animal tension leaving her body. Barbara was beginning to think—to plan. Where were the police? Were they nearby, watching? Waiting?

"Are the lights on in the rest of the house?" she asked.

"No."

"It's all dark? Your whole flat?"

He nodded.

"All right. We're going to turn off the lights in here. Then we're going to go into the living room. Are the drapes drawn?"

"Yes. But—"

"We're going to go into the living room," she said, "and we're going to sit down. We're going to talk. Do you understand?"

"What time is it?"

"About two-thirty. Now move." She raised the pistol, gestured to the light switch. She watched him step back, watched him as he fumbled for the switch, finally plunged the room into darkness. If he came for her, she would club him with the gun. Then she would return to the upstairs flat. On the hallway table in her flat she'd set out the things she meant to take:

her purse, her checkbook, a small satchel of toiletries, a handful of cartridges for the Beretta she'd bought at a pawnshop the day after Lisa died.

The purse—the cartridges—and Lisa's final bequest, the single sheet of paper that meant millions. Combine the page of handwritten instructions with the memorized name—Clayton Wallis—and golden doors came open: millions in tribute, a lifetime of privilege. It was a negligible expense for Wallis but a fortune for her.

"There—" She motioned to an armchair with its back to the windows fronting on the street. "Sit there." He wore only undershorts. She watched him sit down, then cross his scrawny legs, then tug at his shorts, looking down, to make sure his genitals were covered.

His genitals—that contemptible member that was surely shrunken, as ineffectual as Thomas himself. Jamie Thomas, C. J. Kirk—human flotsam.

Outside, the police could be waiting. But waiting for whom? It had been almost one o'clock when she'd returned home. She'd parked her car, walked the block to her building. There'd been no sign of the police. She'd opened the front door and turned on lights, as she always did. Because predictability, she knew, was essential. Therefore, as always, she'd gone to the bathroom, washed her face and hands, put on the outsize T-shirt she always wore to bed. She'd switched off the light—and lain wide awake for more than an hour. Then, no lights showing, she'd gotten dressed in sneakers, jeans, a scuffed leather jacket. She'd gone to the living room, cautiously looked down into the street, trying to discover some movement, some wayward presence at odds with the neighborhood that would give away a police stakeout. There was nothing. The police thought Kirk's death was drug related, just as she'd planned. Case closed.

Next she'd gone into the bathroom. Cautiously, sound-lessly, she'd raised the window that opened on the airshaft leading to the roof. Climbing rungs were attached to the side-wall of the airshaft. She'd climbed out the window, then begun ascending the rungs. Once more moving in extreme slow mo-tion, she'd raised her eyes above the roof level. Again, nothing. But, on the roofs, there were a dozen places of concealment.

She'd returned to her room, stretched out on the bed, closed her eyes, tried to order her thoughts. C. J.—it all pivoted on C. J. He'd been dead for two hours. Long enough, surely, for word of the murder to flash to the policemen watching the building.

Long enough to recall the policemen, case closed.

She'd driven aimlessly for a half hour before she could control herself enough to risk returning home, risk letting anyone see her. As she'd driven, struggling for calm, thoughts of her mother had roiled in her consciousness: that worn-out, self-pitying woman who'd lived from one bottle of cheap gin to the next. And her father, too—images of her father, enraged, beating her mother with a wire coathanger until she bled. Always, long before tonight, long before Lisa had died, that same image of her father had haunted her. She'd been five when the police had taken him away. She'd come home from kindergarten and seen them loading her father into a police van. The charge had been aggravated assault. Later, years later, she'd learned that he'd been killed in a jailhouse brawl while he awaited trial. It had been a broken bottle, her mother told her, jammed into his neck.

"So this man—Wallis, you say—he hired C. J. to kill Lisa. Is that what you're saying?"

She made no reply. Why had she told Jamie about Clayton Wallis? *Why?*

In the darkened living room, their voices were hushed, disembodied. Their faces were in shadow, illuminated only faintly by a streetlamp outside the front windows. Only the gun had substance, still trained on Thomas.

"So you killed C. J.," he said.

She gave no sign that she'd heard.

"Why'd you kill C. J., Barbara? To get off, is that why you did it? Was it a high? That's the way you're acting. You're acting like you're on something heavy, just thinking about killing him."

"As a matter of fact—" Mocking him as he sat so forlornly, tracked by the big, heavy automatic pistol that made him her slave, she nodded. "—you're right, Jamie. You finally got it right. I saw him go down, I felt like the whole world was mine. All of it. Everything."

"Because of you and Lisa—was that it? Is that why you killed him?"

Searching his face in the dim light from the street outside, she made no response. What did he know? What had C. J. told him? Was this the new danger: Jamie Thomas, that narrow, ineffectual spectator, that cowardly boy who'd grown into this craven man? Must he die, too? How? If the police were out there, she couldn't do it now—not now, not here. Not unless there was no noise.

A knife?

Was she capable of plunging a knife into him?

"There's more than that," he was saying. "I know you, Barbara. You didn't kill him just because he killed Lisa— because you loved Lisa. I saw C. J.'s room, after you finished with it. You're after money. That's what it's all about, for you."

She lifted her wrist, caught the dial of her watch in the faint light. The time was almost three o'clock. In five hours, she must begin the pantomime: Barbara Estes, working girl.

242

Barbara Estes, beginning the day's routine, just one day among so many others.

Barbara Estes, dressed for work, leaving the building and walking to her car. If the police were watching, there would be nothing suspicious. Especially if she took him with her: Jamie and she, leaving the building together, both of them going to work. Under the gaze of watchful eyes, they would get into her car. She would drop him at his job, then go on to Jamison Coffee.

Jamie—her insurance. Her edge. If she couldn't kill him to protect herself, then she could use him. She would—

In the darkness, a buzzer sounded. It was the front door. Someone was at the front door. Once more, the sound reverberated. And again. And again, impatiently now.

She sprang to her feet, reached Thomas in three long strides, jammed the pistol barrel hard into the base of his throat. "Who's that? Who's there?"

"I expect," Thomas said, "that it's the police." He smiled at her. Now there was no fear in his face. There was only the small, smug smile. "Who else could it be?"

46

With his right hand on the butt of his revolver, loose in its holster, Hastings exchanged a look with Collier, who stood with her back against the outside wall beside the front door. It was the approved backup stance, out of sight—out of the line of fire. She was watching him intently, fiercely focused. She was ready.

About to push the door buzzer a fourth time, Hastings hesitated. Had he heard the sound of movement from the other side of the door? Once more, he looked at Janet. Yes, she'd heard it, too.

As, slowly, the door began to open.

47 Had it been a poetic fragment, one of Lisa's? Yes, the images returned: years came down to hours, hours came down to minutes, then to seconds. Until finally the cosmic digital counter came up "zero."

Zero for Lisa.

Zero for C. J.

And now, for Jamie, the counter was moving toward zero.

With the steel of the automatic held close against her breasts, cold comfort, she stood in the living room archway, concealed from anyone at the front door as she heard Jamie's voice: "Frank."

Thomas's inflection was unmistakable: the police had arrived, Jamie's old high school friend, Lieutenant Hastings. And, yes, Thomas was terrified.

"Can we come in, Jamie? We need help—information."

We, Hastings had said. Himself, and at least one other, at the front door in the dead of night.

"Yeah—well—" She heard Thomas clear his throat. "Could you—I mean, would you mind if—" He broke off, plainly confused, losing it.

"What's the matter, Jamie? What's bothering you?"

"Please. Don't—"

"Is Barbara upstairs?"

No reply. Was Jamie nodding his head? Or shaking his head? Which? One simple motion, and Hastings would have everything, all the information he needed.

Barbara was moving her own head—one inch, another inch. As the angles changed, the hallway came into view—

—as Jamie was shaking his head. Facing Hastings and a woman, and shaking his head. And now he was moving his head, to indicate the rear of the flat.

Moving quickly, without conscious thought, Barbara was in the hallway, facing the three dim figures. Still without calculation, driven only by a primitive urge for survival, crouching low, she covered the distance to Thomas in three strides. She drove the barrel of the automatic pistol hard into the small of his back with her right hand. With her left hand she grasped his hair, jerked him off balance, back into her.

"This is a gun, Jamie." With all her strength she struck again with the pistol, felt his body spasm, reacting to the pain. *"Understand?"* And to the detectives: "Get back. You've got guns. Drop the guns. Drop them, or I'll kill him. I swear to God, I'll kill him."

Leaving his revolver in its holster, Hastings raised his hands to shoulder height. Beside him, Janet did the same. With Thomas between them in the narrow, dimly lit entry-way, Hastings stepped closer to the wall, made angled eye contact with the woman as he said, "Is that the gun you used tonight on C. J., Barbara?" He spoke softly, evenly. First, he must have her confidence. Then he must try to alert the stakeout team. But how? His surveillance microphone was in his pocket; the surveillance radio clipped to his belt was switched off.

"Where's your gun?" she asked. "I told you to drop it on the floor."

"The gun's right here . . ." Very slowly, using his left thumb and forefinger, he drew back his unzipped jacket to

245

reveal the revolver holstered at his belt, on the left side. "But you don't want me to drop it on the floor. It could go off."

She turned to Collier. "Where's your gun? In the handbag?"

"That's right, Barbara." In the three words, Janet distilled a bitter essence of contempt: two females of the species, squaring off. Watching Janet's face, Hastings realized that he'd never before seen two women confront each other with deadly intent.

"All right," Barbara said, "take the gun out of the bag, put it on the floor. Then step back." As she spoke, still with her hand knotted in his half-long hair, Barbara dragged Thomas back, opening more space to maneuver.

"Hey," Thomas protested. "Take it easy."

"What you're doing," Hastings said, "is making it worse for yourself, Barbara. C. J.—nobody cares what happened to him. He was nothing. But you fuck with us, make us look bad, you'll regret it. Do you understand what I'm telling you?"

"Make you look bad . . ." Each word was heavy with scorn. "I'm talking about my life. And you're talking about your— your image, for Christ's sake." Then, to Collier: "What's your name? I forget."

"Janet Collier."

"Okay, Janet. I want you to put the gun on the floor. Then I want you to—"

"After you killed C. J.," Hastings said, "we found Clayton Wallis's phone number in his wallet. It was Wallis's private number." Covertly watching her face, searching for a reaction, Hastings broke off. Yes, even in the uncertain light, he could see a flicker of fear.

"We went to Wallis's house tonight, got him out of bed. And it turned out that we'd got him just right." Once more, watchfully, Hastings broke off. As, yes, her attention was shifting, focusing on him, no longer on Janet or the revolver still in her shoulder bag.

"Listen," Hastings said, nodding in the direction of the flat's interior, "let's sit down. Let's sit down, talk this over. It seems like we've got a lot to tell each other."

"You've got a lot to tell me. I'm not telling you anything. I'll listen to what you have to say. Then I'm walking Jamie out of here. He's my ticket out. But first I want those guns."

Slowly, with great deliberation—taking the gamble—Hastings shook his head. "No, Barbara. We aren't giving up our guns. No way."

"You son of a bitch. I'll—"

"There're a half dozen policemen, outside. And I'm not letting them see me without my service revolver. I just won't do it. And neither will Inspector Collier."

"Then they'll see you dead, you son of a—"

"Do you want us to tell you what Clayton Wallis said, tonight?" Hastings asked.

Silence. Then, a surprise, Thomas spoke: "Wallis hired C. J. to kill Lisa."

"That's not what Wallis says," Collier put in. "He says C. J. killed Lisa and then asked for money. He says—"

"That's a lie," Estes flared. "That's a fucking lie. C. J. killed Lisa because Wallis hired him to do it. Wallis was be-ing—" Suddenly she broke off, allowing Hastings to finish it:

"Wallis was being investigated by the SEC," Hastings said, "and Lisa knew about it. All she had to do was go to the SEC with what she knew, and Wallis was jail bait. So he hired C. J. to kill Lisa. We've got proof—absolute proof—that C. J. killed Lisa. And we've absolute proof that he was paid to do it."

"Bullshit." This time, Estes spoke almost matter-of-factly.

"C. J. had tens of thousands of dollars on him when he died, Barbara." Hastings spoke in the same soft, compelling voice—the voice of a hostage negotiator. "You should've killed him in a more isolated place. You could've gotten the money that Wallis paid to C. J."

"As it turns out," Collier said, "Wallis is going to jail.

That's what we found out tonight. So there's no more money, not from Wallis. No more cash cow, Barbara."

"That's another lie."

Collier shrugged, pointed to the interior of the flat. "Call him. Ask him whether he talked to the SEC today. Ask him whether he'll be indicted tomorrow."

"You goddam slut. Shut up."

Collier's face tightened; visibly, she drew a deep, furious breath. High on her cheeks, the blood rose. But she made no reply.

"According to Wallis," Hastings said, "you took over Lisa's territory. You're blackmailing him for his insider trading. You got the information from Lisa. It was insurance, probably. She wanted someone to know, if anything happened to her."

"Except," Collier said, picking up the rhythm, "it's all over, now. The SEC has all it needs. There'll be a long, expensive trial. But however the trial turns out, blackmail's a thing of the past."

"You were a week or two too late," Hastings contributed. "The well's dry, Barbara." As he spoke, he began slowly to lower his hands. Instantly, Estes dug her pistol into Thomas's back, producing an anguished protest. In response, Hastings shrugged, raised his hands again, laced his fingers behind his neck. Beside him, Collier was doing the same.

"We're leaving," Estes said. "Get out of my way. If you've got a radio, you'd better tell your people. Tell them to let us through."

"You're making it worse for yourself, Barbara. And you're being dumb. There's no way out. You think a hostage'll help, but you're wrong. You walk out that door, there'll be sharp-shooters on you—rifles, with telescopic night sights. They won't take chances with a hostage's life. But they won't let you off, either. If it comes down to a choice between you and a hostage, you lose. That's not what we tell the newspapers. But that's what happens. Believe it."

"If you think they care about Jamie Thomas," Collier said, "you're wrong."

"Maybe I should take one of you, then," Estes said, speaking to Janet. "Maybe I'll take you. They won't shoot if I've got you."

With their eyes locked over Thomas's shoulder, the two women faced each other. Then, softly, Collier spoke: "You want to take me? Is that what you want?"

Almost inaudibly, her voice clogged by hatred now focused on Collier, Estes said, "Yes, bitch. I want you."

"Janet . . ." Hastings shook his head. "No."

But she looked away. Once more focused fiercely on the other woman, Collier was deliberately ignoring his order. "You want to go outside with me," Collier said, "then let's go. But don't call me any more names, Barbara. And keep your goddam hands out of my hair. You touch my hair, I'll take you down. I promise, I'll take you down."

Slowly, precisely, as if she were responding to an intricate stage direction, Estes trained her automatic pistol on Collier while, with her free hand, she pushed Thomas aside. With the move, Hastings had his first clear look at the gun: a late-model Beretta, nine millimeter. Also moving as if to satisfy some intricate turn in an ancient ritual of mortal confrontation, Janet shifted her stance to square with her opponent. Both women moved as if they were oblivious of Hastings.

"Drop the shoulder bag."

Still with great deliberation, another convention in their deadly ritual, Collier hooked a thumb in the bag's strap, lowered the bag gently to the floor. Still with his fingers laced behind his neck, Hastings shifted, drew a half-step closer to Janet. He spoke in a soft, furious whisper: "Janet. Back off. *Now*. That's an order."

Once more, she ignored him. Instead, to Estes: "Ready?"

"Ready. Open the door. Slowly. Very slowly."

As Collier turned to face the front door, she momentarily

caught Hastings's eye, surreptitiously nodded. Then, facing the door, she put her left hand on the knob as, yes, she felt the proof of the Beretta in the small of her back. Instantly she whirled, caught the gun squarely with her right elbow, sent it crashing into the wall, then falling to the floor. With her body behind the blow, she drove the stiffened fingers of her left hand deep into the other woman's solar plexus. Fighting for breath, Estes fell to her knees, head down, gasping, choking, sobbing. Instinctively, Hastings scooped up the pistol, verified that the hammer was down, uncocked, before he thrust the pistol into his belt as Collier scooped up her shoulder bag. Quickly, deftly, Hastings cuffed the woman as she lay gasping on the floor. Then, furious, Hastings gripped Collier's shoulder, flattened her against the wall close beside the helpless suspect. With his face only inches from Janet's, his eyes ablaze, he increased the pressure on her shoulder until she winced. Fighting for self-control, he spoke in a harsh, ragged whisper: "I told you to back off. Just what the hell d'you think you're doing? You—Christ—you could've died."

"Let go of me, Frank."

Slowly he allowed his hand to relax. But, locked with hers, his eyes still blazed. Standing so close that they almost touched, his body was still drawn taut with fury; neck bowed, feet spread, fists clenched.

"You—" He shook his head, began again: "You could've been killed. What're you—*crazy?*"

Controlling her own anger, she gritted her teeth, pointed to the Beretta in Hastings's belt. "It was uncocked. When I felt her touch me, and I hadn't heard the hammer come back, I knew I could take her. As soon as I saw that the hammer was down, I knew I had time."

"Oh." Grimly, Hastings nodded. Repeating: "Oh. You figured you had a second or two, while she had to cock her piece. Is that it?"

"That's it." Now she, too, was angry. "And it worked."

"Oh. Grace under pressure. Cool head. Departmental citation, is that what you were thinking?"

"Listen, Frank—" Her eyes left his, went to Barbara Estes, then to Jamie Thomas. "Can't this wait?"

He stepped back, took the pistol from his belt, released the clip, dropped it in his pocket. Next he flipped the slide, ejected the live cartridge in the chamber. When the slide slammed forward, he lowered the hammer. Then he held the Beretta up close to her face—and pulled the trigger. The hammer rose, then released, clicking against an empty chamber.

"This," Hastings said, "is a Beretta model ninety-four. And it so happens, Janet, that this model will fire the first shot double-action. So all she had to do was pull the trigger, and you're dead. She didn't have to cock the goddam piece. Just pull the trigger, that's all she had to do."

With obvious effort, Collier transferred her gaze from the Beretta to Hastings. She swallowed once—swallowed again. Finally, very softly: "I'm sorry." She broke off, began again: "I'm sorry—Lieutenant."

As Hastings stepped back another pace, he suddenly felt anger drain away, felt his whole body go slack. If only he could hold her close, feel her body against his. If only he could tell her how terrified he'd been during the few seconds it seemed she surely must die.

Then, once more the officer in charge, he gestured to Barbara Estes, on her knees now, gasping. "You'd better search her and then take her downtown and book her. I'll shut it down here, then go home."

"You mean . . ." She searched his face. Then, tentatively— timidly, almost—she ventured a smile. "You mean it's mine? The collar?"

"When you write your report, say that you persuaded her to give up the gun. Understand?"

The smile widened. "Oh, yes. I understand." A brief, intimate moment. Then, repeating: "Oh, yes."

48

Hastings put the report on his desk and looked at Collier, sitting opposite.

"Did you get any sleep last night?" he asked.

"Three hours. I got home about five o'clock."

"Do you still think you want Homicide?"

She nodded gravely. "You know I do."

"Well—" He gestured to the report. "You're off to a good start. That's one of the best, most concise reports I've seen in a long time. How long did it take to write?"

"About two hours, not counting interruptions. The computer helps." She smiled slightly, impersonally. "You should try it."

He glanced at his watch. "We have to meet with the DA's people at three." He pointed to the report. "I want to ask you about a couple of things, make sure we agree."

She nodded again.

"C. J.'s murder—I just heard from the lab. Everything checks out: the bullets match the Beretta, and two shell casings were found inside Barbara's car. Prints're no problem; her prints're all over. Everything fits."

"Ah . . ." It was a sigh of satisfaction. "Good."

He pointed again to her report. "You don't get into theorizing, which is right. But we should agree between us on theory before we talk to the DA."

"Yes . . ."

"I think . . ." Hastings glanced at his notes. "I think there were two reasons why Barbara killed C. J. First, she was convinced he killed her lover. Second, she knew that, if we arrested C. J., and squeezed him, he'd admit that Wallis hired him to kill Lisa. And if Wallis fell for murder, never mind what happened with the SEC, her golden goose would be cooked. She had a financial interest in protecting Wallis."

"I agree."

"Okay, that's where we stand on the Kirk homicide. What about Lisa's murder?"

"Did the lab find Wallis's prints on the money C. J. had on him?" she asked.

"Not yet. It takes time, when the prints are on paper. They have to use gases, infrared, whatever."

"Well . . ." She broke off, yawned, excused herself. "Well, I think the original theory is still good. Lisa was blackmailing Wallis, and he was scared. So he hired C. J. to kill her."

"Except that there's no way we can get Wallis for her murder. Not with what we've got."

"If his fingerprints are on the money C. J. had, though . . ."

Hastings shook his head. "If Wallis sticks to his story that C. J. first came to him asking for money *after* he'd killed Lisa, then we've got nothing. The DA'll never indict."

"I know . . ." She yawned again, apologized again.

"But we're agreed," Hastings pressed. "We've got our stories straight."

"Yes, we're agreed." Then, bitterly: "We're agreed that the bastard'll probably never pay."

Hastings nodded gloomily. Then he, too, yawned.

"Well—" She sighed. "There's always the SEC."

Hastings made no reply, and for a long moment, both of them exhausted, they stared at each other across Hastings's desk. Finally Collier spoke: "The bad guys don't always lose, do they?"

Hastings snorted agreement, glanced at his watch. In forty-five minutes, they were due at the DA's.

Finally, in a different mood, Collier spoke tentatively: "I—ah—I wanted to ask you, after we see the DA, I'd like to go home, catch some sleep, see Charlie."

"Sure." He nodded readily.

"But—" Now her manner was almost timid. "But before I go home, maybe after we see the DA, could I buy you a cup of coffee? Or tea, maybe, at that Chinese place? Could we do that?"

"Yes," he answered gravely. "Yes, let's do that."

49

"I guess I shouldn't do this when I'm so tired," she said. "But ever since last night—ever since I disobeyed orders, and you slammed me against the wall—I've been thinking about it."

Having already decided not to interrupt until she finished, Hastings took up the porcelain teapot, with the gesture offering her more tea. Almost impatiently, she shook her head. Even though she was pale with fatigue, her gesture was determined, almost harsh. Keeping to his resolve, Hastings said nothing, returned the teapot to the table. And waited until she once more began to speak:

"And the truth is," she said, "that I—I'm attracted to you. I—I guess I'm in love with you, as much as two people can be in love without sleeping together."

Despite his resolve, Hastings smiled. "A hundred years ago—fifty, even—that's the way it happened. First you get married. Then you have sex."

Ignoring the observation, frowning at the interruption, she said, "The easiest thing in the world for us to do, right now, would be to get into bed together—rent a hotel room, have a ball. And, God, I've thought about it, what it would be like.

But—" Now the dogged determination returned as she broke off, then stubbornly began again:

"But then, afterwards, you'd go home to your lady. And—"

"Ann," he said. "Her name is Ann."

She nodded politely, thanking him. Beginning again: "You'd go home to Ann and her two boys. They probably admire you tremendously. Her boys, I mean. You're—God—you're the perfect role model, Frank, for boys. You're calm, and kind, and brave. You're modest, too. And you're good-looking." Now her smile was wistful, whimsical. Or was she teasing him now?

"So you'd go home to Ann and her boys, and I'd go home to Charlie. And we wouldn't be able to forget how it had been, for us. You'd be in bed beside Ann that night, staring up at the ceiling. And me—" The wistful smile returned. "I'd be in my bed, alone. You'd be feeling guilty, and I'd be feeling lost, more alone than I'd been before we made love."

He made no response. It was important, he knew, to look into her eyes, waiting for what must surely come:

"And then," she said, "the next day, we'd be at work. Maybe my desk would be in Homicide by then, every inspector's dream. Except that, for me, there wouldn't be any magic in the dream. Because I'd know what they'd be thinking in the squadroom. Even Canelli, the sweetest guy in the world, I'd know what he'd be thinking." She let a final beat pass. Then: "He'd be thinking that I'd done it on my back."

"Janet, that's just not true. That's just not—"

"Whether that's what he'd be thinking," she interrupted, "that's what I'd *think* he was thinking. Which comes to the same thing."

For the first time looking away from her, he rested his glance on a large ornamental clock on the restaurant's far wall. The time was twenty minutes after five; the meeting with the DA's office had gone on for two hours. In another hour, unless he called, Ann would expect him home, for dinner.

He realized that, between them, a silence was lengthening. She'd said what she'd had to say. Now he must speak. He returned his eyes to hers, let the silence linger one final moment before he said, "The office, that doesn't have to be a problem. But Ann . . ." Once more, he broke off. Until, finally, she said:

"Yes . . . Ann."